SHADOW ANGEL

BOOK ONE

D1604150

SHADOW ANGEL

BOOK ONE

LEIA STONE & JULIE HALL

USA TODAY BESTSELLING AUTHORS

ISBN (paperback): 978-1-951578-17-6

ISBN (hardcover): 978-1-951578-16-9

ISBN (hardcover special edition): 978-1-954510-09-8

Leia Stone (LeiaStone.com) & Julie Hall (JulieHallAuthor.com)

Introducing, Tatum . .

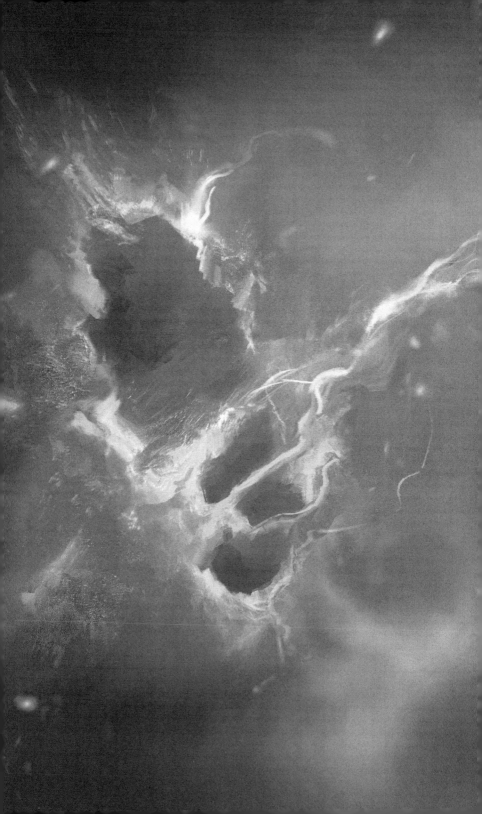

BOOKS BY JULIE HALL
JULIEHALLAUTHOR.COM/BOOKS

FALLEN LEGACIES SERIES

Stealing Embers

Forging Darkness

Unleashing Fire

LIFE AFTER SERIES

Huntress

Warfare

Dominion

Logan

Julie's books have won or finaled in 21 awards.

To our readers.

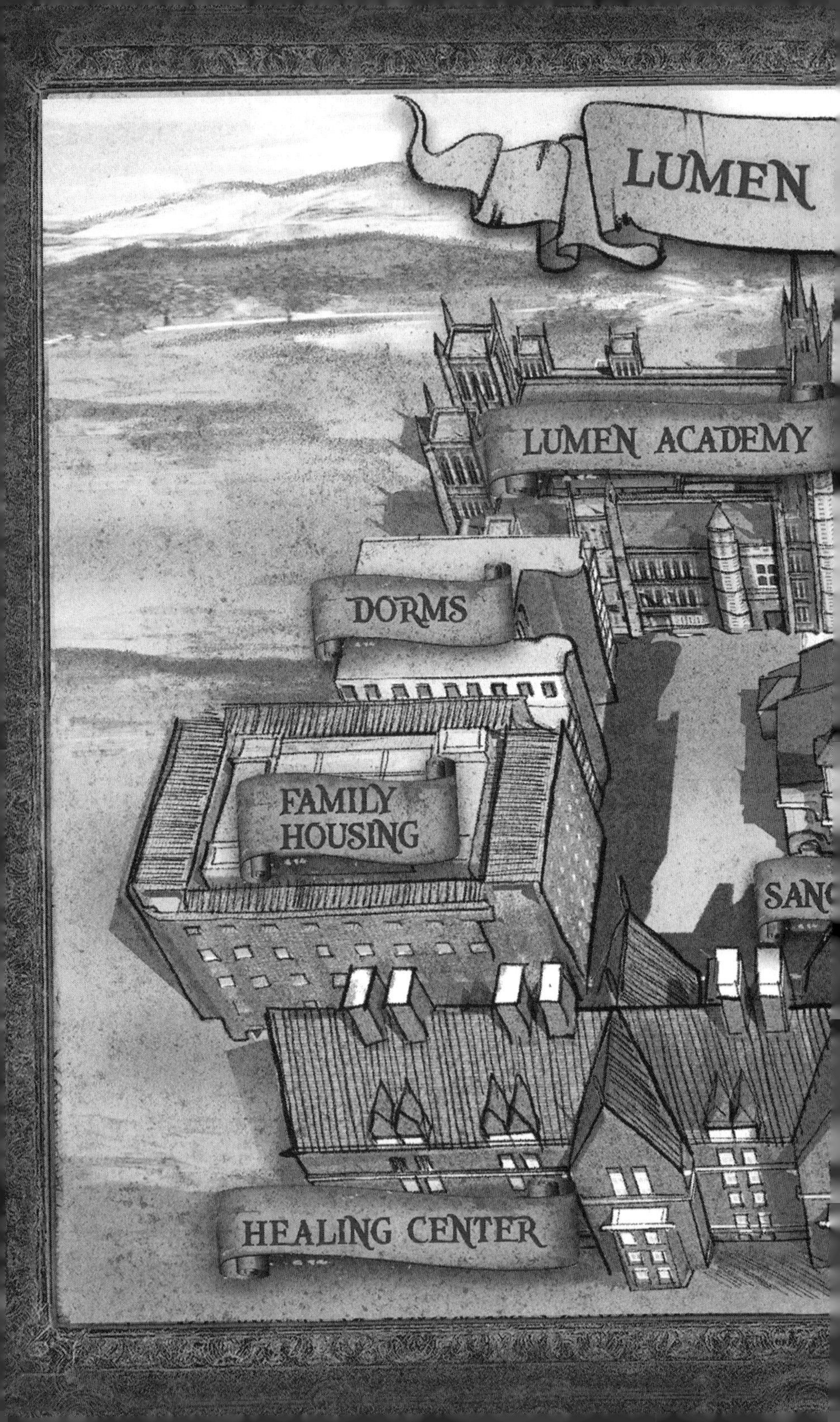
LUMEN
LUMEN ACADEMY
DORMS
FAMILY HOUSING
SANC
HEALING CENTER

The subway car slowly rocked as I leaned my head back against the window, music blasting out of my earbuds, rattling my brain. My body ached so badly I felt seventy instead of seventeen. Today's shift at Sal's Diner had been a long one. I felt like I had bruises on the bottoms of my feet, I'd been standing on them so long. My body might have hated my ten-hour Saturday shifts, but my wallet loved them. I'd made a hundred bucks in tips today. That was groceries for a week for Gran and me.

"Hey, screw you, man!" a lady shrieked, and I yanked one of the earbuds from my ear, suddenly alert.

I flicked my gaze to the back of the car, where a big dude was hassling some lady and her kid. I glanced the other way and realized I was alone—just me and some douchebag trying to touch a lady holding her infant.

Reaching into my purse, I pulled out my purple can of pepper spray. Gran got it for me when I was twelve and started taking the city bus to school. I'd grown up in Brooklyn but never actually had to use this. Sometimes the mere act of pointing it at someone would make them change their behavior. I'd done that twice.

I stared at the guy, hoping he was going to back down so I wouldn't need to insert myself into this drama. I was too tired for this crap.

"I said what's your name?" the guy growled, grabbing the lady's arm and not letting go. The hairs on the back of my neck stood straight up. His voice didn't sound normal. It was scratchy and animalistic.

Flicking the safety off the nozzle of the pepper spray, I pulled it from my purse just as the woman looked at me. Her face was marred with fear, and my heart jackknifed in my chest.

Okay, this was happening.

I stood, planting both feet onto the floor, and aimed the purple spray can. "Let her go, man. We don't want trouble."

He whipped in my direction, and I stared into... two glowing red eyes?

What the heck?

I shook my head, trying to dislodge the illusion. I'd woken up early today to take care of Gran and got her settled before my one p.m. shift. The train from Brooklyn to Manhattan was a long haul. I was a night owl; sleeping in was my thing. But clearly only five hours of sleep was getting to me.

I swallowed hard when he let go of her arm and she

bolted from him, clutching her baby to her chest, over to me. Once she was safely behind me, I readied myself to pull the trigger on this thing if he took even one step closer.

I realized that I would essentially be gassing myself as well, but we could pull the emergency brake or...

I blinked rapidly. His eyes weren't going back to normal.

Tatum, you need more sleep and less Red Bull!

The man widened his stance. Cocking his head unnaturally to the side, he inhaled deeply through his nose.

Dude was tall. Like *Do-you-play-basketball-professionally?* tall. But also big, like *Do-you-snack-on-small-children-for-fun?* big. I was pretty sure if nothing came out of this expired purple can when I pushed the button, then this was how I died. Saving a woman and her baby.

There were worse ways to go, I guess, but seventeen was young. I was hoping to travel the world, get married to the man of my dreams, and open my own restaurant before I died, but here we were.

"Shadowling," he growled, his lips curling into a snarl.

Dude was high, that was the only explanation. High on some new drug that made his eyes glow.

"Don't. Move," I shouted in a voice I imagined a cop would use.

He was grinning and the baby started to cry behind me, and now I was sweating like a pig.

The train announced the next stop, and my body nearly sagged with relief. The second the doors opened, the lady and I would get out and push the help button on the platform.

There was a blur of movement to my left, and then the guy launched himself at me. One second he was standing twenty feet away, the next he was barreling down on me.

"Spray him!" the lady shouted behind me, and I squeezed the button, praying that crushed-up jalapeño juices, or whatever they put in these things, would explode into his open, snarling mouth.

A red stream shot from the purple canister, and I waved my hand in a wide arc covering the man's entire face.

Success!

He fell backward, coughing and sputtering just as the train started to stop. My eyes burned as the mist made its way to the back of the car. I pulled my shirt up to cover my mouth and tried to take small breaths.

The train stopped just as the lady and I began to cough. Peering behind me, I glanced down at the man to make sure he wasn't going to attack. He was on one knee, scratching at his face and wheezing as the doors finally flew open.

Tears wept from the corners of my eyes as I made sure the woman and her baby got off first. There was an older couple about to get on, and I shook my head, hoping the alarm on my face conveyed the situation. They took one look at the man on the ground and backed up as I stepped off and spun around to make sure he wouldn't follow us off.

When my gaze landed on the would-be assailant, the breath hitched in my burning throat.

What. The. Hell. Is. That?

The man was still on one knee, coughing into his shirt, but on his back was...

No. I'm tired. This isn't real.

The inky black creature attached to the man's back looked up at me, and I stumbled backward. Semi-translucent and humanoid, the monster was more shadow than corporeal. But even so, it was a shadow with horns, and claws that were dug into the man's shoulders. A barbed tail whipped back and forth behind the pair.

The man lifted his head and glared at me. Red eyes blazed from both man and beast.

I was paralyzed in fear, locked in my position with a layer of sweat chilling my skin as the doors slid closed between us.

"You really saved us. Thank you," the lady said, pulling my gaze away from the now retreating train and whatever the heck that *thing* was.

No more horror movies for me. Gran was right, they were putting scary thoughts in my brain. I needed to watch more cartoons with cuddly talking animals. I would totally be down for hallucinating about talking bears or giraffes.

I turned to the woman, whose eyes were red rimmed, probably from my accidentally macing the both of us. My heart was thumping, but I tried not to let my fear show on my face. I didn't need to freak this poor lady out more than she already was.

"I'm just glad you and your baby are okay."

She looked on the verge of tears, and now that I saw her losing it, my throat started to tighten with emotion.

How close was she to getting attacked? I shivered just thinking about it.

Without warning, she pulled me into a hug, her arm going around me with her baby pressed between us.

"Seriously. *Thank you,*" she murmured in my ear.

I reached around her and squeezed, looking down at the little baby blowing spit bubbles between us, oblivious to what had just gone down.

When the woman pulled back, I really examined her face and realized she was older than I had previously thought. Maybe in her late thirties? Fine wrinkles kissed the edges of her eyes.

"How far do you live? Let me get you a cab," she offered, and started to lead me away from the subway, but I waved her off.

"No really, this is my stop. I'm just off Prospect."

Concern etched into her features. "You sure?"

I nodded.

Her gaze went to the pepper spray can in my hand and then to my grease-stained apron, which I still had on from work.

"I... thanks again," she said, and I nodded.

We'd shared something serious. One of us should probably call the cops and report the dude, but I was too tired, so I was going to leave that to her discretion.

With a final wave, I went left toward my street, and she went right to hail a cab.

I looked over my shoulder and realized I didn't even ask her name, but something about what I'd done, saving her from God-knows-what, made me feel good inside. My heroic deed nestled deep inside my soul, and I smiled knowing that I'd made a positive difference in someone's life.

By the time I spun back around to face forward, I was on a collision course. I knocked into a lady's shoulder, muttering an apology for not paying attention, and then looked up into her eyes.

Red.

I stumbled backward, holding in a gasp as I blinked rapidly. Glancing back at me—her eyes now a perfectly normal shade of blue—she scowled and muttered a choice word before moving on.

Okay, no more *Supernatural*, it was *SpongeBob* before bed or nothing.

I ran the rest of the way to the apartment I shared with Gran, hoping to push this night from my memory and sleep for twelve hours straight.

CHAPTER
TWO

The sound of something shattering jolted me awake from nightmares of shadow creatures and red eyes. *Gran!*

The thought of her hurting herself took me from out-cold to fully awake in an instant. I tried to jump out of my makeshift bed on the couch, but the blankets were twisted around me, suctioned to my legs like tentacles. With a yelp, I flopped to the floor in a heap.

"Don't touch anything. I'm coming," I called, and quickly worked to untangle myself.

Once on my feet, it only took a handful of rushed steps to get from the couch to the small galley kitchen, where Gran was hunched over picking up pieces of porcelain shards from a broken teacup.

Dropping to my knees, I moved to grab as many bits of the shattered cup as possible. I didn't want her to cut herself again. Gran was only in her early sixties, but arthritis had started to set into her fingers, stealing some of her dexterity.

"I got this, Gran. Don't worry about it."

"So clumsy. I'm sorry I woke you, sweetie." Using a chair as leverage, she pushed herself to her feet; her knee joints cracked and popped like popcorn.

I frowned. She used to be so mobile. Less than a year ago she was doing yoga in front of the TV and hauling groceries up to our fourth floor walk-up. Now her back was hunched like someone twenty years her senior, and she barely made it out of our apartment.

I glanced at the wall clock. Six thirty-six. Ouch. I only got about four hours of sleep. A far cry from the twelve I was hoping for, but that much rest was wishful thinking anyway. Gran was an early riser.

"It's okay. I was basically awake anyway." A lie, but only a white one.

Gran puckered her lips, seeing through me easily. The woman was sharp, except when she wasn't, which was happening more frequently than I'd like lately.

"What would you like for breakfast?" I asked as I dumped the porcelain bits into the garbage.

She waved me off. "I can feed myself."

I held my breath, only releasing it when she went for the milk and box of cereal rather than eggs or oatmeal. She used to be an amazing cook, but with her mind going in and out these days, the kitchen was a dangerous place.

Gran settled into the two-person bistro table adjacent to the kitchen, and I noticed a pink roller still in her brown and gray-streaked hair.

"How was work last night?" she asked. She held her spoon over her bowl of raisin bran, waiting for me to respond before digging in.

A vision of the man on the subway with the red eyes and shadow creature on his back flashed through my mind. I forced the memory of my hallucinations—most likely brought on from sleep deprivation and too many horror movies—from my mind. Stress made Gran's early onset dementia worse. Today was a good morning, and I wanted to enjoy it. Besides, the only issue to come out of last night was that I needed a new can of pepper spray, so I wasn't going to worry her over nothing.

I shrugged and forced a smile. "Same old, same old." Grabbing my own bowl of cereal, I joined her at the table. "Did you sleep well?"

She huffed out a breath. "I wish you'd let me sleep on the couch," she said rather than answer.

"What? And give up that prime real estate in front of the TV? Never!"

The truth was, I missed having a bedroom. Our old apartment wasn't much, but it was home and at least I'd had my own space. But this place was cheaper, which meant we could afford it, so I liked it well enough.

I enjoyed a solid half hour of conversation with Gran before she started to slip and called me Emery, my mother's name. I didn't correct her. I'd learned that only confused and upset her. To Gran, realizing I wasn't her was like losing her all over again.

"If the darkness eclipses the light, we're all lost." Gran looked into my eyes with so much terror that chills ran down my spine. "You have to hide Tatum, or he'll come for her one day."

I nodded, trying not to cry. "Okay, I will."

Sometimes I played into her delusions just to keep her calm. I had no idea what she was talking about, but in her own mind she believed every word she said, and that caused my blood to ice over.

I spent the rest of my day like I usually did: looking over bills I couldn't pay, calming Gran down when she got confused or scared, running quick errands, and trying—unsuccessfully—to get my homeschooling done.

I'd dropped out of public school at the beginning of the year to take care of Gran full-time. At this rate, it was going to be a miracle if I graduated next month, but not finishing high school wasn't what kept me awake at night.

Gran's episodes were getting worse. Her outbursts about darkness and light and some make-believe shadow war were getting more explosive by the day. Everything I'd read on the internet about paranoia in dementia patients said it was a sign of the late stages of the illness.

I didn't know how long I could keep this up. She needed around-the-clock care that I couldn't provide, but I didn't have the money to hire someone for when I wasn't there. If I took her to the doctor, I knew they'd put her in a state-run facility. Gran was the only family I had; it had always been us against the world. I just couldn't see that happen to her. I intended to keep us together as long as I could.

Five o'clock rolled around all too soon. My feet started to ache at the mere thought of being on them for eight hours straight again, but it was a paycheck, so I wasn't going to complain... much.

I made sure Gran took her bath, got an early dinner, and was settled in front of the television in her bedroom before I'd have to leave. When she wasn't looking, I also unplugged the stove so she couldn't use it—thank goodness it was electric instead of gas. When I'd gotten home last night, I'd found a bowl of cottage cheese with a fork in it sitting in the microwave. If she'd turned it on, the metal fork could have started a fire. The thought of her in a fire stabbed a spike of dread right in my heart.

Remembering that, I went back and unplugged the microwave too, just in case, and then hid the steak knives as well. It might be overkill, but better safe than sorry.

Maybe I should pour all the bleach and chemicals down the drain too.

Pushing everything from my mind, I headed out to work. The walk to the subway station was only two blocks and completely uneventful. It wasn't until I stepped onto the train that the weird incident from the night before broke through my mental blocks. I did my best to push it from my mind and made a point not to look too closely at anyone the whole way to work. If I spotted any glowing red eyes, I was going to need major therapy, and that wasn't something I could afford.

The little bell over the entrance to the diner chimed as I pushed the door open. It was the beginning of the dinner rush, so it was busy. I dodged customers and waved at a few co-workers as I headed to the back to clock in and throw on my apron.

The next several hours flew by in a blur of serving greasy burgers and milkshakes. It wasn't until after nine when things finally calmed. I actually preferred the dinner rush because it made the time fly. It was when customers trickled in that I got bored and questioned my life choices.

Right now I was bored.

I was refilling the coffeemaker when Stella nudged me. "Looks like you have an admirer." She wiggled her eyebrows and shot me a sly smile.

Admirer?

"So, who is he?" she asked. "A boyfriend you haven't told us about?"

A boyfriend? Ha, that was a joke. Who had time for guys? Certainly not me. I hoped someday I'd have the luxury of going on a date, but the thought of doing something so frivolous was laughable. My priorities were paying the bills—at least the important ones—and keeping Gran safe. I was currently on a self-imposed boy ban.

"What are you talking about?" I poured the grounds into the top of the machine, only half paying attention to Stella. She liked to mother me, and it was her thing to try and set me up with cute customers.

"Mr. tall, dark, and mysterious over there. He's been watching you for the last ten minutes at least. I assumed you knew him." The smile slipped from her face. "But if you don't, that behavior definitely registers on the creep-o-meter. Shoot. Maybe we should tell Sal someone's stalking you."

Once the coffeemaker was topped off, I wiped my hands on my apron. "Nah. It's probably nothing. Where did you say he was?"

Stella pursed her lips and gestured toward the back corner of the diner.

Tilting my head, I snuck a peek. Sal's Diner wasn't known for its amazing lighting, but some of the overheads must need to be replaced, because shadows darkened the customer Stella was talking about.

He sat at a table by himself, his long legs stretched out in front of him. He was built enough to fill out his long-sleeved shirt and dark washed jeans, but he held his head in such a way that most of his face was shaded.

From the angle of his body, though, it was clear he was staring at me. Now that I was aware of him, his hooded gaze was like a physical touch.

"I don't know him."

Even half obscured, the guy had a presence. I'd remember if I'd met him before.

"I'm getting Sal," Stella said, but I caught her arm before she ran off to the diner owner. Sal was probably in the back working on a stack of bills. There was no need to get him.

"Has he ordered yet?" I asked her. He was sitting in Stella's section. After the train attack last night, I should have been super wary of the attention, but something about the guy intrigued me.

She shook her head. "He said he was waiting for someone. I was going to suggest you wait on him, but if he's a creeper…"

There was a full cup of water on the table in front of him. The diner menu was pushed off to the side.

I got hit on regularly enough to know that I was attractive, but with my blond hair piled in a messy knot at the top of my head, hamburger grease smeared over the front of my apron, and my face scrubbed free of makeup, it's not like I was catwalk ready. The way the guy across the room was studying me seemed a little extreme.

Maybe it was curiosity—or maybe it was something else—but I had a sudden urge to go to him.

"Yeah. I've got this," I told my concerned friend.

Grabbing a menu, even though he clearly already had one, I started toward him. He held himself still, his gaze never leaving me as I crossed the diner.

By the time I reached his table, I'd half convinced myself he was a creeper like Stella suggested.

"Can I help you?" The question was polite, but my tone wasn't. The guy tipped his head back and the light from the dimmed overheads finally illuminated his face.

Day-um.

Chiseled jaw, high cheekbones, thick black brows hanging over forest green eyes, and a mop of black hair so shiny it would make a supermodel jealous. He was hands down the hottest guy I'd ever laid eyes on. I was suddenly less concerned he was a serial killer and more worried about the bacon grease and my lack of makeup.

I discreetly ran a hand over my hair to smooth it. Maybe I needed to rethink that no dating rule.

"That's what I'm trying to figure out." His voice brushed over me like a caress, deep and dark and smooth, making me shiver. The cherry on top was the slight accent. Not full British, but like he'd spent time in the UK as a child, or one of his parents was from there. He looked about twenty years old and had that edgy bad boy vibe going for him. Guys like this were dangerous. Guys like this got whatever they wanted.

"Huh?" I said, still in a bit of a fog. The combo of his looks and voice must have temporarily short-circuited my brain.

"You asked if you could help me," he reminded me. Was he trying to hide a smirk?

Gah, how embarrassing. I shook myself and then cleared my throat. "Right. So… do you want to hear the specials?"

Settling back in his seat, he crossed his arms over his

chest, and my eyes flicked to a brown leather wrist cuff he wore.

"What's your name?" he asked.

I frowned. Good-looking, but perhaps not too bright? I tapped my finger against my name tag that clearly said, "Tatum."

He didn't bother glancing down, his eyes stayed locked on mine. "What's your *last* name?"

Umm, excuse me? What kind of question was that? *A stalker question, that's what.*

"None of your business." I tapped my pen on my order pad and released a disappointed sigh. Why were all the hot ones weirdos?

He knitted his brows in frustration. "Your parents' house, then? Shade or Lumen?"

Shoot. I could have worked with good-looking and stupid. Good-looking and *crazy* was a bit too much for me. Pity.

I slid the menu in front of him as a not-so-subtle hint. "Yeah, so… did you want to order anything?"

He rubbed two fingers over his bottom lip, drawing my attention to his mouth. That did funny things to my belly, so I quickly refocused back on his eyes, which was almost as bad. Thick black lashes framed his emerald-green gaze, and I had to stop myself from fanning my heating face.

Mesmerized, I just stood there as his gaze leisurely traveled down to my toes and back up again. When his eyes connected with mine, I would have sworn the lights overhead flickered, but then his mouth twisted into a half-snarl. "On second thought, it appears you don't have anything I want."

A bucket of ice over the head couldn't have cooled me off quicker. The dude was *not* talking about food off our menu. I knew an insult when I heard one.

Jerk!

I didn't know what his game was, but I'd had enough.

Planting my hands on the table, I leaned forward, not quite breaching his personal space, but getting close to it.

"Listen, Linda," I said, and he lifted his eyebrows. I'd surprised him. Good. "This table is for paying customers. So if you're just going to sit here like a creeper in the corner, I'm going to have to insist that you get up and find somewhere else to park your ass."

The corner of his mouth twitched, and a glint of interest shone in his eyes.

Dude liked a girl with sass? I'd show him sass. Gran always said I was sharper than a knife when I was fired up, and this guy's weird behavior and unveiled insults had awoken the beast. He was about to get verbally filleted.

I opened my mouth to start my rant when a pop outside the diner caused both of us to look to the window.

The lamppost outside the diner had gone dark. There was another pop, and the light at the end of the street went out too, plunging the entire block into darkness.

The guy cursed under his breath. At the same time, I noticed something move under the unlit posts, but between the glare from the diner's lights on the window and the dark night, I couldn't see much.

Probably a car accident, or teens smashing the bulbs for fun. *Idiots.* That was going to make my walk to the subway extra fun tonight. *Goodie.*

I turned my attention back to the table, but the guy's seat was empty. He was just… gone.

The bell above the entrance chimed, and I twisted in time to catch a glimpse of his black shirt before the door swung shut behind him.

I glanced back and forth between the table and the entrance. *How did he get to the door so fast?*

Whatever. Maybe he was a ninja? Jerk hottie ninja with a sexy voice and crazy vibes.

Shaking my head, I grabbed the water glass Stella had brought him and noticed a crisp fifty-dollar bill under it.

Well, that was quite a tip from a guy who basically told me I was ugly.

Stella walked over with a rag to wipe down the table.

"You okay?" she asked.

"Yeah, yeah. Here." I tried to hand her the tip—it was her section after all—but she waved it off, insisting I take it. I only debated a couple of seconds before shoving the bill in my pocket. I wasn't going to get out of this pile of debt by turning down fifty-dollar tips.

It was bright in the corner table again, and I made a mental note to tell Sal the overhead lights were glitchy back there.

"So, who was that?" Stella asked as we made quick work of cleaning the table.

I cast another glance at the entrance. "I don't know, but I hope he doesn't come back."

But oddly, that might not be true, because I couldn't get those burning green eyes out of my mind.

CHAPTER THREE

I spent the entire rest of my shift glancing at the door and expecting the hot part-British guy to come back. The lights kept flickering over his booth, even though Sal came out and replaced the bulbs. It was past one a.m. by the time I'd cleaned my station and was ready to go home.

Gran had one rule about me working the diner late at night: if I got out past ten p.m., I had to take a cab home. In theory, this was great, but Gran didn't seem to realize that I worked in Manhattan and we lived in Brooklyn. A fifty-dollar cab ride home every late-night shift and we would never eat again. What Gran didn't know wouldn't hurt her, and with the big tip from the hot rude guy, I was going to buy a new can of pepper spray in the morning.

Walking the three blocks to the F-train, I kept looking over my shoulder, paranoid I was being followed. But every time I did I only saw the usual young partygoers making their way home from bars, three sheets to the wind.

The subway car I hopped on was occupied by a small group of teenagers. I only relaxed when I confirmed that none of them had red eyes. My recent cartoon binge was doing its job.

I put in my earbuds and let the beat of Above and Beyond work its way into my bones.

The group on board were talking animatedly, and I couldn't help but wonder what they were saying. Home-schooling and working all the time had left me little time to make friends. I wondered what normal people my age did at one a.m. on a Sunday morning. Pausing my music, I listened in.

"Shut up, Jacob, that's not how it happened!" The beautiful brunette with cherry red lipstick and blue eyes grinned as she swatted a good-looking guy with shaggy, dirty blond hair. She had some weird metal lasso whip attached to a thigh holster on her leg. I guess I wasn't really hip to the current fashions.

He grinned at her. "Oh really? I killed that de—" He shot his gaze over to me. Tucking my chin, I made it look like I was really intensely listening to my music. Jacob's voice lowered, but it was still loud enough for me to hear him say, "…demon before you even got there."

My eyes must have widened, because the short Asian girl with a waterfall of black hair flowing to her waist, and a giant tattoo of a sword on her arm, shushed him, and they all looked at me.

Curling my shoulders and hunching down into my seat,

I did my best to school my features. This conversation was getting interesting. Killing demons? Was that code for drugs nowadays? Like snorting cocaine? I killed a demon?

Oh man, maybe me not going to public school anymore was a good thing.

"She heard you," the highlighted brunette hissed.

Busted.

Grimacing, I flicked my gaze to them. I was about to look away when the guy she'd called Jacob stood and a giant set of golden *wings* sprouted from his back. They were feathered, and they shimmered as the light hit their solid form.

My mouth dropped open, a squeak leaking from my throat, and I squeezed my eyes shut.

"She sees!" the pretty black-haired girl shrieked.

"No way. She can't," the winged guy said.

I opened my eyes and the dude had stepped closer. He cocked his head as he regarded me closely. The ginormous wings at his back took up the entire width of the train car, but I could still see the startled gazes of his friends beside him.

I swallowed down a scream. *Someone put LSD in my water bottle. This isn't happening.*

"Hey, you okay?" he asked.

I stood, pulling out my empty purple can of pepper spray, and aimed it at him.

"Stay away!" I shouted, looking frantically at his golden wings. When I thought it couldn't get any weirder, tattoos began to form on his skin. White and pearlescent, they moved and glowed.

No.

No.

No.

"I'm telling you. She sees!" The Asian girl stepped forward and slapped a hand over the sword tattoo on her arm. When she pulled it back, a steel sword materialized as if coming to life and jumping off of her arm.

Fear choked me, freezing my vocal cords. Backing all the way up to the far corner of the train car, my arms shook as I held up the purple can, a paltry defense against wings and a sword. A tear rolled down my cheek.

"That's enough! Put it all away." A girl with tight curly brown hair and bronzed skin pushed to her feet and then nudged her way through the trio. I hadn't noticed her and another guy with a hoodie seated a little behind the others before, but they looked to be part of the same group. The guy in the back didn't bother to move; he just tilted his head in my direction. His hood covered his face, so I couldn't make out any of his features. For a split second I thought he might be the same hot guy from the diner, but his stature was leaner.

"She sees and you're terrifying her," the curly-haired newcomer said, gesturing toward me.

Just like that, the golden wings and glowing tattoos sucked into Jacob's body at the same time the sword in the girl's hand vanished into a puff of smoke.

The blue-eyed brunette plopped her hands on her hips. "That's impossible, Drea. We know every Shade or Lumen coming of age from here to Los Angeles."

I froze. Shade... Lumen... hadn't the guy from the diner used those same terms?

"Unless we don't?" the girl, Drea, told her firmly, and then glanced back at me with a furrowed brow. "Are you about to turn eighteen?" she asked.

Shock ripped through me. I was less than three weeks away from my eighteenth birthday—but what did that matter?

The train started to slow, and with it I glimpsed my salvation. I was nowhere near Brooklyn, but when the doors opened I leapt out, making a run for it to ground level.

The F-train was cursed, or possessed or something, and I was totally going to spend fifty dollars on a cab ride.

"Wait!" the teens called out after me, but I ignored them and booked it as fast as possible. My feet felt like they were going to fall off, but I took the stairs three at a time, my heart beating frantically in my chest.

"Hold up! We just want to talk!" Drea yelled.

Were they following me? I didn't dare look over my shoulder, I just ran as fast as I could to the ground level and popped out onto Bleeker Street. I went left and booked it toward a bodega, only to find out it was closed. Turning right, I found myself down an alley, and realized this was a *really* stupid idea.

I spun to head back out onto a lighted street, just in time to see five shadows enter the alley and cut off my escape.

No.

Gripping the pepper spray, I shook it, wondering if maybe there were some drops left.

Drea stepped forward and held her hands up in front of her. "We aren't going to hurt you."

I was panting, still trying to catch my breath. She didn't even look winded.

"Then stop following me!" I snapped.

She nodded. "Fair enough."

She looked behind her, and the four remaining shadows disappeared. Did two of them go up into the sky?

I whimpered, fully freaked out.

"My name is Drea, and I'm a Lumen," she stated with a kind smile.

"I don't know what that is!" I shouted, "but I want you to leave or I'll…" I bent down and picked up a loose brick. "I'll hurt you, okay."

Her lips curled into a quick smile, then her face took on a very serious expression. "If you can see and you are not affiliated and trained, that could be dangerous."

Affiliated? Like with a political party? That couldn't be what this was about. Politicians would do anything nowadays to get a vote, but slipping people hallucinogens to get them to register made no sense.

"Go away." I shook the brick at her, and she sighed, reaching into her pocket.

Pulling out a small white card, she laid it on the ground in front of her. "I just want to talk. About the things you've been seeing. Probably scary things."

I paled, chills running the length of my entire body. My tongue stuck to the roof of my mouth in fear.

"But I can see my presence is causing you more anxiety, and that's not what I want. Just call me, okay? Tomorrow?" Her voice was so kind, I felt myself growing confused.

"Just go!" I shouted.

She gave me a curt nod and then backed out of the alley and disappeared.

Holy hallucination hell.

I sighed in relief when I finally found myself alone. Walking over, I picked up the white card with a shaking hand.

There was a gold feather emblem on the front, and underneath was a phone number. No name, no other writing. My thoughts went to the dude in the train car, Jacob, and his wings. The feather on the card reminded me of them. I ran my fingers over the design, and it felt downy.

With a sigh, I walked to the end of the alley and hailed a cab. As he pulled away, I stared at the card, questioning my sanity, my life, my everything.

Did that just happen? Was the card even real? Was I losing touch with reality like Gran?

By the time we pulled up to my building, I decided I needed the cabbie to help me do a sanity check.

"Excuse me, sir. Can you see this? What's on it?" I held up the card.

He took it, smiling. "Cool feather. This some kind of underground club invite?"

It *was* real.

Reaching out, I took it back before paying him, and left a generous tip. "Thanks."

After letting myself into the apartment, I checked on Gran. She was sound asleep. I washed up and then made my way to the couch. Wrapping myself tightly in the blankets, I tried to go to sleep, but whenever I closed my eyes, visions of the guy's green eyes from the diner, or the golden wings and swirling tattoos, swam in my mind, keeping me wide awake.

A new thought struck me then.

What if Gran wasn't crazy? What if her rants about good and evil were real all along?

It was a long time before I slept.

CHAPTER
FOUR

I was paranoid for the rest of the week. How could I not be? I'd hallucinated on the subway two days in a row. Combine that with Gran's strange ramblings about forces of light and dark, and the bizarre half-conversation I had with the guy from the diner, and I was barely sleeping. I'd put myself on a strict visual diet of cartoons and *Animal Planet*, but that didn't help.

I hadn't stepped back on the subway for a full seven days. As much as I hated it, I now took the bus to work. I had to switch lines three times, and it added an extra forty-five minutes to my commute, but it was worth it. I only had one scary instance this past week. I thought I saw another shadowy creature attached to the back of a woman on my way to pick up groceries two days ago. It was in broad daylight. She was going into a building, so I'd only snagged a glimpse of her, but it was enough for the icy fingers of fear to grip my heart and squeeze.

One thing you want to be when you travel the city is aware, but I'd started keeping my gaze fixed on the ground in front of me whenever I ventured out. I was also jumpy at work, and Stella and the other wait staff had noticed. They shot me worried glances throughout my shifts. Yesterday, I'd dropped a tray full of food on a customer because I'd thought their eyes had flashed red, but when I was cleaning ketchup off the front of his shirt—as he was cussing me out —his eyes were a perfectly normal shade of mahogany brown.

Part of me feared I was losing my mind. If I could afford a therapist, I'd have already booked an appointment. The other part of me feared that I wasn't, and everything I saw was somehow real. Both options were terrifying and kept me up at night.

I had to do something about this. I needed help, but I didn't know who or where to go for answers.

I chewed my lip as I waited for my next order to come up. Reaching into my apron pocket, I absently brushed my fingers over the business card with the wing that Drea had given me. I'd started to do that for comfort a couple of days ago, and I'd almost worn a hole in it from repeated rubs. The card reminded me that those teenagers I'd met on the subway were real, and that frightened *and* reassured me.

I hadn't worked up the guts to call the number yet, but this push and pull inside of me was ripping me apart. Was I seeing things, or was there more to this world than I'd ever known? I wanted to know the truth, but I also wasn't ready.

Suddenly, the hairs on the back of my neck prickled and a chill ran down my spine.

Someone is watching me.

Holding my breath, I scanned the diner. Nothing looked out of the ordinary. The dinner rush was over, so there were only a couple of late-night regulars seated throughout the restaurant. None of them were looking my way, but I couldn't shake the feeling of being watched.

I glanced toward the windows, trying to see the street past the glare of the diner lights on the glass. I couldn't make out much. The streetlamps that exploded last week still hadn't been replaced, but as I squinted I caught something shift in the darkness outside. Taking a shallow breath, I focused on the dark shape, but still couldn't see any details.

Drifting away from the order counter, I walked slowly toward the entrance. Like a moth drawn to a flame, I kept moving until my nose skimmed the glass door. Bracing my hands against the handle, I peered into the darkness.

There was definitely something on the other side of the street. It looked a little broader than a person, but maybe that was just the shadow playing tricks on me.

Could it be a homeless person? Maybe someone waiting for a ride-share? But what if it was something else altogether?

As I watched, darkness spread behind the form, stretching and unfurrowing in a way that reminded me a whole lot of Jacob's wings, but these appendages were made of shadows and mist rather than solid golden feathers.

My heart pounded against my rib cage like it was trying to escape. I started to get lightheaded and dizzy, and so I sucked in a deep dredge of air.

One breath, two, three...

A hand landed in the middle of my back, and I screamed, backpedaling away from the door and smashing into the person behind me. We both went down in a heap of limbs.

"Tatum, geez. What has gotten into you?" Stella said as we untangled.

I pushed to my feet and snuck a quick look around the restaurant, mortified to see I'd captured the attention of every patron. Sal popped his head out from the kitchen and yelled, "Everything all right out there?"

"Yeah, we're okay. Sorry," I said as I reached a hand out and helped Stella to her feet. Sal shot me a frown, but then went back to the grill.

Stella's brows were pleated as she brushed herself. A few wisps of her reddish-brown hair had been pulled from its topknot, framing her heart-shaped face and making her look a bit younger than her thirty-five years.

I grimaced. "I thought..." I snuck a glance at the street, but there was nothing there. "Sorry. I'm just a little jumpy."

Pursing her lips, Stella planted her hands on her rounded hips. I knew that look. She'd slipped into mother mode. "You look pale. Are you feeling ill? Have you been eating enough?" Pity filled her gaze, softening her features and her tone. "Is it your gran? Is she getting worse?"

Stella was the only one who knew about Gran's deteriorating memory.

"Actually, Gran has had a great couple of days," I told her, and that was the truth. There were several times this past week that Gran had been lucid enough that I considered asking her about some of the things I'd seen, or her confusing ramblings. But I was too worried about sending her spiraling and losing what little time we had.

Stella sighed. "Then what's going on with you, Tatum?"

I shook my head, a pang of guilt gnawing at me for worrying her. "Really, it's nothing," I lied. "You just startled me. I've been watching too many scary movies."

She tilted her head and narrowed her gaze, a clear sign she didn't believe me. "Why don't you take a fifteen-minute break. I'll cover your table."

I opened my mouth to argue, then thought better of it. Maybe I did need to take a breather. "That would be great. Thanks."

There wasn't a break room in the diner, only Sal's office. He let us hang out in there if we wanted, but I needed a little fresh air to center myself. I walked past the kitchen and Sal's office and pushed through the back exit into the alley behind the restaurant. Cigarette butts littered the ground, and there was a definite funk coming from the dumpster, but it was quiet, and most importantly, well lit.

I leaned against the brick wall, hardly feeling the rough texture at my back. The warm late-spring air feathered over me, and I sighed, pulling the white card out of my apron.

Just do it, Tatum. At this point, what do you have to lose?

Taking a deep breath, I shoved my hand into my back pocket and grabbed my cell. The screen was cracked, and I'd already used what little data I could afford for the month, but it still made and received calls.

It took three tries to type the number in correctly because my hands were shaking so badly. With a hard swallow, I hit "send" before I could second guess myself.

The phone rang twice, and then the line picked up, triggering an automated voice message. "Thank you for calling Lumen Academy. If you'd like to speak to the front desk, please press one. To reach a member of the faculty, please press two. To report demonic activity in your precinct, please press three. To be connected with…"

A buzzing started in my ears, and I didn't even register the rest of the options.

Demonic activity?

Nope. *So.* Much. Nope.

I ended the call and almost dropped my phone when I tried to jam it back in my pocket. Calling that number was such a bad idea. This wasn't happening.

I slid to the ground, planting my butt on the dirty asphalt and not caring a lick that I was getting all sorts of gunk on my jeans and probably making my cell's cracked screen worse.

One minute leaked into five, and then ten. My breath came out in short rasps, and I knew I was on the verge of a panic attack. As I neared the end of my fifteen-minute break, I wasn't in any better shape than when I walked out into the alley.

Groaning, I shoved to my feet. I was about to head back inside when a voice sounded behind me.

"Hey!" The voice was feminine and familiar, but I couldn't quite place it. With my hand on the door, I turned to glance over my shoulder.

Drea, the girl from the subway, strode into the light. She was out of breath, her wild brown curls windblown; a fine layer of sweat glistened on her forehead.

"Oh good. I caught you. Give me a second," she said as she bent over to collect herself. Glowing tattoos appeared on her arms and started to swirl but disappeared quickly. When she straightened, she looked rejuvenated.

What the...?

I white-knuckled the door handle, wanting to go screaming into the diner, but also needing answers I was starting to worry only she could give me.

"How did you find me?" I demanded to know.

"Your phone call," she said. "Our dispatch tracked your location."

Dispatch? "You tracked me?"

"Yeah. We were a couple of miles away, and I figured running here would be quicker than a cab."

"We?"

"Geez, Drea," said another voice from beyond the ring of light. "Did you have to take off like that?" The pretty blue-eyed brunette girl from the subway joined Drea a moment later. The smaller, black-haired girl, the guy in a hoodie, and Jacob followed in her wake.

My anxiety skyrocketed.

Seeing my distress, Drea took a step forward and softened her voice. "We're here to help you. I promise. I'm Drea," she said, pointing at her own chest. "This is Skye..." She pointed to the brunette. "Marlow..." The girl with the sword tattoo waved. "Dash..." The hooded guy just grunted and nodded his head. She finally indicated the golden wing guy. "...and Jacob. We're Lumens. Do you know what that means?"

I shook my head, not feeling capable of words at this point.

"I still can't believe it," Skye said as she flipped her sleek ponytail over her shoulder and gave me a once-over. "How is it possible she was missed?"

"If her sight just kicked in, it explains the spike in energy we registered a week back," Marlow added, glancing down at some sort of device in her hand.

I had no idea what they were talking about, and I seriously wanted to run back inside, but my body wouldn't let me. I stood there frozen, listening.

Drea held up her hands. "Let's not jump to any conclusions. We'll get her back to the academy and they can do a lineage test and figure out—"

Lineage test? Nah-ah. I was out.

Lurching backward, I yanked open the diner door, ready to bolt back to the relative safety of the diner.

"Wait!" Drea called, but I ignored her.

Arms banded around my waist when I was already halfway over the threshold. I was yanked backward and up into the air. In a blink, my feet dangled at least ten feet off the ground, and a shriek tore from my throat.

What just happened?

Survival instinct kicked in. I thrashed. Freeing an arm, I jabbed my elbow up and it connected with my captor's face. I heard the satisfying crunch of bone, and a muttered curse, but the hold around my middle didn't loosen. If anything, it restricted even more.

"Get down here, Jacob!" Drea demanded from below. "You're just scaring her even more."

Oh no. Winged boy had me.

I'm flying!

Glancing over my shoulder, I could see his feathered wings flapping to keep us airborne. That's when I went berserk, attacking Jacob like a feral cat.

I had one arm and two legs free, and that was enough for me. Swinging and kicking wildly, I mostly connected with air, but occasionally clipped one of his body parts. Twisting, I managed to rotate in his embrace, which gave me more leverage and a better range of motion.

"I was only trying to stop—" Jacob's words cut off when I kneed him in the groin.

His arms instantly loosened, and I slipped from his grasp. I clearly didn't think this through. Even though we weren't more than a story off the ground, the fall was going to hurt and possibly break a bone or two.

The light bulb in the alley exploded, raining down a shower of sparks as I fell, plunging us into darkness. I hardly had a moment to brace for impact before strong arms wrapped around me, stopping my fall. The air was forced from my lungs, but besides that, I was unharmed.

I blinked and looked up into a pair of vibrant green eyes, lit by the few light bulbs that had yet to shatter.

It was *him*. The maybe-British rude guy from last week.

"You," I said, the weight of accusation heavy in my voice.

His eyes were hard, just shy of unfriendly, as he swept his gaze over my face. He set me on my feet and then stepped in front of me.

The alley was now dim but not completely dark. I looked around the guy to see the others getting to their feet. Had rude-guy somehow blasted them all to the ground?

"Gage," Jacob spat, and took a hostile step forward. "What are you doing here?"

The guy in the hoodie, Dash, moved quickly in front of Jacob, placing two hands on his chest to stop him.

"Not worth it," Dash said, his voice a low rumble that echoed off the brick alleyway walls. I realized with a start that that was the first time he'd spoken in my presence.

Jacob sneered at Gage over Dash's shoulder and then flexed his wings in an obvious show of aggression. The hard look on his face said that he and my would-be-rescuer were far from friendly with each other.

Gage. I looked over at him. The name fit him. It was strong and unique.

In front of me, Gage rolled his shoulders and then darkness sprang from his back, forming two giant wings made of shadow and smoke that were nothing like Jacob's. Black as night and closer to bat wings than birds', the ends touched the brick walls on either side of us.

Holy mother of all things scary.

I gasped, putting a few extra feet between us.

Hearing my retreat, Gage glanced over his shoulder and pinned me with a hard stare.

The look was serious enough to freeze me in my tracks. When he was satisfied I wasn't going to bolt, he turned back to the others.

"You want to rumble, Jakey? Because if so, I'm ready." Cracking his neck, Gage squared up and arched his shadow wings in the same aggressive manner Jacob had.

I didn't mean to notice, but Gage's wings were definitely bigger than Jacob's. Not that size mattered.

"Don't be stupid," Jacob spat. "You're outnumbered. We'd take you down in under five seconds."

Gage glared at the group and then chuckled. "Nah. I like these odds. I'd be happy to take you all out... *again.*"

Dash turned, facing Gage. He stepped out of Jacob's way and crossed his arms over his chest. With the lights blown out and that dang hood up, I still couldn't see what he looked like.

Drea moved forward, pushing between Jacob and Dash. "Okay, guys, take it down a notch. We're not here to fight. This is neutral territory. We're just trying to help Tatum."

The breath caught in my throat. How did she know my name?

Gage turned his head so he could see me from his periphery. "Were these four *helping* you?" he asked.

"I… um… " My heartbeat was intense before, but now it raged. "No?"

"There you have it." I couldn't see his face when he looked back to the others, but I could hear the smirk in his words. "Besides, there is no need to help her. She's a Shade, just like her mother. So she's under *my* jurisdiction."

Chills ran the length of my entire body. My *mother*?

Drea sighed as Skye and Marlow exchanged a glance.

Pearlescent tattoos appeared on Jacob's arms, brightening the air around him. "No. She has a choice, and you *will* let her choose," he growled.

Gage snarled as dark tattoos snaked over the exposed skin on his neck and forearms, disappearing under the leather cuff he wore on his right wrist before popping back up on the backside of his hand. The tattoos leaked smoke and made the area around him grow even murkier.

Without warning, Gage rushed Jacob, who sprinted forward to meet him. They collided, and the world exploded into arcs of light and shadow.

Either this was by far the most detailed hallucination I'd ever had, or it was real.

Gage and Jacob were a tangle of shadows and light, up in the air one second and down on the ground the next. The streetlights at the far end of the alley pulsed ominously from bright as the sun to pitch black. I thought for sure Dash would join in if a brawl broke out, but he just stood there and watched.

"Knock it off, you idiots!" Marlow stepped forward and slapped the sword tattoo on her arm. It peeled from her body like a sticker, before puffing up into a three-dimensional object.

Skye rolled her eyes as she inspected the ends of her hair. "I say let them kill each other. I'm sick of the pissing match between these two."

Drea glared at Skye. "We need to keep the peace." She was clearly the team leader of whatever their little angel gang was. "Gage Alston and Jacob Carter, you will stand down right this instant or I'll electrocute you both!" She clapped her hands and every light in the entire city block illuminated so brightly I had to squint to continue to look at her.

Whoa.

"Way to keep the peace," Skye snickered.

The boys untangled, and I was about to ask them what the heck they wanted with me when someone inside the diner let loose with a bloodcurdling scream loud enough to be heard in the alley.

My heart leapt into my throat. Was that Stella? Had Drea's light display freaked her out?

Before I could wonder further, the lights went out. Not just the alley streetlamps but the little light bulb over the Coach Purse billboard above us, the apartment lights in the building next door, and the whole diner. *Everything* was plunged into an eerie darkness.

"Cut it out, Gage, you've made your point," Drea growled.

Gage looked slightly unsettled. "That wasn't me."

"If that wasn't you, that means..." The moonlight across Drea's face showed her angry expression instantly drain, replaced with a look of horror. She snapped her gaze to the diner as something crashed behind the closed door. I tore across the alley and into the restaurant.

"Stella!" I shouted, knowing in my gut that something was really wrong.

The interior of the diner was pitch black. Screams and the crash of tables being tossed over made the hairs on the back of my neck stand up.

"I've got this," Drea called from behind me, and a blinding light appeared within the diner so suddenly that I winced.

The second the light reduced to a normal wattage, my gaze fell to Stella, who stood by the coffee cart next to the cash register.

My tongue stuck to the roof of my mouth, and my muscles locked. The ugliest, most horrifying creature stood behind Stella as she cried and shook in fear. The monster was so tall that if it weren't hunched over my friend, its curled horns would have pierced the ceiling. One of its charred and peeling arms was looped around Stella's waist, the other was pressed against the length of her arm. It had wrapped a clawed hand around her fingers, forcing her to keep hold of the bloody pie cutter in her hand.

For the first time, I noticed the man at Stella's feet. A bloom of red was spreading on the tiles beneath him.

"He's a level five. I've alerted the senior Lumens." Marlow stepped up next to Drea with that same strange black device in her hand. It was like an old school phone with a tiny screen and buttons, but also had dials. The number "five" scrolled across the screen as it beeped incessantly. "We're supposed to refrain from engaging. They only want us to secure the diner until they get here. Their ETA is five minutes."

"This ought to be entertaining," Gage said as he sat on a barstool and leaned back against the counter.

Ignoring Gage, Drea nodded to Marlow in understanding. "As long as the level five doesn't start feeding, she won't sustain any permanent damage."

Feeding! Did she just say *feeding?*

"A little help please!" Skye's voice rang through the diner from deep in the alleyway.

The back door was propped open, and there, in the alley, were more of the creatures, but these were hunched over on all fours and going after Jacob and Dash like wild animals. The boys were fighting the beasts off with swords of light.

With a gasp, Drea took off in their direction.

Releasing an annoyed sigh, Gage rolled his eyes, barking at me, "Stay put," and then stomped off after her.

"Crap!" Marlow hissed, reaching to touch her forearm and coming away with a shining gold dagger.

As Marlow moved to the diner's alley doorway to help her friends fight the creatures, I heard Stella whimper.

I spun and met my friend's horrified expression. She looked so scared, but I didn't think she could see the creature holding her in its grasp. She certainly wasn't acting like it was there. The way her body trembled, I began to worry she was going into shock.

"Tatum!" Stella whined. "He... attacked me." She pointed to the man on the ground, whom she'd diced with the pie cutter.

Stepping backward a few paces, I glanced through the open kitchen door to see Sal unconscious on the ground, scrambled eggs and slices of ham strewn across the floor.

Reaching out, I grabbed a frying pan and a kitchen knife, the closest objects to me, and turned to face my friend.

She looked incredulously at the unconscious man at her feet with the pie cutter head wound, but all I could focus on was the creature plastered against her back. With the head of a horned goat and three eyes, it had the body of a person, but it was made of shadows, like Gage's wings.

I shivered as it leaned forward and bit into Stella's neck. She didn't move, didn't seem to notice as it... fed off of her?

Oh hell no. I burst into action, running forward with the knife and pan raised high.

"Stella, there's someone behind you!" I yelled. "Lie down and cover your eyes!"

She screamed in terror at the prospect of another assailant and dropped to the ground next to the man she'd knocked out. At least I hoped he was only unconscious and not dead.

When I reached Stella, the creature was still attached to her, having followed her down to the ground. I could barely make out Stella's shaking form through the grotesque smoke and shadowy body of the monster covering her. Lifting its head from her neck, it looked up at me and its eyes flashed red.

I'd always been a pretty chill person—it really took a lot to rattle me; a side effect of growing up with an elderly woman who talked to herself half the day—but when that monster looked up at me I'd never been so mad in my entire life. I saw red.

I quickly came to terms that this monster was real, and I wanted the bastard off of my friend.

"Get. Off. Of. Her," I growled through gritted teeth.

The goat-headed creature grinned, flashing sharp teeth in my direction, then it stood up, moving away from Stella who still lay flat on the tiled floor, bawling uncontrollably.

I was just wondering how I was going to stab a shadow when it swiped at me with a clawed hand. It knocked the knife from my grip, and the blade slid across the floor.

Oh crap.

Even transparent, these bastards could move objects?

I reared back, stumbling away to put distance between me and the monster as I tried to come up with a plan, but there was no time for strategy, so I gave into instinct.

With a battle cry, I lashed out with the frying pan, cracking one of the creature's horns with more strength than I thought I had in these tiny arms, and it broke right off.

"Yes!" I shouted.

The horn hit the ground and then disappeared into a puff of smoke. The creature tipped back its head, roaring in a voice that was not animal, nor human, but wholly evil and beyond this world.

When it snapped back to face me, I wasted no time lashing out with the pan again, going for its face this time. It dodged, avoiding my makeshift weapon, and I lightly grazed its chest, just pissing it off further.

It lifted one hoofed foot and kicked outward, slamming me right in my chest, and I went flying.

Definitely did not plan this well, was my last thought before my head cracked into the wall and everything went black.

CHAPTER
FIVE

I came to feeling like my skull had been cracked in two and my eyeballs had a heartbeat. I moaned, daring to open my eyes and let the light filter in.

What the...? Where was I? Not in my apartment, that was for sure.

I was cushioned on a soft mattress. I ran my fingers over the charcoal-colored silk sheets, looking out at the amazing city skyline from the floor-to-ceiling windows and groaned. The giant room had black striped wallpaper running vertically from floor to ceiling. There were twin nightstands on either side of the king-sized bed, a large black wardrobe, matching dresser, a fancy looking sofa chair, and a side table. In the corner was a desk with some books on it. I scanned the titles: *Demonology, Shadow work, Portals.* Panic flooded my system as the memory of last night came rushing back to me.

Stella!

I bolted upright, regretting the quick action when dizziness washed over me and my vision blurred. Standing gingerly, I got my footing and then ran to the other side of the room, where my cell phone and shoes lay. Turning my phone on, I saw ten missed texts.

One was Gran saying she left me dinner, the rest were Stella wondering if I was okay and asking where I was.

Crap. Crap. Crap.

Where was I? What time was it? I had to get back to Gran.

There were two doors, one on the far wall that I assumed led to a bathroom, and one nearest me that I was hoping got me the heck out of here.

Going to what I prayed was the exit door, I twisted the handle and peered out into a hallway.

Whoa.

I'd assumed I was inside of a bedroom in an apartment but no, the hallway was over a hundred feet long and filled with numbered doors. It was like a fancy dormitory or hotel.

"Tate?" a familiar deep voice called out behind me, and I jumped, spinning and slamming against the door so that it snapped shut.

Holy nearly naked dude.

Gage stood in the doorway to the bathroom, the towel tied around his waist accentuating the V-shaped muscles at his abdomen. But instead of lingering there, where any normal girl's eyes would, my gaze flew to the three deep gashes across his chest.

"You're hurt!" I stepped closer to him.

He looked at me behind those thick dark lashes and waved me off casually. "I've had worse."

My eyes widened. "That needs stitches—I can see your organs," I blurted. Okay, maybe a slight exaggeration, but there was definitely stuff showing that shouldn't.

He chuckled, walking over to a dresser and pulling out clothes. "I've got an appointment with the healer," he said with his back to me.

I looked from him and then to the bed, wondering if we'd shared it last night. I was about to ask, when my gaze fell on the folded blanket and pillow on the floor at the end.

Phew. Did not randomly share bed with scary hot guy with shadow wings.

"What happened last night? Where am I? How did I get here? And by the way, my name is Tatum, not Tate."

He threw a shirt over his bloody chest and then started to pull his boxer briefs on under his towel.

Okay that was going to fall and show his—

I looked away, but not before I caught a hint of butt cheek.

This guy was clearly comfortable around the ladies. I wouldn't be caught dead changing in front of some dude I'd just met.

Once fully dressed, he turned to face me.

Sighing, he looked me up and down. "You were attacked

by a level five demon last night. I saved your life and brought you here to Shade Academy. You're welcome."

He certainly wouldn't be winning any personality awards anytime soon.

Demon. He'd said *demon*. That goat creature was a—

Shade Academy. My mind bounced to the recording from the phone number I called on the white card. Lumen Academy. Rival schools maybe? There was definitely some bad blood between Jacob and Gage. At this point, that was the least important bit of information I needed, so I shelved my questions about Lumens and Shades until later.

"What happened to my friend, Stella? Is she okay?"

"She's fine. Her memory's been wiped. She thinks there was a power outage and some thugs tried to rob the restaurant."

Memory wiped. That was a thing? My head was going to explode, but I plunged forward anyway.

"Okay, so there are demons in the world. No biggie. I can accept that." I was trying to sound nonchalant, but I think it came off as a little crazed. "But why can I see them all of a sudden?"

Leaning back against the dresser, Gage crossed his arms over his chest. "Because you're a Watcher and almost of age. Your sight is finally kicking in."

I frowned. "What's a Watcher?"

"An earthbound angel," Gage said matter-of-factly.

There was a beat of silence where we just stared at each other. His gaze was wary, watchful as I digested his answer.

"And so… you're saying I'm an angel?"

He nodded slowly.

I laughed then, like a full-on chortle. He was crazy.

His expression didn't change. He looked like he wasn't in the mood for this. My laughter trailed off and morphed into a strangled choking sound. He was serious.

I sucked in a deep breath through my nose, and then counted to three before releasing it. "No, that can't be right. How is it possible to be some sort of angelic being and never know? That doesn't make any sense."

"We function mostly as human until we come into our full powers at age eighteen. It's very uncommon for one of our novices to be unaware of their lineage." He raised one eyebrow, the shadow of a smirk dancing on his lips. "Here's another pill to swallow. You'll only have until the night of your eighteenth birthday to decide whose team you want to be on. Shades or Lumens. That gives you, what…?" He looked at his naked wrist, pretending there was a watch there. "…all of nine days to decide?"

Yes, he was right. It *was* nine days until my eighteenth birthday. How did he know that? My heart pounded so hard I feared it would punch a hole through my chest.

Okay, Tatum. Don't freak out. If you play it cool you'll get more information.

"You expect me to… pick a team? How am I supposed to do that? I don't know anything about Shades or Lumens."

"Right." He pushed off the dresser and prowled toward me, his long legs eating up the space between us quickly. I backed up until I bumped into the wall. Gage stopped a foot in front of me. "You'll have the opportunity to tour both academies. Those are the rules."

"And if I don't want to choose? If I just want to go about my life like I used to?" I asked.

A wicked smile stretched over his mouth; he ran his tongue over his top teeth. "If you don't pick a side by your eighteenth birthday, the demons will be able to sense you. You wouldn't last a week without a house affiliation. The demons would hunt you down. They like nothing better than to feast on Watchers' flesh and soul."

He stared at me with those searing green eyes and the room suddenly felt so much smaller. He was trying to scare me, I knew he was, but I also believed he was telling the truth.

My phone buzzed, breaking the tension between us, and I glanced down at the screen. There was a text from Gran.

Gran: *I can't seem to get the stovetop to work. I'm going to call a repair man.*

Oh no. No, no, no, no. If she figured out that I unplugged it, she was going to burn the place down.

"Listen, this has all been super fascinating, but I can't stay. I have to get back or my gran will call the cops." Only a slight bending of the truth. If Gran was lucid enough to realize how long I'd been gone, then she might think to get help.

He jerked his chin, indicating the cell in my hand. "Just call her and tell her you're at that greasy diner. That's usually where you are when you leave your apartment anyway."

O-kay, that was creepy. "How do you know where I go when I leave my apartment?"

A muscle in Gage's jaw jumped. "Just call her," he ordered.

I narrowed my eyes, instantly suspicious.

We met at the diner over a week ago. Had he been following me the whole time? And if so, why wouldn't he have made himself known? Why wait this long to reveal the truth to me?

The phone buzzed again, and I peered down.

Gran: *Never mind, I got it working.*

Shoot.

I quickly dialed Gran's number and she picked up on the third ring. "Tatum! I got the range working. It was just unplugged. Are you in the mood for raspberry muffins or blueberry? I'm about to make a batch."

"No, Gran, don't make muffins. I, ah…" Although her muffins were delicious, I had to think up something to keep her from using the stove or oven. "I'm bringing home a treat for breakfast. Can you just have some cereal until I get back?"

I hated lying to her.

"You're coming home this morning?" She sounded confused. "Aren't you working?"

Right. Gage wasn't wrong about me usually only being at the diner or apartment. When Gran woke up this morning and I wasn't there, she probably assumed I was working. And if I was working the morning shift, I wouldn't be back until well after lunch. Argh. This was one of the problems with lying; it was too easy to get caught in your own web.

"I mean a treat after lunch. I'm only working a half-shift. Can you hold off on making anything special so we can bake it together?"

She grumbled a bit before agreeing. Baking with Gran when I was little was one of my fondest memories. I ended the call as quickly as possible, relieved that she seemed to be having a good morning. I'd been absent since late afternoon yesterday. It made me twitchy to leave her alone for this long.

Next, I quickly sent off a text to Stella, letting her know that I was all right. I didn't care what Gage said, I still wanted to check in with her.

Once that was done, I closed my eyes and bumped the back of my head against the wall. When did life get so complicated?

Something brushed against my cheek, and I snapped my eyes open in time to see Gage pull his hand away from my face. He'd tucked a lock of hair behind my ear.

Okay, I'm awake.

He puckered his eyebrows like he was confused by his own action, but then wiped all emotion from his face.

"Tate, your days of hiding are over," he said. The words

were particularly ominous uttered in his deep and accented timbre.

"It's Tatum, *not* Tate," I said, unsure on how else to respond.

"Yeah, I heard you the first time." He leaned forward and a full body flush washed over me. He was inches from my mouth, and God help me, I couldn't look away from his lips. I knew I needed to move—or deliver a well-placed throat punch—but I just stood there, in silent anticipation.

"You're blocking the door," Gage said, chuckling darkly, telling me he knew exactly where my thoughts had gone.

Embarrassment reddened my cheeks and slowed my response time. Gage tugged on the door handle, and it popped open, pushing me forward. He shifted to the side when I stumbled.

"Look, I've got a busy day. I was instructed to make sure you didn't die, and I did that. Now I'm going to go to my healer appointment while Indigo gives you a tour, and then you can make your choice. Makes no difference to me." He brushed past me into the hallway.

I'd been dismissed.

Rude!

"You're a class act," I snarled. "You know that."

He shrugged as if he didn't care. "See you Monday. Or not. Whatever."

He walked over to a door across the hall and knocked twice. A girl with a black pixie cut popped her head out and he whispered something to her before striding off down the hall.

Ugh, what was his problem?

I crossed my arms and glared at his retreating back, suddenly hoping his cuts got infected.

"Tatum Powers?" Indigo looked like a young college student, maybe eighteen or nineteen, and wore ripped jeans and a cut off Beatles t-shirt, showing her belly. She stepped out into the hallway; her messy black hair all spiked up.

"Uh hey." I waved at her, totally weirded out that she knew my last name.

She gave me a kind smile and then looked at Gage, who had just reached the end of the hallway.

"Don't worry, it wasn't anything you did. He's had a stick up his butt since he moved here from London when he was twelve."

I snort laughed, glad that she thought the same about Grumpy Gage that I did. "You've known him since he was twelve?"

I tried to envision a middle-school-aged Gage and couldn't.

Indigo nodded, rocking on her heels. "My parents were friends with his... mom."

Were.

My heart stopped. Either her parents were dead, or his mom was. Or maybe they had a falling out, but I didn't think so.

I cleared my throat. "So, I'm pretty new to all this..." I

gestured to the hallway. "Can you explain more about the Shades and Lumens?"

Indigo nodded, starting to walk down the hall. "It was during the Black Plague of 1348 in England that the first recorded demon attack happened."

I skidded to a stop and looked at her with a slack jaw.

Indigo paused with me. "Twenty-five million people died in Europe alone. About a third of the continent's population. We think that much death opened the first portal to the Netherworld and summoned the demons somehow."

She resumed walking, and I struggled to keep up with her, chills running the length of my arms. Netherworld?

Holy crap.

Indigo gave me a side glance. "Watchers have lived on Earth since the beginning of time. Blending in with humanity over the millennia, like perfect sleeper agents. But it wasn't until the first portal opened that they started to awaken to their powers—they started to *see*."

I was so enthralled in the little history lesson that I didn't notice the girl coming down the hall until she muttered, "Excuse me" and I had to flatten myself against the wall so that she could pass.

I inhaled as she did and got a whiff of sulfur and oil.

Yuck.

"What happened when they started to see?" I prodded her.

Indigo grinned, enjoying my amusement of her storytelling. "They were visited by both the archangel Cael, *and* the fallen angel Apollyon, and given a choice. Whichever side they chose would determine where their power was rooted and which gifts they inherited."

Archangel? Fallen angel? I wanted to push everything she said away as fiction, but what I'd seen over the last twenty-four hours alone made me believe her in my heart of hearts.

Indigo took a right at the end of the hallway and led us to a cafeteria. There were long, rectangular tables spanning the large space, and a countertop at the far end. Various students milled about eating and drinking.

"The ones who chose Cael," she continued, "were later called the Lumens and tasked with fighting the demons who never seem to stop coming to Earth. For every one they kill, three more pop up."

Shivers ran down my spine at that.

"And the Shades?" I asked, getting the impression I was currently in the belly of the beast.

She grinned. "The Watchers that chose to be gifted by Apollyon were not only blessed with power beyond that of a Lumen, they were given riches beyond their wildest dreams."

Interesting.

I wanted to hear about the riches she spoke of, but there was something more important on my mind. "If the Lumens were tasked with fighting demons, what were the Shades tasked with?"

"Guarding the portals and keeping Lumens from interfering with the demons' work."

"Wait." I stopped dead in my tracks. "You *work* for those creatures?" My stomach rolled at even the thought of it. Disgust must have been written all over my face because Indigo immediately went on the defense.

"What, they don't hurt anyone," she said.

I reached up and gingerly prodded the knot at the back of my head. The demon I'd come up against had kicked me clean across the diner and into a wall. That had hurt plenty. Not to mention it had been feeding off of Stella.

Indigo's gaze tracked my movements, and she went on to say, "Well, I mean not really. Most of them can only physically actually touch the Watchers. The vast majority of them ghost through regular humans and can only influence their behaviors. It's not that big of a deal."

Yeah. No. I wasn't buying that. "The one that had my friend last night did *not* just ghost through her. It was holding on to her. It bit her. It was feeding from her."

Indigo grimaced but tried to cover the look quickly. She cleared her throat and then shrugged like it was no big deal. "Most humans hardly notice when a demon feeds from them."

Hardly notice. Pfft. I didn't know much about this world, but even I could tell there was a lot of gray in that sentence.

"It's just a job. One we get paid really well for." She grinned at the mention of money.

I didn't want to care about the money, but… "How well?"

"Starting salary for a first-year hunter is six-figures. It goes up from there. Some of our best hunters clear up to nine figures a year."

I choked on my spit, hacking into my hand and sputtering as I tried to breathe in fresh air. Nine figures was in the hundreds of millions of dollars.

"That much money for playing a glorified security officer?" I wheezed.

I mean, I didn't want to work for the bad guys, but with cash like that, even the starting salary would put Gran in the nicest assisted living facility money could buy. It was tempting. It's not like I would be spawning demons, I was just protecting the entrance to their home, in what I assumed was Hell. Or the Netherworld. Or whatever they called it.

Yeah, that was bad.

Hell, bad. Demons, bad. I scolded myself.

I cleared my throat. "And I have to choose?"

Indigo nodded and moved us to the food line. "If you don't, the demons will be attracted to you, and if you have no house affiliation..." She dragged a finger across her neck.

Yikes. Okay. Gage hadn't been exaggerating about that bit.

We both grabbed a breakfast burrito and then kept walking. I remembered something from the night before. "Umm, Indigo, Gage said my mom was a Shade?"

Indigo grinned. "Emery Powers was the most fearsome Shade the academy had seen in years. The coolest part was she came from a long line of Lumens and switched sides. We love when that happens."

A pang of sadness sliced through my heart at that. I never knew my mother, but it was hard to believe anyone that Gran raised would choose to work for demons.

Long line of Lumens… did that mean that Gran was a Watcher? No. No way. Gran baked cookies and liked to binge watch reality shows. She couldn't be an angelic super-soldier, could she?

"And what about my dad?" I asked, the ball of emotion lodged in my throat making it hard to speak.

"That I don't know," Indigo said.

I choked down the disappointment. I never knew my dad, and Gran wouldn't talk about him. I supposed it was wishful thinking to hope I'd get all my questions answered today.

"But your mom was definitely one of us."

"I need proof." I could barely find my voice. They knew her name, they knew so much. It had to be true but still, I needed to see it for myself. A registration form, a picture, something that would link her to Shade Academy.

Indigo nodded, taking a bite of the breakfast burrito. Leading us out of the cafeteria, she traversed a maze of hallways as I nibbled on my own burrito. My head spun.

An instant six-figure salary.

My mom had probably been a Shade.

Work for demons.

Breathe.

Everything about Shade Academy was top-notch and expensive looking. White marble, stainless steel, all glass, and from what I could tell right in the heart of Manhattan. When we reached a library and Indigo pushed the doors open, I wrapped the rest of my burrito and held on to it as I scanned the space.

Wow, now *this* was a library. Floor-to-ceiling bookshelves were crammed with leather-bound tomes. Two large sliding ladders were leaned against the shelves.

Round tables were scattered about the room, and a tall, lithe woman sat behind a desk. As we approached, she looked up and waved at Indigo, who strolled right past and over to a back shelf that was encased in glass.

My phone buzzed with a text from a number I didn't recognize. I frowned, opening it quickly.

Unknown: *Hey, it's Drea. I'm outside Shade Academy waiting for you.*

My eyes widened. Drea was outside right now? I peered out the tall floor-to-ceiling windows and spotted her across the street at a coffee shop. Skye was by her side.

Maybe I should excuse myself and go talk to them?

My phone buzzed again.

Drea: *Don't believe a word from their lying mouths. And don't agree to anything until I talk with you!*

I swallowed hard. I didn't know what she was talking about, but even her text sounded frantic.

"Your mom," Indigo said, interrupting my thoughts.

I looked up to where she was pointing, and the breath

was stolen from my lungs. Tears immediately started to well in my eyes.

It was her. Just like the pictures Gran showed me with her long blond hair and upturned nose. She was smiling, standing with some other students, and holding up a trophy of some sort. She looked so happy, at least for a Shade.

How could you help protect demons and be happy was beyond me. Maybe it was the cash? I loved the diner, but not having to worry about bills would definitely make me happy.

There was text under the photo. A list of names in small cursive script, including my mother's.

I was about to ask something else when a chill came over my skin.

"Tatum Powers," a smooth, deep, male voice called from behind me.

I turned slowly and came face to face with the spitting image of Gage, only older. The man was tall, with dark hair feathered through with gray at the temple; there was a hardness in his green eyes that made me leery of him. This was without a doubt Gage's father. Next to him stood a woman with long red hair that fell to her waist in waves. She gripped a notepad and had a sugary smile that seemed as fake as her overly plumped lips.

"Everyone knows my name here," I squeaked, suddenly wishing I was outside with Drea and Skye.

He smiled, but it didn't reach his eyes. "You're the spitting image of your mother. We are so glad to welcome you to Shade Academy. We thought you'd been lost."

A flash of red coated his eyes before it was gone. I wondered if I'd imagined it.

"Yeah... I've just been in Brooklyn." I gave a nervous laugh.

He chuckled. "Wonderful. I'm Arthur Alston, the headmaster. I'm so glad my son brought you home."

Awkward.

"Umm, home? I'm not so sure about that yet."

His eyes narrowed. "Did Indigo not tell you that you would have free tuition, room and board, an expense account, and a generous salary?"

My phone buzzed in my pocket again, and sweat beaded on my brow. "Yeah, I heard. That's... cool." I snuck a glance out the window and saw Drea and Skye staring up at the building.

Arthur's brow knitted, and he pivoted, looking out the window and down at the street where the Lumen girls waited. "I see," he growled.

"Let her tour the Lumen dorm. She'll be back by tomorrow night," the redhead snickered.

It was at that moment that Gage sauntered into the library. His gaze barely skated over me before landing on his father.

"You wanted to see me," he said. I didn't miss the defiant tilt of his chin when he addressed Arthur.

For his part, fatherly affection wasn't radiating from

Arthur either. "You killed a level five demon last night?" he asked his son.

Pressing his lips into a hard line, Gage gave a curt nod.

Gage killed a demon? Was that what he had to do to save me?

"There will be consequences for that. Killing our employers is not befitting of a Shade." His father's voice held the not-so-subtle threat.

Gage shrugged as if that hardly mattered. "Was there anything else you wanted?" he asked as he leaned back against a table and crossed his arms.

I wasn't sure if I was the only one who caught the slight wince when his arms brushed his chest. I wondered if he'd been to see their healer yet.

Arthur frowned at his son, and I would swear the temperature dropped a few degrees.

Gage cleared his throat, the first outward sign that he was uncomfortable in his father's presence.

"As a matter of fact," Arthur started, "I'd like you to accompany Tatum on the rest of her school tour. I'm sure you'll have some fascinating facets of our school and culture to tell her about."

Gage let out a loud breath of air and his nose flared. "Sure," he said, but it sounded like what he really wanted to say was "F-you."

Yikes. This was some serious family drama.

Ignoring his son, Arthur turned to me with a plastic

smile. "It was nice to meet you, Tatum. I hope to be seeing you very soon. I wouldn't want you to make a *mistake*."

The inflection he put on the word mistake had multiple red flags popping up in my head. I couldn't tell if he was trying to make that sound like a threat or a warning. "Thanks?"

With a smile still in place, Arthur nodded at me and then put his hand on the redhead's lower back to lead her away.

Gage might get under my skin, but I instantly disliked his father. The vibes he threw off were creepy and scary, my new least favorite combo.

Ignoring Gage, I turned to face Indigo. "I need to go. My gran is probably worried."

She frowned. "But you haven't seen the gym, or the pool, or—"

"I want to leave." My voice shook. Something wasn't right. Being here felt all wrong. I wanted to leave, and I wanted to leave right *now*.

Indigo's gaze slid over my head, most likely landing on Gage.

"It's okay," his deep voice rumbled behind me, "I'll walk her out."

Indigo chewed on her bottom lip, indecision riding her hard. She finally nodded, and I released the breath I'd been holding. I wasn't wild about being alone with Gage again, but I did want to get back to Gran.

"It was nice to meet you," I said to Indigo. It wasn't a lie. I could see why they chose Indigo to do the tours. She was lovely.

"Yeah, you too." She offered me a tentative smile. "I really do hope you'll come back. This is truly the best place for you."

I didn't know what to say to that, so I just offered my own smile and an awkward wave.

"Come on, Tate," Gage said as he pushed off the table he'd been leaning on.

I huffed and rolled my eyes. "It's Tatum."

"Whatever," he said as he led me out of the library.

I bit my tongue to keep from arguing with him. He could call me the Tooth Fairy for all I cared as long as he showed me how to get out of this maze.

I tossed what was left of my burrito into the garbage on the way out of the library. Gage walked in front of me all the way to an elevator at the end of the hall. After an agonizing wait, the doors finally opened, and Gage waved me in front of him.

Maybe he wasn't completely devoid of manners after all?

When the doors slid shut behind us, he flicked his gaze up to where there was a blinking red light, obviously a security camera.

I gasped when Gage suddenly grabbed my arms and swung me into the corner of the elevator, directly under the camera, and pressed flush up against my body.

"Dude, what the heck are—?"

He dipped his head low, the stubble on his face brushing against my cheek.

"Don't do it," he whisper-growled in my ear.

I swallowed hard. "Do what?"

"*Don't* come back here." His breath feathered over my neck, and a shiver ran down my body. "You're too good for this place."

The lights in the elevator flickered like they did in the diner the first time I'd met him.

There was a ding, and Gage pushed away from me before the doors had a chance to fully open. The lobby beyond was empty but for a single security guard, who was slumped in his seat, snoring softly. I supposed if you weren't afraid of demons, there wasn't a lot in the world you needed protection from.

"See ya 'round," Gage said as he practically shoved me out of the elevator. Still inside the cab, he jammed his finger against a button. We stared at each other, both of us incapable of looking away, until the doors cut off our view.

I continued to gape at the closed door for several long seconds, trying to gather my thoughts. I was absolutely dumbfounded, but sure of one thing.

Gage Alston was the most confusing male I'd ever met.

CHAPTER SIX

D rea spotted me the moment I pushed through the front door of Shade Academy and stepped out onto the busy Manhattan sidewalk. She tugged on Skye's arm, and then pointed in my direction.

I turned and started speed walking toward the nearest subway entrance, away from the girls. Now that I knew I could run into shadow demons anywhere, the subway was no longer off limits. I just wanted to get back to the apartment and to Gran as quickly as possible and pretend none of this was happening. There was no hiding from the inevitable, but I wanted to hit pause for at least an hour and let all the information I'd just learned settle.

"Hey, wait up!" Drea called. She'd waited until I'd hit the end of the block before crossing the street to hunt me down. Maybe there was some rule about not getting too close to their enemy's turf or something.

I threw up a hand, waving her off. "I seriously can't take this right now. You're going to have to give me some space."

She'd been nothing but kind to me, but I didn't have room in my reserves for niceties this morning.

If Drea was surprised or put off by my behavior, she didn't show it. She leaned over to Skye as they kept pace with me and whispered something to her. I glanced at them out of the corner of my eye and saw Skye pull a sore face.

"You sure?" she said to Drea, who nodded back. With a shrug, Skye peeled off from us and was lost in the pedestrian foot-traffic within moments.

Drea stayed silent until we reached the F-train. While we were waiting on the platform for the train to arrive, I finally turned to acknowledge her. "Are you really going to follow me home?"

"We don't have to talk about any of this stuff just yet. I get that you seem to need a little bit of time, but yeah, I'm going to follow you home. It's for your protection."

Now I needed twenty-four seven protection? This day just kept getting more and more awesome.

I sighed and rubbed the pulse point at my temple. A monster headache was forming.

"I know this must be hard for you," she said, compassion in her voice. "I get it."

Hard didn't even begin to cover it.

"Do you, though?" I snapped. "Did you find out a little more than a week before your eighteenth birthday that you weren't... human?" I had the sense to lower my voice. "Did you find out you were an entirely different species and then only have nine days to decide which weird angelic cult you wanted to join?"

A frown pulled down the corners of Drea's pretty mouth. She shook her head, and her brown curls bounced, brushing against her russet cheeks. "You're right. I don't know what that's like."

I scrubbed a hand over my face, knowing I wasn't being fair to Drea. It wasn't my M.O. to spit my words at people like venom, but maybe since I was descended from a Shade, evil was in my blood or something and it was coming out now. A chill slithered down my spine at the possibility. I really hoped that wasn't the case. My thoughts went back to the picture of my mother in the Shade Academy library, and I felt sick.

I really looked at Drea then. She was wearing the same clothes from the day before, which meant she'd probably stayed outside Shade Academy waiting for me all night. There were faint smudges of darkness under her eyes that showed just how exhausted she probably was. It was more than clear she was only trying to look out for me.

And I had immediately jumped down her throat.

I'm a jerk.

I groaned. "I'm really sorry. I apparently don't people well after I've heard life-altering news. I'm having a hard time processing everything, but I shouldn't have snapped at you like that. You've done nothing wrong."

"It's okay," Drea said gently, and then placed a

comforting hand on my shoulder. "You've got to talk to someone about all this, right? I'm happy to be that person."

Gah. She was so nice. I already felt like I didn't deserve her. My throat tightened with emotion at her kind offer.

The train rolled into the subway station, and we both hopped on. It was late in the morning, so there weren't too many commuters, and this time of day people were usually headed into Manhattan, not out of it.

I flopped down into a plastic seat, and Drea lowered herself into the one next to me. I zoned out for a bit, and she let me. A comfortable silence hung between us until I broke it by asking, "Did Gage really save me from that goat demon at the diner?"

It wasn't an important detail, but I still wanted to know the truth.

Drea's eyes widened, and she nodded. "I'd love to tell you that it was one of us, but really it was all him. First, he helped us in the alley against the level threes, and then all of a sudden he took off into the diner. I barely figured out what had happened before he was decapitating the level five with his shadow blade. It was… surprising."

I barked a half laugh. "Surprising because he was able to take down a demon on his own?"

He talked a good game, but maybe that was all it was, talk?

"No." She shook her head. "Surprising because he's not supposed to kill demons at all. Even helping us stay alive against the group of level threes was gutsy, and definitely out of character for a Shade. He's going to be in big trouble if the Shade masters find out."

I grimaced, remembering his father's chat with him in the library. "They definitely already know."

Drea whistled. "I don't envy him right now."

I chewed on my bottom lip, deep in thought. Why *did* Gage fight the demons if he was supposed to be working for them? Was it just because he'd been ordered to protect me? I didn't know him nearly well enough to guess at his motives, but I felt kind of bad that he was in trouble for it.

I'd feel worse if he wasn't such a douche.

The train rolled to a stop in my neighborhood, and we got off. I asked Drea little questions on the quick walk to the apartment and she rattled off the answers.

I learned that there were ten levels of demons. The highest level she'd ever fought was a level four. I'd also asked why their arms lit up with weird swirl tattoos, and she told me that it was one of the powers all Lumens got when they took their oath. It helped rejuvenate their strength.

When I jammed the key into my front door lock and turned it, I was surprised to find I wasn't ready to stop talking. But it was better to put off the supernatural talk until I could be alone with Drea again. Chatting about angels, shadow demons, and angelic powers was sure to trigger Gran's delusions.

"Gran, I'm home," I called, and then waved Drea into the apartment in front of me.

Drea frowned and glanced down. I knew why a second later when I stepped into the room and my feet squished into soggy carpet.

"Tatum, I didn't expect you back so quickly," Gran said as she exited the kitchen. She had a cookie in her hand, and wet slippers on her feet.

"Gran, what happened?" I asked as I shot past her and into the kitchen. The sink was overflowing and flooding the apartment. I quickly shut off the faucet, but the damage was done.

Drea came up behind me. "I can help you clean this up," she said, but the grimace on her face said she knew how bad this was. If the carpet in the entrance was saturated, the water was probably leaking into the apartment below us.

Gran shuffled into the kitchen where there was barely room for the three of us, oblivious to the flooding. "Tatum, introduce me to your fr—" Gran froze mid-sentence. Her brown-eyed gaze bounced over Drea's face, and she went stock-still. Raising her hand to cover her mouth, her fingers spasmed and she dropped the half-eaten cookie.

"Aurelia?"

Drea glanced between Gran and me, eyes wide with surprise.

"Aurelia is my mom," she finally said.

"Gran, do you know Drea's mother?" If Gran knew Drea's mom, did that mean she really was a Watcher? That she knew about the demons. About everything?

"It's not safe," Gran suddenly yelled and then ran to the

windows as fast as a sixty-three-year-old woman could, yanking the curtains closed. She turned back to Drea with wide eyes. "We hid because we had to. You have to understand, it was the only way. But I know he'll come for her one day, and she's not ready."

Oh no, it was happening right now. She'd slipped into one of her delusions quicker than usual. I hadn't even given Drea a heads-up about Gran. This was awkward.

It took me ten minutes to calm Gran down enough to get her settled in her bed and resting. She was watching her favorite baking show, and I promised we'd make some cookies together later. With any luck, she'd be napping within minutes.

When I returned, Drea was on the ground trying to mop up some of the water with bath towels.

"Your landlord stopped by while you were getting your gran settled," she said, chewing her lower lip.

That wasn't good. Mr. Daniels had said one more strike and we were out. But maybe it was just a random drop-by and he hadn't noticed the soggy carpet.

"The water leaked to the apartment below. He said you had a week to clear out and you weren't getting your deposit back. Flooring guys will be by later today to rip out the carpet."

My heart sank. I couldn't find a new place in a week. At least not a decent place I could afford. We were going to be homeless.

I covered my face with my hands and rubbed my eyes. What was I going to do?

"Tatum?" Drea said.

I dropped my hands. Anxiety practically seeped from Drea's pores. It was a tad concerning to see her so unsettled. I'd watched her face off against monsters with less anxiety. "About your gran..."

Gran's episode had clearly spooked her. "She's just confused. She gets this way sometimes. Actually, a lot of times these days," I confessed, and then paused, hesitating to reveal the extent of Gran's illness, but then my gut told me I could trust Drea. "She has dementia."

"She's your blood relative?" Drea asked, unfazed by Gran's diagnosis.

I nodded. "Yeah."

"Are you sure?" she pressed.

I bunched my brow. "Yes, I'm sure. She looks *just* like my mom." It was a little weird she was being so nosy. "With dementia, confusion is normal. Paranoia too."

"No, you don't understand." Drea took a step toward me. The expression on her face was about as warm as a doctor who was about to deliver the news that you'd lost a loved one. "I called my parents. They'll be here shortly," was all she said.

"Wait a second," I protested. "That's not cool. I don't want any more Watchers in our apartment. I told you I need a break from all this."

"Tatum..." Drea crossed the room to stand in front of

me. "Watchers can't reproduce with humans. Which means that if Gran's your biological grandmother, then she has to be a Watcher too. We were created to have a relatively human lifespan so that we would blend in with other humans, but we don't get sick from human diseases and our bodies don't deteriorate in the same way either. Whatever's happening to your gran, it's not caused by dementia."

My heart sank into my stomach. What was she saying? "Then what's wrong with her?"

"I don't know. That's what we're going to find out when my parents get here."

A moment later, a soft knock rapped at the door, and I stiffened.

"It's going to be okay. We're going to get through this together." Drea gave me a small smile as she walked over to my front door and opened it.

Why were my palms sweating? I felt like I couldn't breathe. One sentence just kept looping through my head.

Whatever's happening to your gran, it's not caused by dementia.

Gran was sick. What other explanation was there?

When the door pulled back, a tall, lithe, older version of Drea walked into the room. She wore black leather pants and a halter top. Her hair was twice the size of Drea's and bounced as she walked over to me with a kindness in her gaze I hadn't expected. My eyes fell to the tattoos on her arms. Swords, knives, throwing stars, an axe. All of them weapons she could no doubt make real as Skye did. The white swirl tattoos were also there, hypnotizing me with their glowing movement.

A man stepped in behind her, towering over all of us, and gave me a curt nod as Drea shut the door behind them.

The woman smiled. "Hello, Tatum. It's nice to finally meet you. I'm Aurelia, and this is my husband, Theo. We're here to help your gran."

For some reason I wanted to cry. I think I'd reached my maximum level of new information I could handle. But I sucked the dampness at my eyes back and nodded. I wanted to help Gran, if there was a way. I would power through it and have my much-needed breakdown later.

"Where is she?" Drea's dad asked.

Drea pointed to the back room, where Gran slept, and her dad pulled out a device, much like the one Marlow had at the diner last night. He extended an antenna out of it, and they waltzed into Gran's room like they owned the place.

I tore after them. "Hey!" I whisper-screamed. "She's resting. I just got her calm!"

By the time I turned the corner and charged into her room, Theo was waving the antenna thing over Gran's sleeping body.

What the heck?

The device in his hand beeped, and he sighed, shaking his head. He turned to his wife. "It's as we feared."

Aurelia looked down at Gran and shook her head, a single tear sliding down her cheek. "She's older, but she looks the same. Oh, Joelle." Her voice was wistful, and hearing her call my gran by her first name shook me.

"You're scaring me. What's happening?" I realized then that I was sobbing. I couldn't deal with reality anymore. I'd finally cracked.

Aurelia turned, placing her hands on my shoulders. "Your grandmother was my mentor, a teacher at Lumen Academy. She disappeared the same time your mother did. I looked for them for years, but…"

Gran? A teacher at Lumen Academy?

"Someone needs to tell me what's going on. Right. Now," I ground out between clenched teeth. My sobs had evaporated and now I was just angry. My brain was short-circuiting, and I was riding the roller coaster of emotions.

"Honey…" Aurelia peered down at me with compassionate brown eyes. "Your gran is cursed."

The breath flew out of me as I gasped.

Cursed?

This wasn't happening, this couldn't be real, but in that moment my mind went to all of the things she said in her moments of despair: speaking of darkness and light, shadows and demons. A curse was more believable at this point, that's how crazy my life had become.

"Can we fix it?" I asked.

Drea's mom winced, which told me I wasn't going to like the answer. "It's been getting worse lately? Started off years ago? More mild?"

Chills ran up my arms and I nodded. Gran's first delusion was in her early fifties. I'd thought it too early, but my research told me early onset dementia was possible.

I just nodded.

Aurelia's face fell. "Then, my dear, we have nine days to figure this out, because she will get worse until the curse kills her on your eighteenth birthday."

No! Her words sliced through my heart until I couldn't take it anymore.

"Why on my birthday?" I asked, feeling the heavy weight of depression sink into my bones.

Aurelia shared a look with her husband. "It's a choosing curse. I've seen it once before. It expires once you've chosen."

"Chosen what?"

"Chosen your side," she said. "Shade or Lumen. She'll live if you pick the right side."

I gulped. "Which side is the right one?"

Aurelia frowned. "I don't know yet. I'll have to take a deeper look. A curse like this is forbidden for both Shades *and* Lumens."

Was she saying that a Shade or Lumen cursed my gran so I would choose to join them?

I simply sank down onto the floor and went numb.

CHAPTER SEVEN

"I want Joelle constantly monitored. Text me hourly updates please," Aurelia said to the nurse who wheeled Gran into her new room. Gran was asleep again. She'd roused only to get into the wheelchair Drea's dad had brought up to the apartment. Gran had merely looked at him and said, "Oh hello, Theo," before falling back asleep.

I'd been in a bit of a catatonic state after hearing my beloved gran was going to die in nine days. We were in a care facility that the Lumens' owned for hunters who were injured in battle. It was a hospital of sorts that Drea said was on the same block as Lumen Academy. The sign at the door had merely said *Private Healing Center*.

It was a small building, only two levels, and the doctors and nurses wore blue silk cloaks instead of white coats, but they seemed to know what they were doing.

"Would you like to lie down in an extra room or go and

tour the Lumen campus? Grab an early dinner?" Aurelia asked, clearly trying to read my mood.

Gran seemed safe here, and I had way too much on my mind to sleep right now. We were basically homeless, so I'd need to make my decision sooner than nine days if I wanted a place to live. Unfortunately, the Shade Academy salary was looking nice now that we were about to be evicted, and I'd need a place for Gran to live while I went to school.

"Campus tour sounds nice," I told her.

She nodded, placing a warm hand on my shoulder. "They are going to run some tests. I'll get word to you as soon as I find anything out. She's safer here than anywhere. I promise."

I had to bite back tears. With a nod, Drea stepped up to my side. "Come on, the academy is just a couple of buildings down."

She led me out of the hospital, which was in Midtown, not too far from where the Shade Academy was in Soho. Still, there was a different vibe here—where Shade Academy was full of steel and glass, Lumen Academy had carved stone and wrought iron. It was somehow warmer, homey, and inviting, like the living heart of a community thriving on this block.

We passed a couple of squat buildings full of old-world charm and character that Drea identified as the academy dorms and family housing. On our short walk, she explained that unlike Shade Academy, which housed every-thing in one sleek high-rise, Lumen Academy was spread out over a small city block and comprised of several smaller buildings with a courtyard in the middle.

We stopped in front of a turreted building at the end of the block that was the official academy location. It wrapped around the corner and ran down the adjacent side street. Six or seven stories tall, the exterior was a patchwork of white, gray, and tan stacked stones with arched windows. Two aged cement statues stood on each side of the front stoop: angels, wings spread wide as they gripped swords. The statues made chills race down my spine.

Watchers.

This morning was the first time I'd ever heard that word, but now it somehow felt so familiar, as if I'd known it my whole life.

"This is it!" Drea bopped on her heels excitedly. We stepped up to the door, and Drea pushed the single red button on the call box.

"Lumen Academy," a scratchy male voice said over the speaker. His New York accent was thick.

"Vinnie, it's me!" Drea waved to the upper corner of the door, where I noticed a red flashing light on a small camera.

When the door buzzed, Drea pulled it wide, and I stepped inside. In contrast to the intricate exterior, we entered into what looked like a totally normal apartment building foyer. There was a stocky man sitting behind a desk wearing a security guard outfit, and a wall of mail-boxes on the far wall. I was expecting to see soaring ceilings, stained glass, and giant murals, so it was a tad disappointing, but even though the stone floors were chipped and in need of repair, this place already had a much better feel to it than Shade Academy.

Drea walked past the guard, Vinnie. He gave us both a curt nod. I followed her down a long hallway until she stepped into an ancient elevator that was basically a wood box inside of a metal frame. The accordion metal door squealed as she pulled it shut behind us. She then hit the button labeled "seven." It was a moment before the lift jerked into motion, and I tried hard not to let my apprehension for being in this death box show on my face.

"First two floors are faculty offices," Drea chatted excitedly, completely oblivious to my discomfort. "The academy classes, cafeteria, and training areas are on levels three through seven. The gyms and training centers in this building are only for students, but there's a community center on the opposite side of the courtyard that has a gym that's available to all Lumens. The compound also has a library and armory on the other side of the block."

My eyes widened at the last building she threw out like it was commonplace. Armory. Was it weird I wanted to visit that next? Like what kind of weapons did angels have?

I scanned the row of buttons on the elevator wall as we made the slow trek up to the top floor, my gaze catching on the one at the very bottom.

"What's floor SB?" I asked just as the lift lurched to a stop. The whole box bounced slightly a few times before Drea could safely haul the metal grate back open.

A look of nervousness flashed across Drea's face, and she jumped out of the cab and into the hustle and bustle on the seventh floor without answering me. "Oh look, we're here!"

Young teens walked briskly by as they talked and laughed, bookbags slung over their arm or swords on their hips.

"Jasmine!" Drea hailed a girl with long brown hair. She turned, and upon seeing us walked over with a young guy, who stood a foot taller than her but had the same chocolate brown hair and olive skin. They looked like siblings.

"Jasmine, James…" Drea looked from them to me. "This is Tatum. She's a prospective student."

Jasmine smiled, giving me a wave. "Hey, Tatum. You should totally grab a chocolate chip cookie from the cafeteria before you leave. Miss Freese makes the best."

I returned her smile, feeling at ease here and digging the nice demeanor of the students versus the chilly air that sat around the kids in Shade Academy.

"I'll do that, thanks," I told her.

A bell rang and students cleared the hallways, ducking into various classrooms or running down a wide set of stairs that zigzagged around the elevator shafts, presumably to the ground floor. When the area was clear, I noticed an illustrated poster on the wall across from us.

DO YOU KNOW YOUR
DEMON LEVELS?

LEVELS

1-3

GRAB YOUR LIGHT WEAPONS!

These small creatures often present as shadowy versions of bats, birds, or snakes. Bring your light swords because many of these demons can't be destroyed by traditional weapons.

4-6

ALWAYS DOUBLE TAP!

These large demons are a mash-up of different animals. They aren't the smartest, but what they lack in strategy they make up for in brute strength and savagery. Remember to double tap!

7

REMEMBER YOUR TRAINING!

These animal-like creatures stand upright and often have a single humanoid feature. Be on guard with these demons. They're the muscle of the Netherworld and they pack a punch!

8

DON'T GET DISTRACTED!

These demons will have a strange and jarring mix of human and animal features, but getting distracted by tails, scaled skin, or multiple heads could cost you your life!

9

FIND A MASTER LUMEN!

These creatures look mostly human in appearance with only minor deformities such as fangs, pointed ears, small horns, or clawed hands. If you pass one of these on the street, report it!

10

RUN FOR YOUR LIFE!

Run for your life. Completely humanoid and can touch the mortal world with no problem. You only know you are in their presence if you are a trained Watcher and can sense the darkness within.

♥ SHARING IS CARING

It read: *Do You Know Your Demon Levels?*

Moving away from Drea, I stepped closer and studied what looked to be a diagram of ten levels of demons. There were black silhouettes of the various demons, along with their attributes, powers, and strengths.

It looked like the higher up the demon level got, the more they looked human.

"There's one on every floor. They practically wallpaper the dorms with those," Drea said. "As if anyone here could actually forget the different levels." She started to laugh, and then cut it off abruptly. A grimace replaced her smile as she remembered that I didn't know them. But I wasn't offended. How could I know the demon levels? I only found out what I was less than twenty-four hours ago.

"Sorry," she said. "It's just really rare for a Watcher to grow up outside either of the communities. I didn't mean to make you feel bad. I'm sure you'll catch on in no time."

"It's okay." I waved her off and then refocused on the poster. It was wildly helpful. "If there are extras of this, I wouldn't mind having one. I could carry it with me on the subway as a cheat sheet."

I was half joking but Drea didn't smile. She nodded. "Yes, definitely. Let me show you around, and then later I can get you one out of my dorm room. I'm sure I have one floating around somewhere."

Starting from the top floor, Drea took me around each of the academy levels. The classrooms were on floors five, six, and seven. They were modest rooms. The professors taught off chalkboards, and lessons ranged from normal educational topics such as math, science, and English, to the more bizarre curriculum such as demonology, angel powers, and portal studies.

Drea explained that Watchers attended the academy from age twelve until twenty-two, with on-the-job training starting their first year. The parents were responsible for their children's education before that, so many of the students went to human schools before coming to Lumen Academy.

She also mentioned that most of the Lumens didn't receive a salary to do the job the angels had charged them with. Many of them still worked full or part-time jobs elsewhere, taking hunting shifts during their off-time. It sounded like a lot of work, but they were doing good in the world, as opposed to the Shades, who seemed like evil's overpaid security guards.

Training gyms took up all of the fourth floor. There was a larger area that reminded me of a regular, if not a tad outdated, run-of-the-mill gym. Students and faculty members were scattered across the room using the standard weightlifting and treadmill equipment to condition their muscles. There were a handful of smaller gyms that lined the hallways where students were practicing hand-to-hand combat, some limited weapons training, and even practicing their powers. Solid metal doors blocked the interior of the training gyms from view, but I could still hear the muffled sounds of fighting from within.

We stopped outside one of the rooms. Drea opened the door and poked her head inside. She waved me in after her a moment later.

Marlow and Jacob were sparring in the center of the room. There wasn't much to the space beyond the four blank walls, but they didn't need anything. As soon as Drea and I settled off to the side, Marlow swept her arms in an arc and then pushed them forward. A shockwave burst from her outstretched palms and slammed into Jacob, throwing him backward into the wall.

I winced at the fleshy splat of his body slamming into what looked to be a wall of solid concrete. He slid down the wall and landed in a crouch. The white tattoos on his arms glowed suddenly, and he shook his head as if clearing his thoughts. A moment later, he popped back up, and with a wicked grin his golden wings burst free from his back. He rushed Marlow, moving so fast he was only a blur. His fist shot out, and she jerked to the side to avoid the blow.

"Nice try, *wings*," Marlow snapped.

"You wish you could fly," Jacob gloated.

They continued to go at it, throwing friendly verbal barbs at each other as often as blows. It was impressive. They were like a pair of suped-up ninjas.

I leaned toward Drea. "I was told Shades inherit more powerful abilities than Lumens."

Drea laughed. "Is *that* what they said? Let me ask you a question. Can you ever snuff out light with darkness?"

I opened my mouth to say, "Sure," but then I thought about it a moment. "I guess not."

"Right, you can't. You can chase darkness away with the smallest amount of light, but it doesn't work the other way around. Light is always more powerful than the dark, no matter what the Shades may tell you. Remember that."

It was a simple truth, but a profound one.

"Hey, Drea." Dash's voice rumbled off to the right, and I almost jumped out of my skin.

He must have been here the whole time, although I don't know how I hadn't noticed him. I guess he kind of blended into the wall with his gray hoodie and dark jeans. The lighting in the room was good, so even with his hood in place I got my first decent view of his face. His eyes were gray and his skin a deep bronze. A chunk of dark hair lay over one of his eyebrows. When he saw me staring, he pulled his hood forward, shading the upper part of his face.

Pity, he seemed like a good-looking guy. Why was he always covering himself like that? It was like he was trying to hide from the world.

"Hey, Dash." Drea waved back to him. "I was thinking of ordering us all pizza and chilling in the dorm lounge. You in?"

He jerked his chin in a quick nod.

"Did someone say pizza?" Jacob asked, halting his sparring with Marlow.

"Come on, now. I was just about to lay you out," she complained. "You can't tap out now."

"She said *pizza* and I can't ignore the boss." Jacob gave Marlow puppy-dog eyes while he rubbed his belly.

She rolled her eyes and relented.

Both of their arms glowed, sending swirls in high arcs up and down their biceps as they replenished their strength.

"Whoa," I said aloud.

Drea grinned. "Light tattoos are cool, right?"

I nodded.

Marlow and Jacob looked fresh as daisies when the tattoos faded. That was a cool trick. Maybe I did want to be team Angel Gang.

"I'll put in an order," Jacob offered as he reached his bag and pulled out his cell phone.

"Just make sure not to order meat on everything," Marlow said. "You know I'm a vegetarian now."

Jacob lifted his eyebrows and dialed. "Yes, I'd like four extra-large meat-lovers pizzas please," he said into his phone. Marlow chucked a sweaty towel at his head, but he dodged it.

"I'm going to show Tatum where the other buildings are. We'll meet you guys in the lounge," Drea said as she tugged at my arm. Marlow and Jacob were bickering, but Dash acknowledged her with another quick nod.

"Where's Skye?" I wondered about the pretty brunette member of their five-some.

"She has a date with a senior hunter." Drea wiggled her eyebrows, and I chuckled.

We took the scary elevator down to the ground floor

and exited the academy, waving to Vinnie as we passed. We then circled the block with Drea pointing out the rest of the buildings in the Lumen compound.

With soaring spires, carved stone, and stained glass windows, the library exterior had a similar Gothic feel to it as the academy. The armory, which I was still super curious about, looked like a giant cement block. It sat right next to the library and was a real eyesore. We didn't peek inside, which kind of bummed me out. The community center was obviously the newest of all the buildings, a simple yet functional design that was about ten stories tall.

We cut in between the community and healing centers to take a shortcut through the courtyard and to the dorms. Right next to the dormitory was a building marked family housing. "I grew up there. All of the master hunters on salary live in the family housing building, but I moved into the student dorm next door when I was sixteen."

An ancient looking structure sat in the middle of the open green space, and I asked Drea about it.

"That's the Ascension Sanctuary," she said.

"The what?"

I eyed the small two-story stone building as we passed. It was devoid of windows, and the center of the roof came to a peak, reminding me of an old church.

"It's the first building the Lumen erected in New York City almost four centuries ago. The rest of Lumen Academy was built around it slowly over the years," she explained.

It did look like the other Lumen buildings were protecting this one in the middle.

"It's where Watchers go for their ascension ceremonies when they choose to be Lumens," she continued. "It houses a permanent portal to Avalon."

Peeling my gaze off the Ascension Sanctuary, "Excuse me?" I asked. "Did you say there's a *portal* in there? And what's Avalon?"

Drea smiled. "Avalon is where the angels live. It's a whole different world, unbelievably beautiful. All Lumen visit there to get blessed with their gifts and abilities once they make their choice. Permanent portals are really rare. There are a couple more at Lumen academies around the world, and all heavily guarded."

"Where do the Shades go to get their powers?" I asked, although I was scared I already knew the answer.

Her smile faded. "Shade Academy has their own portal, although I don't know where they hide it. My guess is its deep within the ground somewhere and they built their high-rise on top of it. Their portal leads to the Netherworld —the Hell dimension where demons are from. Watchers go there when they choose to become a Shade, and Apollyon gives them powers and juices up their talismans."

Talismans?

Whoa. This was making my head spin.

We reached the dormitory, which was sandwiched between the academy and the family housing building, and I followed Drea up a few flights of stairs in a haze. My mind was blown. Portals to Hell and Heaven-like worlds. How much more could I absorb in a single day?

Skye, Marlow, Jacob, and Dash were already lounging in the dorm's common area when we arrived. Four pizza boxes were spread out over a coffee table, and Jacob had a half-eaten slice of pepperoni in his hand. I was surprised to see Skye. She waved when we entered.

"What about your date?" Drea asked.

"He got pulled out on a call. Level six in Harlem." She frowned, looking down at her cute outfit that had gone to waste.

"Sorry," Jacob told us around a mouthful of food, holding up his half-eaten slice. "I couldn't wait."

The rest of us dug in when Drea and I were seated. The common area had a college vibe to it. There was a smattering of mismatched and stained furniture, a small basketball hoop stuck to one of the walls, several defaced *Do You Know Your Demon Levels* posters, and a bit of a funk that even the smell of pizza couldn't mask.

I munched on my slice of Hawaiian pizza happily as I listened to Marlow and Skye talk about their upcoming trip to a small thrift store Skye had discovered the week before. I'm pretty sure they were plotting how to buy out the whole shoe section.

My phone buzzed in my back pocket, and I pulled it out and checked it while I ate.

I didn't recognize the number.

Unknown: *Hey, are you coming back to Shade Academy*

tonight? You're welcome to stay with me until you get a room assignment.

My stomach dropped, the invitation causing a weird fluttering in my gut. Was Gage asking me to come back to Shade and sleep in his room again?

Another message came through.

Unknown: *BTW, this is Indigo.*

Oh.

A rush of embarrassment flooded my system that I'd thought the message was from Gage. I quickly programmed her number into my phone, shaking my head at where my thoughts had gone.

"Why are you blushing?" Skye asked, her keen eyes seeing too much.

"No reason," I said quickly, and sent a note back to Indigo that I wasn't going to crash there. She'd been nice to me so I didn't want to hurt her feelings, but if I could help it I'd never set foot in that place again. I shoved the phone in my back pocket, anxious to put it away. I don't know how Indigo got my phone number. It seemed to be available to everyone these days.

"Was that Gage?" Jacob asked, a dark look sliding over his face.

"No, of course not," I said even as my heart rate spiked. "Is there any more pizza?"

Drea shot me a weird look and then pointed to my plate, where there was still a slice and a half uneaten.

"Oh, right." I picked up the food and shoved it in my

mouth. Hearing it wasn't Gage was enough to bring back Jacob's good mood, and he went back to trying to sink shots with the small basketball as Dash heckled him.

I waited until Marlow and Skye went back to their conversation about fashion, and then leaned closer to Drea.

"What's the deal with Jacob and Gage?" I asked in a low voice. "I know Shades and Lumens probably don't like each other, but is there more to the story?"

I'd already watched Gage and Jacob come to blows in the alley behind the diner, and I wasn't vain enough to think that was just over me. Then there was the look on Jacob's face a minute ago when he thought Gage was texting me. There was some bad blood between the two, and I was curious to know what went down.

Drea flicked her gaze to Jacob to make sure he wasn't listening before dropping her voice and answering. "You're right, we have a natural rivalry with the Shades, but Jacob's dislike goes a lot deeper than that. There was a girl named Britt. She was Lumen-born, from Upstate New York, and Jacob was *really* into her. Rumor has it, before she chose her house, Jacob and Gage both went after her. When she had her obligatory tour of Shade Academy, she fell for Gage instead and eventually decided to become a Shade. Jacob's always felt that Gage played on her emotions to get her to join their side."

I gasped. It wasn't loud, but noisy enough to draw some of the group's attention. I patted my chest and pretended I'd choked on some of my food, and they went back to their separate conversations.

"Is that true?" I whispered to Drea, my stomach souring with the thought of Gage pretending to be into a girl just to trick her into picking Shade Academy. That was disgusting.

Drea shrugged. "Who really knows. I don't follow Shade gossip, but I don't think Gage and Britt were ever officially an item. Or if they were, it wasn't for long. How it all went down certainly doesn't make Gage look good though."

I glanced at Jacob laughing with Dash because he'd just sunk a shot by ricocheting the ball off the ceiling.

Would Gage really do something that despicable? The truth was, I didn't know him well enough to say that he wouldn't.

I felt for Jacob though. I hoped it was just a small crush and not more serious. Watching someone you cared about pick a different house had to be painful. I didn't know the full story about why my mother decided to leave the Lumens and become a Shade, but it probably broke Gran's heart.

I knew it was going to be hard for her to talk about it, but I had to confront Gran the minute she was lucid enough to do so. Now that I knew what I really was, Gran was the only person who could help put the rest of the pieces together.

CHAPTER EIGHT

Rather than returning to our soggy apartment, I stayed by Gran's side at the healing center all night long, dozing in a ratty orange tweed chair next to her bed. Aurelia said her healers were trying to analyze the energy they pulled from Gran to decipher who'd laid the curse on her. She was apologetic about it taking so long, and offered me their visitors' room in the dorm, but I turned her down, wanting to be near Gran if she woke up. She'd been asleep since we brought her to the healing center, and that scared me.

I was stretching when Drea poked her head into the room. She winced when she watched me try to work a kink out of my neck.

"Rough night?" she asked, looking over at Gran.

"It wasn't the best night's sleep of my life, but I'll live."

Drea offered me a small smile. "Hungry? We could grab

a late breakfast in the cafeteria, and you can go to a couple of classes with me today."

I glanced at Gran. I'd been with her all night and morning, and nothing had changed. Leaving her for a little while would probably be okay.

"I think I need to run back to the apartment and get changed," I said.

"I'll go with you," Drea offered.

"You really don't have to. I've been navigating New York and its five boroughs practically since birth."

"If you don't mind the company, I'd like to come."

I shrugged. Company wouldn't hurt.

It took almost an hour to get from Lumen Academy to my apartment. One of the subway lines was closed for maintenance, so we had to take a circuitous route. Bonus, I didn't see any demons on the way, but it was still a long trip.

Once inside the apartment, I stared at the torn-out carpet and padding. The rattle of the box fans drying everything out drowned out the noise from the busy street below. The landlord must be so pissed, but there was nothing I could do now. I changed quickly while Drea tried positioning some of the fans to dry out the bottom two inches of the couch I normally slept on, but it was a hopeless task. The musty smell of mold had already started to set in. In truth, I wasn't sure how much of our furniture was going to be salvageable.

The uncertainty of life pressed down on me, sitting

heavily on my chest and making it hard to feel like I could take in a full breath of air.

Before we left, I took a moment to call Sal and tell him I needed to take a week or two off work. It was a bad time to take off, we certainly still needed the money, but I didn't know when I'd be able to make it back in. I'd worked at the diner for the last three years. Sal took a chance on me when I was only fourteen, letting me bus tables after school. I owed it to him to let him know I wouldn't be in for a bit. I'd given him a vague explanation of family issues. I didn't think telling him that I'd recently discovered I wasn't actually human and that I needed the time to figure out how to lift a curse from my gran was a good idea. He was understanding and wanted to make sure I was all right, which I assured him I was, and asked him to pass the information along to Stella for me.

We were leaving the apartment when I ran into Mr. Daniels, my landlord. I stood there and took it while he reamed me out for five straight minutes, yelling about how much damage the water had caused to our apartment and the one underneath it, and how I was lucky we were only being evicted rather than sued for damages. I had to hold my tongue when he reminded me that I had only six days to clear out.

My jaw hurt from gritting my teeth when he finally stomped away. I was both appreciative for Drea's presence, and embarrassed. It was humbling to have to go through all of this in front of another person, especially one that I'd only known a short amount of time.

"Attacking humans is against our credo or I would have definitely given him a well-deserved knee to the groin," she said when he was finally gone. I gave her a small chuckle but was too depressed to genuinely laugh.

"Are you doing all right?" she asked on the subway ride back to Lumen Academy.

I sucked a breath through my nose and held it for a beat before releasing it out my mouth. "Honestly, I don't know."

"You know we will make sure you and your gran have a place to live, right? You can stay in the dorms with us, and the family housing building is right next door for your gran. Lumens don't have the same abundance of resources that Shades do, but we take care of our own. We won't let you two be homeless."

I looked at her, tears collecting in my eyes. It had just been Gran and me for so long that I hadn't realized how lonely I really was. The thought of having people I could count on, people who cared, cracked the shell on my heart I'd formed over the years. I didn't want to freak Drea out, but the feels were hitting me hard right now.

Clearing my throat, I tried to inconspicuously brush the wetness from my eyes.

"Thanks," I croaked.

Drea laid a hand on my arm and nodded. "You're not alone anymore, Tatum."

Aw man, why did she have to go and say that? My eyes

instantly filled and spilled over. There was no stopping it this time.

Reaching over, Drea wrapped her arms around me as my body shook with the force of my sobs. I'm sure we were getting looks from the other passengers on the train, but whatever, we were having a true friendship moment over here.

Drea didn't say anything as I wet her shoulder with my tears. She just let me get it all out. I'm pretty sure I cried through all of lower Manhattan, but the flood started to dry by the time we reached our stop in Midtown.

When I finally leaned back and gave Drea a grateful smile, I knew my face was splotchy, my eyes were red, and I needed to blow my nose, but I felt so much better I didn't care at all.

It was well into the afternoon when we emerged from the 33rd Street subway stop. We'd skipped breakfast and missed lunch, so my mind was fixated on getting food into my belly. We walked at a brisk pace until we had reached the Lumen Compound and Drea slipped between the healing center building and family housing as I followed her into the courtyard. I was just going to suggest we hit up the cafeteria when Drea's phone started buzzing and beeping. It wasn't a normal text or call chime. It sounded like an alarm.

Drea pulled the phone out, glanced down at it, and the color drained from her face, making her look ashy.

"Black alert," she said with a mixture of awe and fear and then took off running.

I frowned, not knowing what that meant, but realizing it couldn't be anything good.

I followed, hot on her heels as she sprinted across the garden and right to the armory.

"What's a black alert?" I yelled as Drea and I ran through the back door of the armory. Lumens loaded with weapons ran past us with serious expressions.

Drea dragged me into a large open room. Her hands shook as she pulled swords off of the wall and tapped them to her arm. The second they touched her skin they disappeared, becoming tattoos.

Okay, I *really* needed some of those.

"Drea?"

She turned to face me, knowing she wouldn't be able to keep me from the truth any longer. "A black alert means that a demon portal has opened somewhere inside the compound."

My eyes widened.

"A demon portal?"

She nodded. "Directly from the Netherworld."

I grabbed a small dagger, then another one the same size. No way was I facing another demon weaponless.

"Do you know how to use those?" Drea asked.

I nodded. "Stab and repeat."

It was a knife. How hard could it be?

A grin pulled at her lips.

The door slammed open then and Jacob, Skye, Marlow, and Dash burst into the room, panting. They were armed to the teeth with swords, daggers, and even bows and arrows.

One by one, their phones buzzed with alerts.

"We've got our orders," Drea called out to the group. "The novice hunter teens from the middle school are being brought up to the gym in the community center. The junior hunters are to defend them there. The senior, principal, and master hunters will find the portal, killing any demons that come through it until my mom can get it closed."

They all nodded and then looked to me.

"Hey, Tatum," Marlow said as she pulled a blade from the tattoo on her arm.

I cleared my throat, gripping the handles of the knives as my heart jackknifed in my chest. "Hey. Just a regular day in the life of a Lumen?"

"Not exactly," Skye said as she secured a whip to her belt.

Now loaded with weapons, the others left, and Drea turned to face me. "If you want to hide in here, I can come get you when—"

"No way!" I admonished. "It sounds like there are children to protect. I want to help."

Drea grinned, a dimple popping out in her cheek. "Let's go, then."

We jogged out of the armory and across the courtyard to the back entrance of the community center. Red lights flickered at the top of the hallway when we entered the building, but no sound was made. It was a silent warning.

Families ran to and fro as we burst into the stairwell,

taking the steps two at a time. The gym was on the tenth floor, so it took a while to get there.

"Does this happen often?" I asked, trying to sound less out of breath than I was. I really needed to take up running if this was going to be a common occurrence.

Drea shook her head, her curls bouncing around her face. "The entire Lumen compound is warded to prevent portals from opening here, so I don't know how this is happening."

I stumbled a little. The first black alert and it was my second day at Lumen Academy. Crappy odds.

We burst out into the hallway and through the double doors, and I skidded to a stop. Hundreds of middle schoolers and early high school aged kids were all huddled in the far right corner of the gym. Those must be the novice hunters Drea mentioned.

About fifty older teenagers, the junior hunters, saddled with every weapon possible, stood in a living wall before their younger counterparts. The mere sight of it made goose bumps rise on my arms.

Drea walked up to Jasmine and James, the siblings I'd met the day before, giving them a nod, and then we found our place among the wall next to Skye, Marlow, Dash, and Jacob.

Some kids were sobbing, others just clung to each other quietly.

There was an eerie silence, broken apart only by the

children's sniffles as a few of the older hunters tried to console them in hushed tones.

It was there, standing in front of innocents to protect them from unseen dangers, that I made my choice. I could not join with a side that protected these monsters, knowing they tortured the innocent and caused children to weep and cower in fear. Not for all the money in the world.

I was a Lumen, through and through. I didn't know what made my mother change sides, but that wasn't me. I wasn't her.

Gage's words played out in my mind now.

Don't come back here, you're too good for this place.

I didn't think I was too good for anything, but I would rather die than serve demons.

The lights went out suddenly. We were cast into total darkness for a moment, until the dim emergency lights turned back on.

Children screamed in fear as Drea stepped forward, obviously the leader among us. She clapped her hands together and every single bulb flared to life with the intensity of the sun.

There was a loud thump, and the floor shook a little, like an earthquake. I could tell from the widening of Drea's eyes that she was afraid, and this wasn't normal.

"Fighting formation!" Drea cried as each warrior teen stepped forward brandishing their weapons and formed a zigzag pattern.

I might not be a trained demon hunter, but I wasn't a coward, I wouldn't stand back while something awful happened to these children. I found a place among the formation and gripped the handles of the daggers. An electric current buzzed just under my skin as adrenaline rushed through my body.

Every single phone beeped and buzzed and Drea looked down, her face falling into a look of defeat.

"Cover the kids' eyes! Turn them away," she called out to the hunters who were standing with the youngest among us, and a pit formed in my stomach.

What did the text s—?

The double doors burst open. Bile rose in my throat as sheer terror gripped my heart and nearly caused it to stop beating.

Holy hellfire and brimstone.

I'd seen some scary things over the last week, but this was by far the most terrifying. A vortex spun at the room's entrance. Sulfuric smoke billowed from the opening, and flames shot out of its depths. The shrieks of unseen creatures pierced the air, and I had to stop myself from dropping my weapons to cover my ears. Dread churned in my gut and held my lungs in a vise-like grip. It was like looking into the beating heart of the Netherworld.

Serpentine shadows flew from the vortex, attaching themselves to the walls and ceilings as they slithered their way toward us, popping every bulb in their path and raining glass down upon us.

Several of the junior hunters around me manifested semi-transparent wings and shot into the air. Producing swords of light, they swung their weapons at the darting shadows, which turned to ash whenever they came in contact with one of the Lumen's bright blades.

"Get behind me. Those are level twos, only light blades affect them," Drea yelled as she shoved me back. Pearlescent tattoos appeared on her exposed arms, and with a flick of her wrist a light blade materialized in her hand as well. She stood at the ready in front of me, quickly dispatching any of the serpent-like shadows in reach.

I scanned the room. Children shrieked and their protectors shouted for them to bunch together. The junior Watchers' objective was simple: keep the shadows from reaching the younger kids. At first, they were successful at their mission, but it wasn't long before a sleek shadow serpent made it past the aerial blockade and zoomed toward the closest grouping of kids.

A Lumen warrior with a dark brown ponytail darted in its path—Jasmine. Holding daggers similar to my own, she slashed at the inky substance, but her blades, which were clearly not made of light, glided through the darkness without slowing it. When it reached her, the shadow serpent peeled itself off the floor and wrapped around her leg, winding its way up her body.

Dropping her weapons, Jasmine batted at the shadow, but her hands went through it as easily as her blades had.

Like sharks smelling chum, other shadow serpents

leaked through the blockade and darted for her. Suctioning around her limbs and torso, they twisted around her body as they climbed higher.

Panic radiated from Jasmine's face. She screamed right before her head was fully covered. Her calls for help abruptly cut off, and she fell to the ground, convulsing.

Fear gripped me. She needed help, but what could I do?

I looked down at the small daggers in each of my palms, realizing they'd do no good against these creatures. Grunting in frustration, I started in her direction anyway, knowing I at least had to try and help.

I didn't make it two full steps before I was cut off by two Watcher warriors. Rushing to her aid, the Lumens used their light swords to cut the darkness off of Jasmine. She stopped convulsing but lay motionless as the remnants of the shadow serpents turned to ash and floated to the ground.

What had those serpent-like shadows done to her?

A roar blasted behind me, mincing my eardrums, and I swung my head back toward the entrance. I watched a demonic beast emerge from the spinning portal. It had the chest of a man and stood upright, but that was where the similarities to a person ended. Burnt and cracked flesh covered its muscled torso and animal appendages. Tuffs of black fur hung off parts of its arms and legs. Lifting its bull-like muzzle, it roared again and the windows along the exterior wall shattered. He was the first solid demon I'd seen, and it horrified me to think of what he was capable of.

Its horned head grazed the nine-foot-high doorway as it stomped into the room, the very foundation of the community center shaking with each hooved footstep it took. Smoke billowed from its animal-like mouth when it exhaled, the dark substance swirling around its head.

The beast's red gaze swept back and forth, not resting in any one place until its eyes found me, and then held.

Crap. It's looking right at me.

"Shadowling," it growled, it's multi-tonal voice raking over me like a barbed whip shredding through flesh.

That's what the demon from the subway had called me, but I still didn't know what it meant. A bolt of fear struck me right in the chest, and I stumbled backward a step. The demon's eyes tracked my movement, and then with another mighty bellow it rushed toward me. Other Lumen fighters tried to engage the beast as it steamrolled forward, but it swatted them out of the way with ease. Lumens flew ten and twenty feet from a single shove of this beast, and my throat went bone dry as I watched.

The moment the bull-like creature was in reach, instinct had me dropping low, daggers held in each hand ready to slash out.

My nostrils flared as I sucked in a breath of sulfur-tinged air, and I realized with sudden clarity that I was probably going to die today—I wasn't anywhere near all right with that.

Determination to stay alive drove out the terror that had been riding me since the Netherworld portal appeared. I wasn't going out quietly, and if possible, I was taking this ugly demon with me, or at the very least one of its creepy red eyes.

My hands gripped my weapons so tightly that my fingers went numb. The monster was only steps away. I lifted my arm, ready to swipe at the beast, when I was tackled out of the way.

I hit the ground hard, absorbing not only my own weight, but that of another on top of me.

"Stay down," Drea shouted as she popped to her feet.

I rolled over and watched the demon ram into a group of Lumens battling shadow serpents. It took them out like bowling pins, but rather than finishing them off, the beast stopped and searched for me. It spotted me right away, and with another mighty bellow, headed back in my direction. It was a clear shot between me and the demon. Only Drea stood in its path.

I shoved to my feet, already having seen what this beast did to Lumen warriors in its path.

"No!" I screamed, throwing my hand up in the direction of Drea as if I had the power to stop the inevitable with sheer willpower alone, but of course that did nothing.

With a blade of light in one hand and what looked like an electrified whip in the other, Drea looked ready to take down the monster, but when it neared her it swung its massive arm at her, its fist on a collision course with her temple.

Drea tried to dip and twist out of the way, but she wasn't

fast enough. The demon's meaty paw clipped her shoulder, sending her flying into the wall. Her body hit the cinderblock wall, and then slid to the ground.

I scrambled for her, stumbling and dodging battles between Lumen and shadow serpents along the way. When I reached the spot where she was crumpled on the ground, I dropped down next to her.

"Drea," I shouted over the battle noises. I didn't want to jostle her if she had a spinal injury or something.

She groaned, and her eyes fluttered but didn't fully open.

Another roar shook the community center and ceiling dust trickled down on us. I looked over my shoulder to see the giant bull-like demon fix its red-eyed gaze on me.

This demon was relentless. What was its deal? Was I secreting some weird "attack me" pheromones? Why was it so fixated on me?

Kids shrieked, Lumens shouted commands, and the sounds of battle echoed in all directions. The room was in chaos, but my attention was singularly focused on the beast barreling toward me. The dark monster wanted me and had already proved it would destroy everything in its path to get me. The only way to protect everyone from its wrath was to lead it away.

"You want me?" I whisper-growled. "Fine. But you're going to have to catch me first."

Pushing from the ground, I took off for the emergency exit on the far side of the room. I didn't have to glance behind me to know that the nether-beast was following because I could practically feel its smoke-filled breath on the back of my neck as I ran.

Shoving through the door, I spiraled my way down the narrow staircase, not stopping when the beast smashed through the emergency exit behind me, taking down part of the wall in the process.

My feet barely touching each step as I bounded toward the first floor, I tried to formulate a plan, but the only thing my mind could come up with was, *Run faster!*

My lungs burned and my legs felt like Jell-O as I flew down the multiple floors taking three steps at a time. The sounds of the beast tearing after me gave me the endurance I needed to push through the pain. I had one more floor to go.

As if knowing he was about to lose his prey, the beast roared angrily. The vibrations shook the stairwell, and I lost my footing. Pitching forward, I tumbled down the last set of steps, my shoulder, knee, and thigh all taking painful impacts as I rolled. Sharp stabs of pain ripped through my body as I slammed into the door at the bottom landing and spilled out of the building and into the courtyard.

I'd lost my daggers somewhere in all that rolling, and there wasn't time to go back for them. Bruised and bloodied, I heaved myself off the ground and took off again, sprinting through the open gate that encompassed the entire compound and toward the alley between the Healing and Community Center. It was only three beats before the monster Hulk smashed through the exit after me.

I neared the mouth of the alleyway at an all-out sprint. Grabbing one of the metal bars from an open gate as I passed, I used it to help me veer around the corner, so I didn't run into oncoming traffic.

There was a group of teenagers on the sidewalk that I nearly took out. They cussed at me as I barreled through them. I glanced back and caught a glimpse of the demon hot on my tail, but it phased right through the teens like Indigo had told me they could. If I wasn't running for my life, I would have sighed in relief. If she'd been wrong about that, it would have meant I would have just unleashed a nether-beast on the unsuspecting people of New York City.

"Tate!" a familiar voice called out.

Jerking my head forward, I saw Gage running toward me. His eyes widened when he caught sight of the demon behind me. He mouthed a silent curse and skidded to a halt, then changed course so we were both racing in the same direction.

"Follow me," he yelled.

Gage was a Shade, and I didn't completely trust him, but I was out of options. I kept my gaze locked on his back as he sprinted ahead of me. He glanced back more than once to check that I was still keeping up. Sweat dripped down my face, and my lungs were about to explode, but there was no way I was slowing anytime soon.

"Shadowling!" the creature bellowed another time, and I ran even faster, catching up to Gage. Grabbing my hand, he yanked me down a narrow alley. We were through it and at the next block in seconds.

Gage tugged me to the right. "The cemetery," he said. "Demons can't set foot on the resting places of the dead."

He pointed to a small patch of green a block away that was sandwiched between two high-rise apartments. As we neared, I looked for an entrance and noticed the gates were shut, a length of chain holding them closed. The cemetery was ringed by a spiked metal fence that was at least eight feet tall.

Reaching the fence, I tried to scale it, but it was just too high and the decorative fleur-de-lis spikes at the top made it awkward to try to climb over.

Gage cursed. Knitting his hands, he bent over and gestured for me to put my foot in his hold. When I did, he boosted me up high enough that I could scramble over the top.

I dropped to the ground on the other side, and a burst of unfamiliar energy flooded my body. It felt like lightning bugs were zipping back and forth under my skin, but I pushed the sensation to the back of my mind and spun just in time to see the beast only a handful of steps from Gage.

Facing the approaching monster, Gage held a sword that was easily the length of his arm. Dark tattoos pulsed over his forearms, and smoke poured from his clenched hand running up and down the length of his steel blade. I had a sudden flashback of Drea's body flying through the air when the demon had swatted her away to get to me. I didn't want to see the same thing happen to Gage.

Just like before, I yelled and put my hand up in the air, but this time, something *did* happen. I felt a rush, a pulling and tugging inside me, and then it released with a snap. The strange energy that had entered me a moment before fled my body, feeling like it was shooting from my palm. A fissure appeared in the air, tearing the fabric of reality right in front of Gage. It leaked sulfuric smoke and glowed red from deep beyond.

Gage fell back a few steps in surprise. Unable to stop its momentum, the creature collided with the fissure and then seemed to be sucked into it.

With a gasp, I stumbled backward, dropping my outstretched arm. The red slash disappeared with a snap, sealing instantly. The only evidence that it had been there at all was the tinge of sulfur that hung in the air.

I stood frozen to the spot, still panting from the sprint through half of Midtown, unable to tear my gaze from the place the demon had vanished.

Gage turned slowly, shadows still licking up and down his arms, sword clenched in his fist. There was a haunted look in his eyes as he took me in, almost as if he were seeing me for the first time. His gaze swept from my head down to my feet and back up again, but then he shook his head, and his face cleared of all emotion.

With a flick of his wrist, the blade of his sword folded

three times and then retracted into the handle, which he shoved into a sheath at his side.

Walking up to the metal fence, his dark shadowy wings sprang from his back, and he looked over his shoulder for anyone watching before flying himself up and over with ease. The second his boots hit the hallowed earth, he flinched as if in pain, his wings disappearing instantly.

"What just happened?" I asked when he reached me. I swayed a little as a strange wave of exhaustion rolled over me.

Instead of answering, his brows knitted, and he brushed a clump of hair off my forehead, inspecting what I assumed was a wound. He prodded it lightly with his finger, and I flinched involuntarily.

"Did I do that?" I pointed at the place where the demon had disappeared into the fissure.

Gage glanced over his shoulder and then back at me. "No," he said with authority. "Watchers can't create portals, and I've never seen one that looked like that."

Relief rushed through me. I didn't know how it all worked, but perhaps whoever, or whatever, sent the creature had suddenly called it home. If so, that was lucky timing for us.

But if that's what happened, then what was that energy burst I felt?

Gage turned my arm to inspect another injury. I had a gash that was dripping blood. I probably got it when I tumbled down the stairs, stabbing myself with my own daggers like an idiot.

"This one might need stitches," he said.

I knew I was banged up, and now that I wasn't running for my life, all the bumps and bruises were starting to throb. All. Over. My. Body. I was also depleted of energy, but that was probably normal after an adrenaline rush. I'd get some stitches, heal, and recover, but figuring out what just happened was way more important at the moment.

"Are you *sure* Watchers can't open portals?" I pressed, looking back at the place the demon disappeared, because it kinda felt like some energy had burst out of me the second the rift was created, which was freaking me out.

He grunted and then nodded. "Positive. We can't create portals. Shades only get notified when one is about to open, Lumens can sense when they are near one, and only a Portal Master can close them. That's it."

Portal Master? What was that?

I narrowed my gaze, my thoughts suddenly drifting toward Gage's involvement in today's incident. "What were you doing outside of Lumen Academy right when we were attacked?"

He sighed. "When I heard the demons were going to open a portal inside the academy, I had—"

"You knew?" I reared back, ripping out of Gage's grasp, a ball of disgust growing in my belly. "There were kids in there! People got hurt. Some Lumens may have even died.

You knew it was going to happen and did nothing to stop it? Did nothing to warn them?"

"I couldn't get through," Gage gritted out, and then ran a hand through his hair. He started to pace. "Once we declare our house affiliation, we're not allowed on each other's property anymore. Wards are put up around both Shade Tower and the Lumen Compound to keep the other side out."

"Don't try to act like there was nothing you could have done. You could have warned someone. They could have evacuated the building," I growled.

"I—" Gage stopped pacing and clamped his mouth shut. A muscle flexed in his jaw as he ground his teeth together. "It's just part of the job. Shades and Lumens aren't friends— we're enemies. You'd do well to remember that."

"So you just stand by while people get hurt?"

His nostrils flared. I thought for sure he was about to say something, but he just glared at me.

"I could never be part of something like that," I spat. I was sick just thinking that my mother had made the decision to be a Shade. What could have possibly convinced her that was the right thing to do? Was she really shallow enough to be swayed by money and a fancy school? That didn't sound like the person Gran told me about. But what did I really know about her?

"Good. You aren't cut out for it anyway," he growled.

I forced out a humorless laugh. It sounded a bit like a strangled hyena. "If that's your idea of an insult, it's weak."

Gage took a step toward me, crowding me. His chest puffed out, and there was a wild look in his stormy green eyes. I almost retreated, but instead held my ground, straightening my spine to my full height, which meant I only came up to Gage's Adam's apple. His eyes flared when I refused to back down, the green in his irises so bright they looked lit from within.

Inhaling deeply, he held the breath for several beats before letting the air leak from between his lips. As his lungs deflated, his stony expression started to melt, as if his tough exterior was a façade he could no longer hold on to.

"It wasn't an insult," he said softly. His accented voice rolled over me like a caress.

A switch flipped inside me, and I went from furious to something altogether different in the span between breaths. Warmth blossomed in my chest as we stood no more than a foot apart, just staring at each other.

"Why did you do it? Why did you choose to become a Shade?" I asked, my voice no louder than a whisper. So far, Gage had been a ball of contradictions, but it felt like there was something inside him that was good. He'd come to my aid more than once, and that was hard to reconcile with everything I knew about Shades.

"When your father is the leader, it's not a choice," he answered honestly, and my heart bled for him. There was so much to that simple statement. I'd been told every Watcher got a choice on how they will live their life, which side they'll fight for, but looking at Gage and seeing the conflict splashed across his face, I knew that wasn't really true.

Time stretched between us. Something raw and powerful started to grow, pulling us together like magnets. I didn't understand it, but that didn't make it any less real.

Gage's body tipped toward me, and I followed his lead. I raised a hand, my fingertips feathering over Gage's high cheekbone, drifting up to brush a wisp of hair off his forehead.

Lifting his own hand, he gently caught mine and tugged me closer. Our gazes collided and held.

For a breath, a single moment in time, I felt like I saw him for who he truly was. It was a near perfect moment in which Gage wasn't a Shade and I wasn't a Watcher who hadn't chosen her house yet. A moment when we were just us.

And then it was shattered.

CHAPTER NINE

"Tatum!" Drea's shrill voice snapped me from my trance.

Gage flinched, and I stumbled backward, away from whatever magnetic pull he had over me. A mask dropped over Gage's features, shuttering whatever bit of vulnerability he'd just revealed to me.

Spinning to face my friend, I sighed in relief that she was alive. She was covered in black soot and bleeding at the lip, but alive. Reaching onto the myriad of tattoos on her arm, she came away with a double-sided axe. With one mighty swing, she broke the chain locking the cemetery gates together and then stowed the weapon back on her body.

Man, I need some magical tattoos asap. Except I needed ones with cookies and pizza.

Gage and my moment had fizzled, and I was back to feeling pain throbbing throughout my limbs as Drea jogged over to us.

"Get that stitched up." Gage's command washed over me before his wings snapped out of his back. Then he kicked off the ground and soared into the air, the darkening early evening sky only half-camouflaged his ascent.

"Hey! You'll be seen," Drea hissed after him.

Ignoring Gage's hasty retreat, I threw myself at Drea, crushing her in a hug. She might be a super new friend, but we'd also been through a lot, and it felt like we'd grown close in this short time. "I'm so glad you're okay."

"Are you kidding? I'm glad *you're* okay. Don't ever do that again," Drea scolded, pulling away from me and checking my wounds with a concerned look.

"Did any of the kids get hurt?" My heart was in my throat as I waited for her to answer.

Drea shook her head. "You led the demon away and then my mom closed the portal. She's the only Lumen in the city with the ability to close portals."

Ah. Aurelia must be the Portal Master that Gage mentioned.

"The level two serpentine demons dissipated when the portal closed," she continued. "They can't exist in our world without a link to theirs."

Relief crashed into me as emotion tightened my throat.

"You're going to make an amazing Lumen." Drea grinned. "You already have the courage part down."

A smile tugged at my lips. "I'm definitely going to need some of those cool tattoos."

"Patience, young Lumen," she said in her best Yoda impression, and then winked. "Let's get you stitched up."

I nodded and followed her out of the cemetery and down the alley, then we made our way through the bustling street and toward the Lumen healing center.

"What was Gage doing here?"

There was an air of annoyance in Drea's tone, and I didn't blame her.

I shook my head. "He knew about the portal, and he helped bring me to safety."

I don't know why I was trying to stick up for him after I'd just reamed him myself. Maybe it was because despite all of Gage's faults, I could see an ember of good in him, the tiniest of sparks I hoped would catch fire and spread.

People stared at the two girls limping past with bloody, dirt-stained clothes, but no one said anything. This was New York City after all. We could be stepping off a post-apocalyptic themed photoshoot.

The entrance to the healing center was packed. Injured Lumens littered the entryway as we passed. I don't know if I was in shock or what, but I didn't feel the pain anymore. I just wanted to see my gran now that I was reminded of her.

"Can I see my gran? Is she awake?" I asked Drea as she wove through the crowded waiting room. Teens and adult Lumens alike sat with bleeding arms and legs, waiting to be seen.

"Sure, after we get you stitched up," she called out. "That one gash on your arm looked pretty bad."

Walking up to a large open window where a nurse sat looking flustered by all the recent activity, Drea signed my name on a clipboard.

"Can I get some gauze? Her arm is bleeding heavily," Drea asked.

The nurse nodded and then disappeared, returning with a roll of gauze. "Stitches might be a wait. We have head injuries and abdominal bleeds we are dealing with first," the nurse told her.

Drea nodded. "Understood."

When she turned around, I waved her off. "I feel fine. Wrap me up and let me see Gran."

Pulling a strip of the gauze out, Drea rolled her eyes. "Okay, tough gi—"

The words died in her throat as she examined the deep gash on my arm.

Oh no. Was it worse than I thought? Pulling my arm up, I peered down, and my stomach dropped.

It was gone.

The deep gash that freely bled was now like new skin, without even a scar or scab to show for it, only some dried blood to indicate that there was once a wound there. I even felt like I had more energy now.

Drea scrambled to grab my other arm and inspect it. Then my forehead. My heart pounded in my ears as my hands shook.

"This is normal, right? A Watcher thing?" I swallowed

hard. This was new. I'd had stitches twice, and several burn marks littered my hands and arms from working the grill at the diner. I'd never healed like this before.

Drea's eyes were as wide as saucers. She indicated the waiting room full of injured Watchers. "Not normal."

Crap.

"Tatum! Drea!" Marlow called out, and we looked up to see her approach with Jacob, Skye, and Dash in tow.

I pleaded with my eyes for Drea not to tell anyone about my magically healed wounds, and she just nodded once, grabbing the pen and scratching my name off the list.

We approached the gang and Marlow squealed. "Holy crap, Tatum! It was a level *seven.*"

"Huh?" My mind was still on the healing wounds and how freaking amazing I suddenly felt after having tumbled down a flight of stairs less than an hour ago.

Marlow grinned. "You chased off a level seven demon. The novice hunters are chanting your name back at the academy."

A level seven. Wow that sounded super bad, and I was super dumb for doing that all by myself.

"Tatum..." Aurelia's voice feathered over me, and I spun to find Drea's mom looking down at me with a compassionate gaze. "Can I speak with you privately?"

My stomach sank. She knew. She knew I was a freak who healed, and maybe now they wouldn't let me into school here.

I nodded, sending Drea an alarmed look.

Breaking away from the hall, Aurelia led me to a quiet room, closing the door behind us.

She turned to face me. "Are you hurt?"

I shook my head.

"That was very brave of you today." She sat down in one of the empty hospital chairs and patted the chair next to her.

Why was she treating me like she was about to tell me someone died?

"My gran...?" I let out a strangled cry, suddenly realizing why she wanted to talk in private.

She placed her palms out, "She's fine. For now."

I chewed on my bottom lip. "For now?"

Aurelia nodded. "Tatum, I've discovered who cursed your gran. A Shade."

I let that sink in, but it only took a single breath to go from terrified to furious.

"Who?" I asked. For a wild second I thought she might say it was Gage.

"Arthur Alston."

I gasped. "How do you know?"

"Every Shade's magic is slightly different, like a fingerprint that's left behind whenever they use it. Most of their magic fades quickly, but curses are different. They linger, and so do the traces of magic from the caster. It took us longer than expected, but we recognize traces of Arthur's magic in the curse."

"But…" My mind was reeling. "So, he cursed my gran so that I would join the Shades no matter what?"

Aurelia nodded. "It looks that way. If you choose to become a Lumen, it will kill her if it's not removed."

My mouth dropped open. "And if I choose to become a Shade?"

Aurelia's lips pursed. "She'll recover fully."

Those bastards. They trapped me. I had no choice.

"Well, then remove it! That's why we brought her here, right?" I jumped up and started to pace the small room.

"A choosing curse is dirty work. They're forbidden, dark magic and one placed by a man as powerful as Arthur—"

"There has to be a way to break it!" I growled.

Aurelia took a deep breath. "Every Shade has a talisman, a necklace or crystal, a ring even. It's something they put a lot of energy into. If we can get his talisman, my healers might be able to reverse the spell using Arthur's energy imprint."

Before I could respond, there was a knock at the door and then a young man entered. He looked about thirty years old and battle weary. His clothes were torn, his hair matted with blood, but he stood erect and addressed Aurelia with the respect of an army general.

"Ma'am, I have the tipoff call you wanted to hear. Our voice identifiers can't place him," he said.

Aurelia waved him in. "Sorry, Tatum, this will only take a minute."

I nodded. I needed to cool down anyway, my mind was

spinning with gruesome murder scenes: Arthur's head torn from his body as I screamed bloody murder.

Breathe. Breathe.

"Play it," Aurelia said impatiently as the dude looked at me and raised an eyebrow, but Drea's mom waved him off. "She's fine."

Walking in, he pulled out his phone and tapped a button.

A woman's voice played out into the room from the speaker. "Lumen Academy, how can I—"

"A demon portal is opening up there right now! Get everyone out." Gage's deep timbre made my entire body lock up.

"Is this a prank?" The woman on the recording sounded pissed.

"No! Sound the alarm. Now!" Gage yelled at her.

An alarm blared and then the call went dead.

"Hmm, I don't recognize him," Aurelia told the man. "Thank you, Timothy."

He tipped his head and left while I stayed rooted to the spot. I'd accused Gage of doing nothing and he'd been the one to call and warn us in time to sound the alarm. Without that alarm we wouldn't have grabbed weapons or gotten all the kids into the gymnasium to protect.

A sob ripped from my throat, startling both Aurelia and me. The past twenty-four hours had been too much for me. I was finally breaking down. My gran, the eviction, the curse, Gage and his damn good deeds! I didn't know up from down.

I wiped at my eyes. "It was Gage Alston. On the call."

Her head reeled back in shock. "You sure?"

"Positive."

"Why would a Shade warn us of an upcoming attack?" she mused aloud.

A light bulb went off in my head. If Gage would warn us about an attack, what else would he do? Help me steal his father's talisman?

I met Aurelia's gaze. "I'm going to get you that talisman."

She shook her head. "Honey, no. It's impossible. A Shade's talisman is their most protected possession. They need it to perform spells. Arthur would kill you before he let you take it."

Okay, that wasn't ideal, but I'm sure I could figure out a way to get it without dying... I hoped.

I swallowed hard. "It's that or I join the Shades to save my gran. I can't exist in a world where she doesn't."

Tears filled Aurelia's eyes and she nodded once, accepting I wouldn't be deterred. "How can I help? Including today, we only have eight days."

I took in a deep breath, swallowing hard. "Hold my spot for me here. I'm going to be a Lumen, but for a little while I need to pretend I'm choosing the Shades."

She raised one eyebrow. "That sounds dangerous, Tatum."

I rolled out my neck. "Take care of Gran. I got this."

Without waiting for her reply, I burst out of the door and ran for the exit.

No one was taking my gran from me. If I had to steal Arthur Alston's talisman, then I would. It was time to test just how much Gage cared if I lived or died.

CHAPTER
TEN

I took the subway to Shade Academy, forcing my eyes to
the floor every time I saw a shadow or beastly creature
on someone's back. I was in a fragile place right now. I
couldn't handle the fact that the world was full of so much
darkness. As I walked from the subway stop to Shade Academy, I planned what I was going to say. I wasn't sure how
much I could trust Gage with the truth about my gran, but I
knew I would need his help if I was going to find that
talisman and break the curse.

I was just wondering if I should walk inside and ask for
Gage, or what, when the man of the hour stepped out from
behind a gelato cart and blocked my path.

"What are you doing here?" He looked at me incredulously. He held a cup of gelato with all the toppings and a
bottled water.

Two other dudes, about Gage's build, stepped up
beside him.

"Hello, beautiful," one of them purred. He was blond and covered in tattoos. Not the light-up Lumen kind, but the skulls and pentagram type. He was smiling, but the vibe he threw off was dark and made me feel like bugs were crawling over my skin. I rubbed my arms to rid myself of the sensation.

"Don't talk to her," Gage growled at his friend.

The dude scoffed, and Gage started forward, forcing me to walk backward and away from his companions lest I get trampled.

"Go home," Gage snarled.

I frowned. "I don't have a home anymore, and I'm here to get the full tour. I'm still undecided."

His eyes thinned to slits. Tossing his untouched dessert into a nearby trash can, he grabbed my arm gently but firmly, and steered me farther away from the other Shades, toward the side of the building. I glanced forlornly at the discarded gelato as we passed the trash can, sad to see the perfectly delicious food go to waste.

"What are you doing here?" Gage demanded to know when we were out of earshot. The rumble of his low voice resonated in my chest.

I swallowed hard, ready to really sell the lie that I wanted to finish my tour here. But lying to Gage felt wrong. "Your dad put a choosing curse on my gran. She'll die in eight days if I don't break it."

Gage ran a hand over his face, rubbing at his lips before

letting it drop to his side. "That sounds like him. Sneaky bastard."

Okay, not exactly the compassionate response I had expected, but at least he didn't try to defend his douchebag father.

"I need his talisman in order to break the curse."

Gage choked on his spit, turning it into a coughing fit, and pounded on his chest. "My father's talisman is his most prized possession. If he catches you trying to steal it, he'll kill you."

"Then help me," I told him.

"So I can die too?" He looked at me dubiously.

I narrowed my eyes, my mind whirling. Gage's help was essential to pulling this off. Without him, I didn't even know where to start looking for Arthur's talisman. I steeled my heart, telling myself that I'd go to any length to save Gran. If I couldn't appeal to that spark of goodness inside Gage, then I'd have to appeal to his sense of self-preservation.

"Interesting. I wonder what Arthur would think about you warning the Lumens about the demon attack at their academy earlier today?"

Gage's face hardened, a murderous look coming over him. "I don't know what you're talking about."

"I heard the call. I *know* it was you." A ball of unease rolled in my gut. I didn't like what I was doing, but I reminded myself it had to be done. "One call to Lumen

Academy and I could get the recording. We could let Arthur decide if it was you or not."

I started to get a little nauseous. This wasn't me. What was I doing?

Saving Gran. Suck it up, Tatum.

Gage regarded me silently. I could see his jaw flexing as he ground his teeth together. His nostrils flared and eyes narrowed. He was trying to keep his emotions under wraps, but anger radiated from him in waves. He stayed silent.

Okay. I was going to call his bluff. If he wanted to play hardball, I could play.

I reached into my back pocket and pulled out my phone. There was a new crack along the back of the case and the old one on the screen was longer, but it still worked. I had no idea how it had made it through the day. Maybe old technology really was the best? I found Lumen Academy's number and stopped with my finger hovered over the "call" button.

"You wouldn't," Gage growled.

I didn't take pleasure in this, and I was really hoping Gage caved soon, because I wasn't sure I could go all the way through with it. But he didn't know that. Pressing "call," I turned on the speakerphone and let Gage hear the operator pick up.

"Lumen Academy off-hours call service, if this is an emergency press one to be connected with a live operator. Otherwise please call back during busin—"

Gage yanked the phone from my hand and ended the

call. He looked at me disbelievingly. "I didn't think you had it in you," he breathed.

Shame burned my cheeks. "My mom's dead, I never knew my dad. Gran's all I have." My voice broke, and Gage sighed.

I realized then that I couldn't blackmail Gage, not after he'd helped us by calling in the warning.

"Fine, I'll get Indigo to help me. I *do* have a tour to finish." I yanked my phone from his grip and blasted past him, knocking into his shoulder and then past the two scary looking dudes he rolled with. Taking long strides across the street, I headed right for the entrance to Shade Academy.

No one was keeping me from saving my gran. No one.

A toxic mix of anger and fear swirled inside of me, but I didn't get half a block before I heard Gage curse and then jog to catch up.

He caught my arm, stopping me, and then growled, "It's late. Don't go in the front door, it will just cause undue attention. You're enough of a handful as it is. The last thing you need right now is for security to wake my dad and tell him you're here."

"So you'll help me?" I tried and failed not to sound desperate.

"If you get that audio call deleted. Besides, nothing would bring me more joy than seeing my father lose his prized possession." Hurt crossed his features then and I wondered how deep their relationship issues went.

Pretty deep, considering he had just agreed to help me steal his father's talisman.

Part of me wanted to smile in victory, but I was too disgusted by my own actions to take pleasure in the win.

We reached the cross streets for Shade Academy, and Gage redirected me down a narrow side street with a flick of his chin.

I reluctantly followed, relatively sure he wasn't taking me to some back alley to murder me. If he wanted me dead, he could have watched me get gutted by demons twice over by now. But I did just blackmail him, so his previous heroic deeds only offered me a small measure of comfort as we walked down the poorly lit thoroughfare. At what point would it just be easier for him to off me and then be done with it?

That utterly terrifying thought only made me more jumpy. New York City never really slept, but right now the only sound was the slapping of our boots against concrete beneath our feet. I tried not to think that every shadow had a sinister slant or held a monster waiting to jump me. Lack of sleep and sustenance weren't helping my mental state.

I squinted, trying to see the number on the building we'd just passed, when the grinding of metal followed by a loud bang had me jumping a foot in the air. I didn't notice Gage had stopped to wrench a door open. He looked at me like I'd lost my mind.

"There was a rat," I lied as I shuffled past him and into the dimly lit stairwell.

"Sure there was," he said, and then brushed past me to lead the way.

Yuck, stairs. I'd already had my share of them for the night. I rubbed the place on my arm where I should have had to get stitches, glad that the deep aches and pains from my tumble went away when my skin had healed.

Gage glanced over his shoulder and caught me rubbing my arm. "Did it need stitches?" he asked gruffly, but there was a glint of softness in his gaze before he fixed his eyes forward and continued climbing.

"Not exactly," I hedged, suddenly wishing I'd had the forethought to throw on a hoody before racing out of Lumen Academy. I didn't have answers about my healing, and I wasn't sure it was something I wanted to share with him.

Gage half turned so I could only see his profile. His eyebrows pinched at my non-answer, but he let it drop.

Shade Academy had entirely too many floors. The more we climbed, the more fearful I got that Gage was going to make me hike all the way to the top floor.

"Where are you taking me?" I asked after we huffed it up eight flights of stairs without talking.

Gage didn't answer. He was probably still stewing that I'd forced his help, but after two more flights he finally stopped when we reached the landing on the tenth floor. Gingerly, he pushed the door open and checked the hall to make sure it was clear before letting me pass.

"Where are we going?" I asked again.

"My room," he simply said.

"Excuse me? Your room? Why are—?"

Spinning, Gage jerked my body close and slipped a hand over my mouth to stop my shrill question. "I'm trying not to wake the entire place and alert them to your presence," he growled.

I licked his hand, and with a grimace, he dropped it.

"Cut it out," I demanded on a harsh whisper. "I don't like being manhandled."

"Noted... *Tate*," he said and then continued down the hall.

I knew he was calling me Tate just to get under my skin, so I almost yelled after him, "It's Tatum," just to be loud and piss him off too.

When we reached his room, Gage punched a code into the keypad next to the handle and then shoved it open. I followed him inside, noting the room looked exactly how I remembered, which shouldn't surprise me seeing I'd woken up in it only yesterday morning.

Gage went to his dresser and started scrounging around in it for clothes.

I planted my hands on my hips. "Can you tell me now what the big deal is about people knowing I'm here. It's going to happen eventually. It might take me a day or two to find Arthur's talisman."

Gage huffed out a humorless laugh and shook his head. "The big deal is that I need to know your plan before we go rushing into anything. If I'm going to help you, and that's a big *if*, we need to get our stories straight and have a rock-solid strategy. Otherwise, we'll both end up dead. You might have a death wish, but I certainly don't."

Right. My plan. My big, elaborate, well-thought-out plan.

I dropped my hands from my hips and some of the blood drained from my face, but Gage didn't notice because he was still opening and shutting drawers, taking out his frustration on his dresser while he searched for something. I started to chew my lip.

With a bundle of clothes clenched in his hand, Gage finally walked back toward me. "So, let's hear it," he snapped. "What's your master plan for this talisman heist? What scheme have you thought up to steal my father's most treasured and highly secured item, and then make it out of Shade Academy alive?"

"Well," I said, and then cleared my throat before going on. "My plan was to get back into Shade Academy so I could search for the talisman."

"And...?" he prompted.

"*And* to enlist your help in stealing it."

Gage blinked back at me, waiting for me to go on, but that was as far as I'd thought ahead. "That's it? That's the entirety of your plan?"

"Well..." I splayed my hands wide to indicate the room around us and then him. "I'm in Shade Academy and you're helping me. Everything is going well so far." I lifted my chin, daring him to contradict me.

Swiping his free hand down his face, Gage grumbled under his breath something that sounded an awful lot like, "She's going to be the death of me."

I opened my mouth to shoot off a pithy remark, but then stopped myself. The reality that I was putting Gage in real danger finally sank in. From what I knew about Shades so far, they did *not* mess around. Arthur was willing to murder my gran to get what he wanted, so what would he do to his son if he ever found out Gage helped me thwart him?

Something bad, that's what.

My stomach decided that was the moment it wanted to vocalize its displeasure and growled loudly. I laid a hand on it, my face reddening.

"That was a tad embarrassing."

Gage sighed. "When was the last time you ate?"

I shrugged. "Dinner… last night."

It had been a long twenty-four hours.

Setting the dark bundle of clothes on his bed, Gage disappeared into the bathroom. A moment later he reappeared with a fluffy white towel and shoved it at me.

"I'll go grab some food downstairs. Get cleaned up." He eyed the crusted blood on my clothes. "You're a mess."

Looking down at myself, I scrunched my nose. He wasn't wrong. I was covered in dried sweat and blood, and my clothes were ripped. I didn't even want to know what my hair looked like.

Reaching forward, he lifted my arm. "There's a waterproof dressing for your wound in—" Gage stopped talking.

It wasn't until his eyes widened that I realized what he was doing and snatched it back.

"What happened to the gash on your arm?" he asked, pointing to the spot where it should have been.

"Er, I don't know. It just… healed," I finished lamely. That was the only answer I had for it. I didn't know what happened any more than he did.

His fingers dusted over my face as lightly as butterfly wings as he took note of all the other places I was injured. His gaze swept me from head to toe and back up again. The intensity of his inspection caused a warm feeling to settle in my gut.

"You just… *healed*?" There was a touch of awe in Gage's tone that made me want to squirm.

"Yep." I popped the "p" and took a step back, wanting to break the sudden tension that hung in the air between us.

"That's not possible," he said.

"So I've been told." I was a little disappointed. A small part of me had hoped that even though Drea hadn't known why I healed so quickly, that Gage would have an idea. But he looked just as confused as she had.

Pressing his lips together, Gage shook his head lightly, clearly not knowing what to do about this particular anomaly.

"Shower. I'll get food so you don't pass out," he finally said. "You can borrow those." He pointed toward the lump on the bed. "We'll talk about your lack of a master plan when I get back."

"Looking forward to it," I said with a cheeky grin.

"I'm not," he grunted, and then left.

When the door clicked shut, I wasted no time grabbing the extra clothes and heading toward the bathroom. Of course it was immaculate, and as lavish as I expected: white marble everywhere; a walk-in shower and separate clawfoot tub; a fancy toilet with buttons that did who-knows-what; even a squatty bidet. It was a bathroom fit for a king, or maybe in this case, a Shade prince.

I shook my head. What a stark contrast to the shared showers and bathrooms at Lumen Academy. I supposed if you were trying to sway Watchers to the dark side, a luxury bathroom wasn't a bad place to start.

Stripping off my clothes, I left them folded in a pile on the ground and set the temperature in the shower to scalding, just how I liked it. I found girlie hair products under the sink and tried not to think about why he had the stash as I scrubbed the filth off me.

I would have preferred to spend an hour or two under the six-jetted shower, but there wasn't a lock on Gage's bathroom door, and I was paranoid about him coming back while I was naked. After I was pretty sure I'd scrubbed off a few layers of skin and smelled like a perfume store, I hopped out of the shower.

I quickly dried off, dressed, and then towel dried my hair. The clothes Gage left me were a pair of basketball shorts and a soft black t-shirt. The tee hung almost to my knees and the shorts more than halfway down my calves, but I couldn't deny they were comfy and smelled great. Shade Academy definitely sprang for the fancy detergent, something I'd always passed on in favor of the cheap generic off-brand.

I was about to head back into the bedroom when something buzzed from my mound of dirty clothes. Reaching down, I rooted through them and pulled out my phone. Now only the top third of the display screen still worked, so I couldn't see who was calling. I hit the answer button anyway.

"Hello?" I asked, holding the device to my ear as I walked out of the bathroom.

"Tell me you didn't return to Shade Academy," Drea barked on the other end of the line.

I winced and pulled the phone away from my ear. It was stuck on speaker, and with the display not working, I couldn't do anything about it.

"Okay. I didn't return to Shade Academy."

Her sigh of relief was audible. "Thank goodness. Tell me where you are, and I'll come pick you up."

"I'm at Shade Academy," I said, and then braced for the fallout.

"You just told me you weren't there!" she shouted.

"I only said that because you told me to."

"Tatum, you can't be there." There was genuine concern in Drea's voice that made me feel instantly guilty for not at least saying goodbye before I bolted. "I thought you were visiting with your gran, but I ran into my mom, and she told me what happened. I know what you're doing there, and it's dangerous. You need to come back to Lumen Academy."

"I agree with her," Gage said from over my shoulder. Yipping in surprise, I spun to face him. He carried a tray stacked with food; my mouth instantly started to water. Did I smell bacon?

Yum.

"Who is that?" Drea asked. "Gage, is that you? If you let anything happen to her, I'm going to rip your guts out through your nose. Do you hear me?"

Wow, that was colorful. Drea certainly had a creative imagination. I should've probably been disturbed by her reaction, but instead I was strangely touched she'd threaten someone's life on my behalf. I never had a friend willing to commit premeditated murder for me before. It actually gave me the warm fuzzies.

I looked between my phone and Gage, waiting to see how he'd react to Drea's threat, but he only smirked and set the tray of food down on one of the nightstands.

"I'm fairly certain that's an impossible task," he finally responded.

"I knew it was you," Drea accused. "I don't know what you're playing at, but I mean it. I will find the most painful ways to pull you apart piece by piece if Tatum gets hurt."

"Is that so?" Gage's smile only kicked up a notch as Drea's temper flared.

It was time to step in. "I'm going to be fine, Drea. I promise. Gage has agreed to help me." Both of them snorted, and I shot Gage a look that promised death if he contradicted me. "I'm only going to be here as long as it takes to find Arthur's talisman. Then I'm headed back to Lumen Academy. Promise."

The line was silent for long enough that I started to worry that she'd hung up. "Tatum, please come back. We'll find another way to help your gran."

"Your mother said that they couldn't reverse the curse unless they had Arthur's talisman. You and the other Lumens can't even enter Shade Academy to search for it, but I can. There is no other way."

Drea sighed. "One of us will be close to Shade Academy at all times. If you need us, just call."

"I will. Thanks for understanding how important this is."

"Family is everything. *Lumens* understand that." When Drea put extra emphasis on Lumens, heavily insinuating family wasn't important to Shades, Gage just rolled his eyes.

"Gage, you take care of our girl. If not—"

"Yeah, yeah, I know." He waved a hand in the air. "Dismemberment, disembowelment, and then death if anything happens to Tate." Reaching over me, he hit the "end call" button, cutting off whatever Drea would have said next. "Little does she know that if we get caught, there won't be anything left of me for her to torture," he said with a chuckle. "Shades are very thorough when it comes to destroying all the evidence."

I bit my lip. I'm pretty sure that was a joke... but then again, maybe it wasn't.

"Your father wouldn't really hurt you, right?"

A dark look crossed Gage's face. "Don't make the mistake of thinking that being my father's son will afford me any leniency. If anything, I'll be punished twice as hard because of who I am."

I'd noticed there wasn't a strong bond between the two of them when I'd met Arthur, but I wouldn't have guessed Arthur would actually hurt his own son. I wondered if that contributed to Gage's frosty personality. This made the stakes of this heist even higher. I needed Gage's help to pull this off, but could I live with the consequences?

While I was lost in my thoughts, Gage grabbed a glass filled with some sort of green substance and handed it to me, and a sliver of the brown cuff he seemed to always wear on his right wrist peeked from under his sleeve. "Green smoothie."

The corner of my mouth twitched. Maybe he was over the whole blackmail incident? "You made me a smoothie?"

"Don't get too excited. They come out of a machine in the cafeteria."

I tilted my head to see around him. "Do I smell bacon?"

"Sure do, have at it. I'm going to shower."

He headed toward the bathroom, pulling his shirt over his head as he went, not bothering to wait to start undressing until he reached privacy. I started to look away, but my gaze caught on the three red slashes that ran across his back.

"What happened?" I gasped.

Gage glanced over his shoulder, his mouth pulling down in a frown. "Punishment for killing that demon at the diner the other day."

"Arthur did that?" I wasn't an expert, but it look like he'd been whipped. The skin wasn't broken, but it was raised and bruised.

"He doesn't tolerate disappointment well," he said flippantly.

Bile churned in my gut, dampening my hunger. Whatever happened, I could not let Arthur find out about Gage's involvement in this heist. If Arthur whipped him for killing a demon, what would he do to him if he learned Gage helped me steal his talisman? It was a chilling thought.

Gage turned to look at me by the bathroom door. "If you fall asleep before I get out, just make sure not to sleep on the left. That's my side of the bed."

I choked a little on the smoothie I'd just taken a sip of.

"You're kidding, right? We're not both sleeping in there." I pointed to the extra-large bed that would probably fit four people comfortably. Since he'd slept on the floor the last time, I just assumed he would again.

Rather than answer, Gage lifted an eyebrow and smirked before shutting the door.

I pushed the sleeping arrangements out of my mind as I dug into the pile of food Gage scavenged for me. I found I wasn't simply hungry, but ravenous. Running from demons really worked up an appetite. Or maybe the self-healing thing burned a crazy amount of calories? Whatever the case,

I had the whole mountain of food polished off before Gage even finished his shower.

Drowsiness set in quickly—food coma mixed with running from a giant scary demon knocked me out. This had to be the longest day of my life.

I lay down on top of the bedding, promising myself I was only going to rest my eyes until Gage returned. We had too much planning to do for me to sleep now, but the lull of oblivion was too strong, and I was out in seconds.

B ang, bang, bang.
"Just five more minutes, Gran," I yelled as I grabbed a pillow and shoved it over my head.

Bang, bang, bang.

The pillow did little to muffle the noise of Gran knocking on my bedroom door. She was persistent this morning.

Wait. I didn't have a bedroom anymore, I slept on the couch—and the soft mattress below me was definitely not a lumpy couch cushion.

I threw the pillow off my head and tried to sit up, only to find a large bare arm thrown across my stomach, pinning me to the bed. Turning my head, I came face to face with slitted green eyes.

"You slept on my side," Gage grumped, his words slow and deep from sleep.

"Get off me," I squawked as I slapped at his hand.

Removing his arm from me, he stretched both of them high above his head, giving me an eyeful of naked man chest.

Bang, bang, bang.

"Don't get your knickers in a twist, I'm coming," Gage shouted, and then slid out of the bed. He walked to the door in low-riding sweatpants, the brown leather cuff on his wrist, and nothing else.

Yikes.

My heart rate spiked, and I had difficulty tearing my eyes from his broad shoulders and muscled biceps. The magnificence of his form wasn't diminished by the red marks that crisscrossed his back, although the slashes made me feel a little bad for ogling him. He'd earned those stripes for helping me.

I shook off those thoughts and tried to make sense of what had happened. I fell asleep on top of the bedding last night, which meant Gage must have moved me under the covers. Why didn't he wake me up when he got out of the bathroom? Maybe he tried and I was too knocked out? It was possible. Even now, I felt like I could sleep ten more hours.

Gage threw the door open and then slouched against the jamb.

"Is the building on fire?" he asked in a bored tone.

I was horrified to see Arthur over Gage's shoulder. With a squeak, I pulled the covers up to hide the fact that I was in one of Gage's t-shirts—as if lying in his now-rumpled bed wasn't damning enough.

"I was notified by security that you slipped in the side entrance with Ms. Powers last night. Is that true?"

Rather than answer, Gage just opened the door wider so Arthur had a clear shot of me.

Arthur cocked a brow. "I see," he said, and then turned back to his son. "You were supposed to bring her to me immediately when she returned," he uttered quietly, but I still heard every word.

Gage shrugged. "We were busy," he said.

Kill. Me. Now.

Just the insinuation that Gage and I were sleeping together reddened my face. It didn't matter that I didn't respect Arthur and was one hundred percent sure he was an evil POS, I still wanted to crawl under a rock and hide. I got that this was probably not a big deal for a lot of kids my age, but it was a big deal to me. I was by no means sheltered. I'd spent the better part of the last year being the primary money earner and taking care of Gran all on my own, but I'd hardly had time for boys, so, romantically speaking, I was a bit stunted.

Arthur made a noise in the back of his throat that was hard to interpret, and then nodded in satisfaction. "Bring her to my office once she's presentable. I'll get her set up in our system and registered for classes." He tilted his head in my direction. "And I'll allocate her a more appropriate room assignment."

He'd said what any responsible adult would say, but was there a glitter of pride in his eyes? *Gross.*

With that, he turned on a heel and left. Several other Shade students loitered in the hall, keen on watching the show.

This was quite possibly the most humiliating moment of my life.

"Do you have Tatum in there?" a familiar voice asked. Indigo peeked around Gage. Seeing me, she smiled and then waved.

"Do you have any extra clothes Tate can borrow? Hers are..." Gage swiveled his head in my direction, a suggestive grin on his face. "Let's just say hers didn't make it through the night unscathed."

I sucked in a breath of air so quickly I started to choke on it.

"No prob. Give me a minute," she said.

Gage closed the door, and I chucked a pillow at his head, which he easily deflected.

Jumping out of bed, I stomped over to him and poked a finger in his exceptionally well-toned chest. He simply looked down at my hand and then up at my face.

"What were you thinking? Now everyone thinks we slept together," I said. Maybe this was payback for blackmailing him. If so, I probably deserved it.

Gage plastered an innocent look on his face—I wasn't buying it—and gestured to the bed. "We *did* sleep together."

"That's not what I meant, and you know it," I snapped.

"Calm down, Tate—"

"It's Tatum."

"It's just part of the plan," he said.

I scoffed. "Convincing your father and the rest of Shade Academy that we... er... that you and I..." I waved my arm toward the bed because I couldn't seem to get the words out. Gage smirked, obviously amused at my distress. "*That* was part of your plan?"

"Actually, it was. Much easier to explain why we're spending so much time together if everyone thinks we're shagging."

I'd gotten so used to his light accent that I'd forgotten he was British until he said things like shagging.

"Ah, you're a pig." I pushed against Gage's chest in frustration, but he didn't move an inch.

"Apologies for the spooning," he said with a broader smile. "I rather like having a warm body next to me while I sleep. I think I could convince Dad to keep the sleeping arrangements the same if you'd like." He raised one eyebrow but there was a playful smirk on his face.

I really wanted to throat punch him. It was going to happen right then and there, and it didn't matter if he'd kinda, sorta, maybe, saved my life a time or two. I wouldn't feel bad about it.

Not one bit.

I don't know if it was the look on my face, or if reality just set in, but Gage finally sobered. "Honestly, it earns me brownie points with my father if he thinks I seduced you into becoming a Shade." I frowned, immediately remembering what Drea told me about the girl Jacob had liked: Britt. Maybe that story was true after all?

Gage continued, oblivious to my judgy thoughts. "He was suspicious after I killed the level five demon in the diner. If we're going to get away with stealing his talisman, we're really going to have to sell this lie. I can guarantee we won't be able to pull this off unless I'm on his good side."

"So you want to pretend I'm your girlfriend?" I crossed my arms and pinned him with a glare.

Gage's eyes bugged. "Girlfriend?" He said the word as if it were something foul and detestable. "Let's not get carried away. I don't do *girlfriends*. I have a reputation to uphold."

"Then what was all that about?" I swung my hand around to indicate the room and the little charade he'd just performed for his dad.

"Shagging and having a girlfriend are two different things."

"You want people to think I'm sleeping with you without being your girlfriend?" I pulled a face. "Who do you think I am? Gross."

Gage crossed his arms over his chest, which drew my eyes back down to his naked skin. He needed to put on a shirt.

"What do you care what people here think of you? You're not planning to stay anyway. And besides, we just met. Saying that you're my girlfriend won't be believable."

I rolled my eyes. "But you think it's perfectly believable that we'd be having sex after only two days?"

Gage shrugged. "Yeah."

I rubbed my forehead. "I can't believe we're having an argument about the status of our fake relationship."

"Just for the record, I don't really like the 'R' word either. Sleeping together, friends with benefits, bed buddies… whatever. But 'R' word and 'girlfriend' are off limits."

I threw my hands in the air, totally exasperated.

"How about we meet in the middle and settle on dating? It keeps things vague while still accomplishing our goals," Gage offered, his lips twitching, but he covered it by going over to his dresser, grabbing a shirt and finally, *finally*, covering his chest.

I narrowed my eyes. Was he enjoying this argument? If so, he was deranged.

Huffing, I planted my hands on my hips. "Seriously. You think this charade will help us find Arthur's talisman?"

I didn't like this persona Gage suggested I project, but he had a point. Did I really care what the Shades thought of me if I was never going to interact with them again?

"Yeah, I have a plan." He paused, considering his next words. "But are you really prepared for the consequences of your actions? You need to know that after you steal my dad's talisman and heal your gran, you'll be hunted. You won't ever be able to show your face around here again. You'll have to watch your back for the rest of your life. His talisman is his source of magical power. He will not let it go lightly."

I swallowed hard. *Yikes.* Maybe he was only playing up the danger to get me to chicken out of the whole thing and get himself off the hook? But if he *was* telling the truth, watching my back for the rest of my life didn't sound ideal... but if it would save Gran, then I would do it.

"I'm okay with that. Gran deserves to get her life back. What's *your* plan?" I hadn't meant to growl the words accusatorially, but they came out that way. His father took years from Gran. It was his fault she had a scrambled mind, so now I was going to take something from him.

"Have dinner with me tonight."

I shook my head. "Gage, focus on the plan."

He lifted a single brow. "That's the plan. We're fake shag... dating, so I'm bringing my newest conquest to have dinner at my father's penthouse to impress her with my wealth and power."

Conquest. Yuck. I think I just threw up a bit in my mouth.

"And how is that going to help us?"

"The most likely scenario is that he stores his talisman in his home office. We'll need to get into his penthouse to search."

"If you think it's there, why don't we just go right now. He's probably going to be busy here all day."

Gage chuckled. "That's cute you think my father would let me in his residence unsupervised... at least anymore. He's well aware of the trouble I could get into. His penthouse is warded with Shade magic, as well as the best human security money can buy. We're not getting in unless he invites us."

Excitement thrummed through me. Sure, I'd prefer to ransack Arthur's penthouse right now, but waiting until tonight wasn't really a stretch when I originally thought it would take me days to find his talisman.

I stepped forward eagerly. "What does his talisman look like? Should I get a gun? Or maybe a sword? I wonder if I—"

Gage groaned, rubbing his face. "Why am I doing this?" he grumbled up at the ceiling in frustration.

I grasped the sides of his face and forced him to look at me. When he did, I was met with two stormy green eyes.

"Because I believe... deep inside... you're a good person," I told him. And I did believe that. Mostly. He couldn't only be helping me to keep me quiet about his warning call to Lumen Academy. There had to be more to him than that.

His face fell, eyes softening. It was like he'd never been told that before and I'd hit him right in the feels. Gage, I was learning, was like a complicated puzzle. Every time I thought I had a piece figured out, there were hundreds more that didn't fit.

"I'm really not," he said, and then his eyes fell to my lips, and I wet them with my tongue.

Full disclosure. Even before I started homeschooling my senior year, I was a bit of a loner, so other than kissing Peter Garrison on the bus sophomore year, I had zero experience when it came to making out or anything of that nature. But

I'd be lying if I said I hadn't thought about what it would be like to kiss Gage.

"Tate." His voice was so soft it feathered over me.

Butterflies took flight in my stomach.

"It's Tatum," I breathed, leaning closer to him.

Sure, I could fake date the giant, ripped, angel warrior. Easy peasy. Totally believable. My street cred for this stuff was legit.

Run. My inner self was freaked out.

What am I doing?

A knock at the door snapped me from my mental breakdown. I dropped Gage's face like a hot stone. Stepping back three paces, I realized I was all but panting.

"Enter," Gage growled, annoyance laced in his voice.

Indigo popped her head into the room and grinned. "Clothes. Wanna change in my room?"

I sighed in relief, nearly fanning myself. "Yes."

I crossed the room so fast I all but ran. It was getting *way* too hot in here.

"Meet you in the cafeteria, *babe*," Gage called at my back.

I cringed. "No pet names!" I snarled back at him.

I could tell by the cocky look on his face that I was in trouble.

Indigo was shorter than me, so her skinny jeans were more like mid-calf capris, and I was totally not wearing underwear, but other than that I was rocking some clean semi-cute threads. The jeans were high waisted, and she'd given me a hot pink crop top so that a few inches of my midriff showed. She'd insisted on doing my hair into a thick side braid, and even putting on makeup.

"If you don't look your best on the first day, the other girls here will eat you alive. Especially Claire."

I paled. "Who is Claire?"

"She's kinda the queen bee around here. Or at least she likes to think so. And she's hooked up with Gage on and off for years."

Great. And everyone thought I was dating—or, ah, doing *stuff*—with Gage now, so Claire would be after me.

"She still likes him I assume?" I raised one eyebrow as Indigo added some smoky black eye shadow to my upper lids.

Indigo snorted. "Still likes him? She's *obsessed* with him. Watch your back."

My stomach knotted. I was getting the very strong impression that Lumen Academy was full of sunshine and rainbows and wholesome students, while Shade Academy contained psychotic unicorns, demons, and worse... evil mean girls.

Oh, how I longed to have Drea at my side. But I had to admit, Indigo was growing on me, and I wasn't sure how easy it was going to be to leave her here when I joined Lumen Academy.

"Hey, thanks for helping me out." I reached out and squeezed her hand.

She smiled. "I was the underdog when I arrived too. We gotta stick together."

Was I the underdog? *Dang.* Wasn't that another word for loser?

Pushing that from my mind, I stood up and got a glimpse of myself in the mirror.

Whoa. I rarely wore much makeup. I was a mascara and lip gloss kind of girl. I was also pretty modest with how I dressed. I liked my body, it was just that I was kinda bashful with all the attention I got when I showed skin, so I stopped doing it. I guessed if I was going to be posing as someone who'd caught Gage's attention, I'd have to dress like this. I needed to be seen as his equal, because he didn't seem like the kind of guy who dated girls that worked at dodgy diners and just wore lip gloss and mascara.

One hundred dollars says Claire wears false eyelashes, I bet myself.

Indigo and I left her dorm room and headed toward the cafeteria. *Just one day.* I only needed to do this for one day so that I could make it to dinner with Arthur tonight. Then I would steal his talisman and book it back to Lumen Academy and save Gran.

One day, I breathed, making it my internal mantra.

When we stepped into the cafeteria, Indigo grabbed two trays and handed me one. I swallowed hard as every single eye seemed to turn in my direction.

You're imagining things. You're not that important, I told myself. But it was hard to shake the feeling that they were going out of their way to stare at me. My stomach grumbled as I piled eggs, bacon, toast, fruit, and a cup of yogurt on my plate. I'd been hungrier lately, like I couldn't get enough calories no matter how much I ate.

When we left the food line, I spun, and Gage was standing right in front of me. His green eyes raked down my body, trailing over my pink top, down the tight skinny jeans and then slowly back up.

Without a word, he took my tray, carrying it for me as we followed him to a table with half a dozen people at it.

Gage is carrying my tray not because he likes me, but because he's selling our lie, I told myself, because the butterflies in my stomach were dancing like they were at a rave right now.

When we reached the table, Gage set my tray down and then sat next to it, patting the seat. There was a challenging sort of glint in his eyes. I imagined making me uncomfortable was his concession for being roped into this heist.

I gulped, sitting as I stared at the group of teens who'd fallen into a hushed silence. Indigo sat on my other side. She shifted and silently dove right into her meal. I got the vibe this crew made her a little uncomfortable as well.

"Everyone, this is Tate. She's new here," Gage said casually, and then slipped an arm onto the back of my seat, clearly staking his claim without using words. "Her mom was a Shade."

"It's Tatum actually." I gave everyone a friendly but probably awkward smile.

Gage reached out, grabbing a piece of bacon from my plate, and bringing it to his mouth. I yanked the strip from his hand and put it back on my plate.

"Get your own, *babe,*" I said sarcastically, and he smirked.

I was starving, and I'm pretty sure *Thou Shall Not Steal Bacon* should be the eleventh commandment.

A gorgeous redhead wearing a black leather corset top and way too much makeup reached across the table and placed a piece of bacon on Gage's plate. "You can have mine, G." She winked.

Jealousy flared to life inside of me as Gage picked up the bacon and ate it.

My gaze flicked to the redhead's, and she smirked.

False eyelashes.

"Claire?" I asked.

She looked surprised. "Gage told you about me?"

I shook my head. "Nope. Just a good guess."

An uncomfortable silence descended on the table as I tucked into my meal. Gage cleared his throat. "Kev, my dad got season tickets again this year. Wanna hit up the Yankee's game opening week?"

The scary dude I'd seen outside the gelato cart last night nodded. "Definitely."

It was hard to explain, but some of these kids had an energy to them that made me squirm. I couldn't put my finger on it, and I was just finishing my last bite of food when my vision suddenly went blurry. I blinked rapidly, trying not to freak out.

Maybe four pieces of bacon was too much salt or something. When my vision cleared, I gasped.

Kev, Claire, and Gage's other friend Shawn all had a dark shadowy snake coiled around their throats.

I yelped, flying off the bench and stumbling backward. Gage turned to face me in surprise. Waving off Indigo, he left the table to approach me where I cowered in the corner of the lunchroom.

"What's wrong?" he asked.

I searched Gage for the same snake, relieved to see it wasn't on him, and then looked back at everyone at the table, who were now staring at me like I was a lunatic. Indigo was also snake free, but the smoky shadow creature slithered from Kev's neck, down his shirt, and out of sight. I blinked and Claire's snake loosened, draping around her shoulders like a shawl.

"Snakes," I whimpered.

Gage frowned. "What?"

I swallowed hard. "Claire, Kev, and Shawn have... demon snakes around them. Don't you see that?" I pointed to the table, glad we were out of earshot.

Gage looked at his friends and then back at me. Surely, if he was a Watcher, he had the same abilities as I did to see demons.

"I don't see anything. Maybe you need more sleep."

No. They were there. I blinked rapidly again, and the snakes turned into black smoke and then disappeared. Shaking my head, I ran a wobbly hand over my arm. Goose bumps covered my flesh.

"Hey. You good?" Concern etched on Gage's face. He reached for my hand.

I'd be touched if I thought it was concern for me, rather than concern that I was ruining his reputation. I didn't know what that was, but it was clear no one else could see it so I was keeping it to myself.

"Just need more sleep, I guess."

Gage peered at me for another long moment, and then pulled a piece of paper out of his pocket. "I got your school schedule, so you didn't have to suffer my dad's company any more than necessary."

That was rather thoughtful. I was instantly suspicious. "Classes already?" I laughed nervously. "Thought I had seven more days."

He shrugged. "Technically, you have until your eighteenth birthday before the Descension Ceremony, but until then I think my dad wants to get you settled."

"Descension Ceremony? As in 'to descend?'" I shivered. That name alone should have tipped every Watcher off to which side they should choose. "Thank God dinner with your dad is tonight, I wouldn't make it a week here." I couldn't imagine being here and having to do that ceremony to save Gran.

Gage looked around the room, reaching up to brush his hair from his face, avoiding eye contact.

"Gage? Dinner?"

"Yeah… about that." A muscle jumped in his cheek. He was annoyed about something.

I growled.

"Do you need more bacon before I break the bad news?" He indicated the self-serve counter.

"Ha ha. Tell me." I mean, more bacon wasn't a bad idea. My stomach grumbled at the thought. Even after all that food I didn't feel full.

"So my dad said he'd love to have you and me over for dinner... in three days when he gets back from an emergency business trip in London."

My eyes widened. "Three days!" I whisper-screamed, causing a few students nearby to stare.

Gage grabbed me by the arm and dragged me to a quieter section of the cafeteria. He backed me up against the wall and then leaned forward, his lips touching my ear, and his clean-shaven jaw brushing against my own. I froze, totally convinced he was going to kiss my neck or something. Maybe that's what he wanted everyone else to think.

Breathe. Think. Focus. Bacon.

"Listen, the plan still holds. You have seven days, and you will have the talisman in three. Just relax and try to fit in." He dragged his lips across my cheek as he pulled away and I lost my train of thought.

"Your skin is really soft," I said stupidly.

A half-cocked grin pulled at his face, and he reached out and dragged two fingers across the one-inch strip of bare skin at my rib cage. "So is yours."

My heart pumped so hard in my chest I was pretty sure he could hear it.

Gran. I was doing this for my gran. "Look, my grandma is in a coma. She's on death's door. Every day we wait is a day she suffers."

The fire behind his eyes died and he nodded. "There's nothing more I can do. My dad is already on a plane, and there's no way the two of us can get into that penthouse without him dropping the wards. Besides, I want that voice call evidence destroyed if I'm helping you, so this gives you time to work on that."

I chewed my lip and nodded. I should be grateful Gage was helping me at all. I told myself it didn't really matter if it was out of the goodness of his heart or to cover his own tracks, but that didn't stop me from secretly hoping it was the former.

"Okay. Three days, no biggie." I cleared my throat, because he was still standing too close.

He tilted his head.

"Come on, *babe.* First bell is about to ring," he said.

He slipped his hand into mine and pulled me across the cafeteria. I knew it was no big deal to him—by the sight of the girlie shampoo under his sink it was *really* no big deal at all—but I'd never been in anything close to a relationship. I'd never gotten that experience working five billion hours to pay the bills with Gran, so even though this was fake, I gripped his hand tightly and decided to enjoy it.

Would-you-like-ketchup-with-that? Tatum Powers, was going to be the popular *it* girl for three days, and I was going to soak it all in.

CHAPTER TWELVE

I sat in a desk surrounded by twelve-year-olds for half the morning. Since I didn't grow up in this world, I guess Arthur thought I needed to catch up, so he'd sent me to sixth grade demon history class. For the first hour I was mortified, then I got interested in the subject. It was fascinating. The teacher was claiming that angels fell from the upper realms, and they were what we call demons—not evil at all, just ugly angels apparently. Holding my tongue was harder than I thought, but I managed it.

"This place is awful," I whisper-screamed to Drea as I hid inside of the broom closet. I'd called Drea to gripe about it. It was just my lunch break, but I needed to talk to someone sane right now. "They teach the kids everything backward."

"Well, yeah. How else are they going to brainwash them to guard portals of evil when they grow up?"

Well, that was depressing. This place was a total lie. I wanted to kidnap all these kids on my way out.

"Look, I'll be back in three days. Just keep a close eye on Gran for me, okay?" I'd already told her about the delay.

She groaned. "You're crazy."

"I know," I agreed.

The closet door yanked open then and I ended the call, coming face to face with Indigo.

"Applying for the janitor position?" She looked at the mop in my hand, which I'd grabbed on reflex as a weapon.

I gave a nervous laugh. "Oh, is that for me?" I reached out to grab the tray full of sandwiches, chips, and three pickles.

She yanked it back. "It's for both of us. Geez, what are you, pregnant?"

My mouth popped open. "No!"

Grabbing one of the sandwiches, I tore into it like a rabid dog, and Indigo's brows drew together.

"Whaft?" I murmured through a mouthful of food.

"Nothing." But I could see she was silently taking notes on me, and I slowed my chewing.

Always hungry, self-healing. It was clear that there were a few things happening to me that didn't seem to happen to the other Watchers.

It dawned on me then, and I set the sandwich back onto the tray. "Is something wrong with me?"

Her face, once concerned, now filled with compassion. "No. You're fine. Come on, Shawn is having a huge party at *Wings* tonight. Come with me?"

I followed her out of the closet, gracefully tripping over

an empty bucket and nearly face-planting. "Say what? Isn't that the eighteen and over club where druggies and dirtbags hang out to get into trouble?"

Indigo pinned me with a glare.

"Oops. I mean, super cool teens who are stand-up citizens?"

She shook her head, chuckling. "Gage knows the bouncer. He'll get you in. I turned eighteen six months ago."

My stomach growled, and I grabbed a pickle, snapping it off with my teeth. "So Gage is going? Will Claire be there too?"

Indigo nodded. "Where Gage is, Claire is."

A stone sank in my gut. I didn't like this game anymore. I wanted Arthur's talisman and then I wanted to go home.

"Where did you get these boots?" I asked Indigo. "I want to snag a pair."

Apparently even being a prospective Shade came with some pretty nice perks. Indigo took me shopping for essentials after school. I almost fainted when she handed me my very own platinum AMEX with *no* limit. I didn't expect the money train to last after I stole Arthur's talisman, but I wasn't going to pass up the opportunity while it lasted. Maybe I could buy some expensive items to sell off later? Sticking it to Arthur in more ways than one was fine by me. Gran suffered for years because of his curse, so if this was his money, I was spending as much of it as I could.

Indigo glanced down at the chunky black biker boots she'd lent me for the night. "They are pretty on-point. You can have them if you want. I have a closet full of boots just like them."

I was still dressed head-to-toe in Indigo's clothes. Along with the boots, I wore the coolest cropped leather jacket. I wasn't as wild about the black spandex lace dress I wore because it showed way more skin then I was normally comfortable with. She'd told me it came to right above the knee, and maybe it did on her, but with my added height it barely covered my butt and suctioned to my curves like cellophane. I had to resist the urge to tug it down every other step. At least—thanks to our shopping outing—I was wearing underwear.

"Thanks, but I'm not taking your stuff." I smiled back to show that I was still grateful.

We turned a corner, and I spotted a small grouping of people waiting in line in front of *Wings*. I assumed we'd fall into place at the end of the line, but Indigo strutted right by everyone and headed for the entrance, which was guarded by a heavily muscled and even more heavily tattooed giant. I slowed, but it wasn't the bouncer's size and ink that caused my hesitation. It was the horned figure hovering behind him and whispering in his ear that gave me pause.

Demon.

Indigo was two paces in front of me before she noticed I

wasn't next to her anymore. She glanced back and forth between me and the gorilla of a man guarding the entrance to *Wings* several times before it dawned on her why I'd stopped. She quickly rejoined me, a look of understanding on her face.

"You'll get used to it," she said, indicating the shadow demon hunched over the bouncer. "I promise."

Tearing my gaze from the red-eyed creature, I blinked at Indigo. "It seriously doesn't bother you?"

She smiled, a dimple appearing in both cheeks. "Nope, not one bit."

That made me sad... for her. This wasn't anything I ever wanted to get used to, ever.

"I get it's going to take a little time though. You can wait here while I go talk to Jett and make sure we are on the list."

"Hey, sweetness," came a slurred voice from behind me. "How about you skip the clubbing and just come home with me? I can show you a real good time."

I glanced over my shoulder to find a twenty-something dude who reeked of alcohol and bad life choices. I sighed. This was the fourth time I'd been approached since we left Shade Academy. My dress was short, I got it, but that didn't mean I was going to throw myself at every creeper who said "hello."

Indigo's gaze slid to the dude who'd just propositioned me. "Want me to put him down for you?" she offered.

There was a sly look in her eyes, like she was joking, but

also hoping I'd say yes. The look matched her off-the shoulder tee that said, "sweet but psycho" a little too well.

I shook my head. "It's not worth the trouble. I'll be fine."

She pursed her lips, but then turned and headed toward the giant bouncer. With her spiked black hair framing her face and her cute punk rock outfit, she looked like a little goth pixie to me, and I was sad that she had already chosen to be Shade.

"Come on, baby. Don't be so frigid," the drunk dude garbled behind me.

I rolled my eyes. As a resident of New York City since birth, I was used to the occasional perv and weirdo. During the night shift at Sal's Diner, we got losers like this all the time. Taking the subway home at two a.m. was always a mixed bag, but this guy was really starting to rub me the wrong way.

A hand landed on my butt suddenly and squeezed. Unbridled rage rushed through me, and all rational thought flew from my mind. I spun so fast the guy didn't even have time to duck. My elbow smashed right into his nose, and I heard the satisfying crunch of cartilage. His body crumpled to the ground with a thud, and I sneered.

"You broke my nose," he wailed with his hands cupping his face. I was pleased to see blood dribbling down his chin.

"You don't grab girls uninvited, *ever*," I yelled at him.

He dropped his hands. His nose was bent at an unnatural angle, and the lower half of his face was painted crimson.

"Look at what you're wearing. You're asking for it," he spat, his features contorted in rage.

I. Saw. Red.

I took a quick step toward him, and he flinched. "It doesn't matter if I strutted down the street naked. That wouldn't give you permission to lay a hand on me."

"Preach!" a female said, and I looked up in time to see a group of girls in line let loose with a series of cheers and whistles.

"I guess you didn't need my help after all. I'm impressed," Indigo said, suddenly appearing at my side. "Come on, we're good to go."

She tugged my arm, and I gave the guy on the ground one more scathing look, tempted to land a kick to his ribs just to make my point. The group of girls who had my back laid into him with boos and verbal smackdowns as he struggled to his feet. There was a trace of fear on his face now that he was outnumbered, and I was satisfied with that.

I gave Jett a wide berth as Indigo shuttled me into the club. I couldn't see the demon anymore; my demon vision was still in and out, but the guy's eyes flashed red as he watched me shuffle past him. I'd be lying if I said I wasn't a little shook. The fact that demons could just *attach* to a human and affect them was beyond unsettling.

Inside the club, the music was loud, and the lighting was dim, making it hard to hear Indigo, and difficult to tell the difference between real shadows and the smoke-like demons that hovered around some of the clubbers near us.

A rock band was playing on the stage toward the back. It was difficult to decipher the words to the song, but the beat was good, and the crowd was into it. I'd always loved dancing—even though most of my raves were solo and held in the safety of our apartment—but something about this environment was oppressive. I didn't like it one bit.

The performers were on an elevated platform, set apart from the mash of bodies on the dance floor, so I could clearly see demons feeding from two out of the five band members as they rocked out. The two musicians' eyes were glazed as they performed, and it sent shivers down my spine.

I wasn't feeling this vibe, and I wondered how long was an appropriate time to wait before telling Indigo I was headed out. Would fifteen minutes be too soon? Ten? I'd never get used to seeing these creatures just hanging off of people like vampires, sucking their energy or whatever it was they did.

"Wanna get a drink?" Indigo shouted above the noise. She tipped her head toward the bar that ran the length of one side of the room.

I took one look at the glassy-eyed gazes around me and shook my head. This didn't look like the type of place that was overly concerned with underage drinking, and I wanted every one of my wits about me.

Indigo frowned, clearly wanting to get something for herself.

"Go on," I urged. "I'm just going to wait over there and watch the band."

She checked the spot I indicated and nodded. "I won't be long. I made out with the bartender last year," she said with a wicked smile and a bounce of her eyebrows. "I've been enjoying the libation perks ever since."

I probably shouldn't have encouraged her, but I couldn't help the surprised laugh that burst from my mouth. I was not expecting that.

With a wink, Indigo dashed away and was quickly swallowed by the crowd. I shook my head as I dodged bodies on a quest to find a space that wasn't as crowded. Several guys tried to lure me in along the way, but I just waved them off and kept moving. Luckily for them, no one groped me, but I still breathed a little easier when I found a spot to stand with a pillar against my back.

Fanning my face, I people watched. I didn't recognize anyone, but if this was Shawn's party, there must be a decent amount of Shades mixed in the crowd.

"I didn't expect you to make it," Gage's low, accented voice rumbled next to me, and I startled. It was too loud to have heard him approach, but I was thrown that someone could so easily make it into my space undetected.

Gage was wearing dark wash denim jeans and a black leather jacket. The charcoal gray crew neck shirt that stretched over his chest made his green eyes pop. I hadn't seen him since that morning at breakfast. Eyeing him now, I wasn't going to deny that he looked good, but I made sure not to let my inner thoughts show on my face. Gage's ego was already properly inflated.

"Why not?" I asked.

He shrugged. "This doesn't seem like your scene."

It wasn't, but he didn't need to know that.

"I guess you don't know all that much about me," I said and shrugged back.

"Hmm," was his noncommittal response. His gaze tracked from my head down to my boot-tipped toes and back up again. "Nice outfit," he said, but the heat in his eyes said he thought it was more than "nice." A warm feeling settled low in my gut, and I fought the urge to preen.

I cleared my throat. "Besides, we're supposed to be selling this thing between us. It would probably look weird if I didn't show up since you're here."

At least, that was the reason I'd repeated to myself for coming tonight, but it was only part of the truth. When Indigo said Gage and Claire would be there, my mind had been made up.

"Right, this *thing* between us," Gage said, and moved in a little closer. Lifting a finger, he brushed a wisp of hair off my cheek that had escaped from my braid and tucked it back behind my ear. His fingers traced down the side of my throat and across my collarbone before he pulled his hand away. The skin he brushed tingled, and a warm sensation traveled through my body. I couldn't say I minded it. In fact I wanted more.

"I'm very good at being convincing," he said, the double meaning of his phrase not lost on me.

I swallowed, wetting my suddenly dry throat, when Gage's gaze dipped to my lips and held. My own eyes strayed to his mouth as well.

How far were we willing to take this fake dating? How far was I willing to go? Would a kiss be too far?

My body swayed toward Gage, but I jerked back when a bottle smashed at my feet, the amber liquid drenching the top of my borrowed boots.

"I said stop looking at my girl!" a male voice bellowed.

Within a half-second a full-blown fight broke out less than ten feet in front of us. Two guys threw punches and insults, knocking each other into the surrounding partiers, which incited the drunk and demon-influenced to join the fray.

Gage stepped protectively in front of me, and I peered around his shoulder to see that thankfully the fight was veering away from us, but the conflict drew shadow demons like sharks to a kill. I squinted as I noticed shadowy black eyes, mangled inky hands. Small demons looked to be egging people on, while the larger ones fed off the aggression, attached to the humans' backs like leeches. It wasn't long before the group became a demon-influenced, red-eyed, smoke-filled mess.

I hadn't learned a lot about the demons, mostly just what I'd learned from that poster at Lumen Academy, but it was clear they could affect humans and cause them to do things, and that thought scared the crap out of me. Had I ever been demon-influenced?

I shivered, feeling bad for all of the unsuspecting humans around who weren't Shades and had no idea what was happening. To them it was just a bar fight.

"Do something," I urged Gage, but he just looked back at me and lifted his eyebrows, stepping away from the fight and settling a shoulder against the pillar, clearly not going to do anything to help break it up. In fact, he looked to be enjoying the show.

"Really?" I said. "I expected more from you." And I did. There was that spark of goodness in him that I kept latching on to.

"You shouldn't," he said, chuckling when the smaller of two brawlers landed a blow to the other's jaw.

"Why not?" I pressed.

Gage trailed his gaze back to me, irritation oozing from him. "Stop trying to make me into something that I'm not."

"What's that supposed to mean?"

Straightening, Gage spread his arms wide. "Take a good look, *Tate*. This is who I am. And if you are hoping for something else, you're going to be disappointed."

"No." I shook my head. "You can put on an act and pretend to be some unredeemable ass, but I don't believe that. I know there's more to you than that. You just stepped forward to protect me from the fight. You saved me from the demon in the diner. You even called Lumen Academy to warn them about the demon attack."

He snorted a humorless laugh. "Yeah, what a mistake that turned out to be. That momentary lapse in judgment is what got me into this mess," he said, gesturing between us.

Okay, technically I'd used his good deed to force him into helping me. I didn't feel great about it, but having it thrown in my face like that annoyed me.

I tipped my chin up high. "I think you would have helped me regardless."

"You think wrong."

I stepped closer, until we were chest to chest. "I *see* you, Gage Alston."

His expression faltered the slightest bit, and I knew I'd gotten through to the one shred of light within the darkness. But he said nothing. *So stubborn!*

Gage and I just stared at each other. Anger sparked, growing big and ugly and filling the air between us.

Just then a feminine hand skated over Gage's shoulder. I noticed the red fingernails were filed to points as Claire shimmied up next to Gage, pressing the length of her curvy body to his side. She wrapped her hand around the back of his neck and toyed with the ends of his hair with her claws.

Watching Claire touch Gage made me sick to my stomach, but I wasn't going to do anything about it if he wasn't.

"Why did you run off, G? Things were just getting interesting," Claire purred.

I narrowed my eyes at her as she shot me a coy smile and then nuzzled his neck, planting a kiss on the spot beneath his ear when he tilted his head to give her better access. Her lips left a red stain on his skin, like she'd marked him.

Gage's gaze never left mine. I knew what he was doing. There was a clear challenge in his green eyes. He was proving to me he wasn't the guy I wanted him to be.

Claire slid in front of him, rubbing her hands over his chest and then down his stomach suggestively, stopping dangerously close to the waistline of his jeans.

My annoyance at her antics and his refusal to stop her advances bloomed into full-blown anger when she tilted her face up, a clear invitation.

He wouldn't, I told myself. *Not right in front of me.*

But then he did.

Lowering his head, he brought his lips in line with Claire's, and kissed her.

It wasn't a long kiss, or even a particularly passionate one, but it felt like a shot to the chest. I staggered back a step at the unexpected burst of pain.

Gage held my gaze as his lips connected with hers, wanting to see my reaction. When he pulled back and let Claire paw at him and rain kisses on his neck, I expected to see triumph in his eyes, but instead it was all dark, emotionless.

Gage was broken.

See, his green depth's seemed to say. *I told you this is who I am.*

Unable to watch any longer, I turned and fled into the crowd.

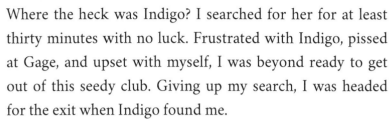

Where the heck was Indigo? I searched for her for at least thirty minutes with no luck. Frustrated with Indigo, pissed at Gage, and upset with myself, I was beyond ready to get out of this seedy club. Giving up my search, I was headed for the exit when Indigo found me.

"Girl, where have you been? I've been looking for you everywhere," she said. She appeared sincere, but I could smell the booze on her and see the slightly glassy look in her eyes.

"I'm leaving," I said.

"No," she pouted. "Not yet. We practically just got here, and we haven't even hit the dance floor together yet."

Just got here? I was sure it had been at least an hour, but even if it had only been five minutes, I was done.

Sucking a deep breath of air, I reined in my ugly emotions. Yeah, I was irritated it took so long to find her, but I shouldn't unload on her. She didn't deserve the full force of my ire.

I dug into my purse and then lifted my shiny new platinum card in the air. "I'll get a cab back to the academy. It's been a long day and I just want to crash. You stay. I don't want to ruin your night."

Chewing on her dark bottom lip, she considered my proposition. She started to shake her head and opened her mouth to respond, but I never got to hear what she was about to say. A gust of sulfur-scented air blew into the room, causing both of us to freeze.

I gasped as a portal opened on the other side of the club, the swirling red vortex only taking a few moments to widen enough for a demon to emerge. This one was the most human I'd seen so far. He had the body shape of a man, but his skin was covered in black scales; he had horns protruding from his forehead, and claws at the tips of his fingers.

The humans in the room seemed oblivious to the creature's entrance, but a handful of heads swiveled in the direction of the portal. Humans might not see what had just happened, but the Watchers could.

"Whoa," Indigo said. "A level eight."

"What the heck? Isn't this Shade turf? What's it doing here?" I asked.

No sooner had the words left my mouth than the creature's fiery gaze landed on me.

"Shadowling," he rumbled, his voice louder than the music, and then headed for me, ghosting through humans along the way.

Not again.

I turned to flee but stopped when I noticed the humans' reactions after the demon phased through them. Each and every person turned instantly violent, attacking whoever was next to them, smashing bottles, throwing punches, chucking chairs. People screamed as a full-blown club-wide brawl broke out.

Indigo grabbed my hand and pulled. "Time to go," she yelled over the shrieks and calls for help.

I snatched my hand back. "Time to go? These people need us. They don't even understand why they're acting the way they are right now."

Someone hurled a bistro table and it smashed to pieces against the wall to my left.

"That's not what we do," Indigo argued. "Demons show up, and so long as there is no Lumen threat to their portal, Shades get out of the way. All things considered, our job is actually pretty easy."

That was so wrong. And that might be how Shades acted, but I *wasn't* a Shade.

Conscious of the large, scaled demon stomping my way, I ran away from Indigo and to the bar. Boosting myself up on top of it, I scanned the crowd.

The club was a madhouse. There was brawling everywhere, and smaller demons poured into the building through the still-open portal. It was easy to spot the Shades because they were the ones skirting the violence and heading for the exit. The cowards.

I racked my brain for what to do. I was utterly weaponless, but even if I had thought to grab a dagger or two before we left Shade Academy, I didn't think normal blades would work on this demon. I needed one of those special light-up weapons the Lumen hunters had used against the shadow demons at Lumen Academy.

Something drew my attention to the ground. There was

a redhead curled into a ball just below me. People tripped over her, and she shook from the force of her sobs. I might not be able to battle the demons, but I could help this girl.

I slid off the bar and reached down to help her up. She screamed and slapped my hands away but stopped when she realized I was only trying to get her to her feet. Her leg was injured, a boot-print bruise was already forming on her thigh. There was no way I could get her to the exit in all this chaos, so after helping her stand, I steered her behind the bar to take cover.

The level eight demon roared, and a tremor shook the entire building. I didn't think the humans could hear the earsplitting noise, but they must have felt something, because the redhead's eyes grew even wider. Letting out a whimper, she pulled her knees to her chest and started rocking.

"Stay here," I said, but I don't even think she heard me.

Popping up, I scanned the room, fully expecting the demon to be right on the other side of the bar, but he wasn't. I grinned when I spotted a small group of teens, their swords and daggers covered in electric light as they battled the monster.

The Lumens had arrived.

Drea, Jacob, and the others slashed at the beast, keeping it from advancing toward me. Relief came fast and sharp, loosening the knot of dread that had settled in my belly. I wasn't alone. They must have been shadowing me this entire time to have gotten here this quickly.

"Drea! Marlow!" I shouted, but they couldn't hear me over the noise.

The Shades and some humans had fled the club, so there were fewer bodies to dodge as I made my way toward my Lumen friends. If I could reach them, maybe they could share one of their weapons with me so I could fight off some of the level one and two demons who were feeding into this anarchy. There were still about a dozen humans involved, and I wanted to help.

Before I could get halfway to Drea, somebody tackled me, and the next thing I knew I was on the ground. While I was still dazed, the guy who had taken me out rolled me on my back and straddled my stomach, pinning me to the ground.

"Get off," I yelled, but the dude just stared at me.

His lips twisted into a creepy grin and his eyes flashed red as he pulled a switchblade from his back pocket.

"I'd like to see if Shadowling blood runs red," he said, his voice a deep and unnatural tone that seemed to echo.

Screw that. This creep wasn't making *me* bleed.

And why did these fools keep calling me *Shadowling*? What did that mean?

I threw a punch that landed on the side of his neck. My leverage wasn't good, but the hit was strong enough to throw him off balance. As he tumbled to the side, I squirmed out from under him and tried to crawl away. I got about a foot before he grabbed my ankle and yanked me back.

Flipping me over, he wrapped his hands around my throat and squeezed. Pain cinched the tender skin at my throat, and I couldn't breathe. I panicked as I tried to pry his hands away. But he was too strong. I clawed at his face, scratching deep cuts into his cheeks, but not even that erased his deranged grin. I could see, just for a flash of a second, the demon latched on to his back before the vision disappeared.

A blur passed overhead and then the guy was off me. I sat up gasping, not understanding what had just happened, but thankful I could finally breathe. I wheezed as I sucked in deep lungfuls of precious oxygen.

My attacker slammed to the ground next to me, and then was hauled back up by a figure cloaked in black shadows. I blinked, and realized the shadows were actually black wings.

Gage.

The wings parted to reveal Gage pounding his fist into the guy's face over and over again. Blood and teeth flew, but I didn't feel sorry for him. That guy almost killed me.

I stumbled to my feet but didn't make it a step before scaled arms wrapped around me from behind and tightened into a vise-like grip, lifting me into the air.

Can't a girl catch a break?

"Shadowling," the demon hissed in my ear, and I gagged. His foul breath was a mix of diarrhea and vomit.

Terror crawled up my throat as I thrashed in his grasp.

My arms were pinned to my side, and nothing I did loosened his grip.

The creature hauled me backward, and there was nothing I could do to stop it.

"Gage!" I screamed, and his head snapped up.

We locked gazes and the color drained from his face. He shouted something I couldn't hear and shoved the possessed guy he'd been fighting out of the way. As he started toward me, he pulled a handle from beneath his jacket that with the flick of his wrist turned into a full sword, shadows licking from the blade.

I almost sagged in the demon's arms, convinced Gage would reach me in time, but the desperate look in his eyes was the last thing I saw before I was sucked through the portal and into an abyss.

CHAPTER THIRTEEN

After spinning in what seemed like a washer and dryer set on high, my feet slammed onto dusty black earth and a scream ripped from my throat. The scaly arms around my body cinched tighter and complete and total panic set in.

Where the hell was I?

I glanced around, praying I'd find that I'd been portaled to Brooklyn, or maybe even the Bronx—I wouldn't even complain about New Jersey right now. When I looked up and saw a giant volcano spewing lava in the distance, I sagged against my demon captor in defeat.

I flicked my gaze to where a bunch of shadow demon snakes slithered along the rocky ground. And then it hit me.

I'd left Earth?

Holy craptastic crap show. This was *not* happening. Was this the Netherworld?

There was barely any light to illuminate the path, but as

my eyes followed the ashy black earth before us, I peered out into a valley of orange veins that looked like they were made of lava. Shadow demons floated about the space, as the earth burped up sulfur and oil.

"Where are we?" I dared to ask.

Hot acrid breath washed over my face as the demon holding me spoke, his voice garbled, as much beast as human. "The Netherworld."

I knew it. The Netherworld was a sugarcoated word for Hell. This monster had *literally* dragged me to Hell.

I whimpered.

He spun me around, and I gasped.

Even though it looked like we were in the middle of a volcanic wasteland, there was a city before us. Skyscrapers, cobblestone roads, and streetlights were enclosed within a soaring two-story wrought iron fence and gate.

I snorted. "You *close* the gates to Hell? As if someone might actually sneak in here?"

Bad idea. Stupid Tatum.

The grip he had on my arms tightened and my hands started to go numb. "Level eight and higher demons only in Shadow City."

He leaned in and brushed his scaly nose across my neck, and I freaked. Bucking backward, I cracked my head into his ear and flailed like a fish out of water. But the creature was strong, too strong. He only tightened his grip, causing me to yelp in pain as he let out a maniacal laugh. "Master Apollyon told me not to kill you." His voice was deep and laced with a darkness that gave me chills. "Pity, because I would enjoy it very much."

My brain short-circuited then. Master Apollyon… *Apollyon*. Where did I—?

Oh no.

That was the fallen angel that gave the Shades their powers.

"Gage! Drea!" I screamed as he dragged me toward the closed gates.

"Shut it or I'll cut out your tongue," the demon growled, and I immediately quieted.

We reached the fence and I stared up at two giant semi-solid shadow creatures standing at each side of the decorative gate. I swallowed hard as I looked up at their horrifying forms. Their lower body reminded me of a bear, but then the fur gave way to scales across their manlike stomachs. When I finally reached their faces, I had to stifle a scream. Lizard skin wrapped around a manlike bone structure, with only two slits for a nose and thin, beady red eyes. A small cluster of horns broke out on their foreheads, and I tried and failed not to stare. I forced my head up trying to appear confident, hoping that would give me an edge somehow.

"Here to see Delilah," my captor told the guards.

"Good work, Trilok," one of them said with a snake-like hiss as he bowed his head. This was so beyond horrifying. I was going to have nightmares for the rest of my life.

They nodded and with a flick of one of the guard's wrists, the gate started to open. Trilok shoved me through the opening and marched me right down the rocky cobblestone road and into the city.

I should have been scared, I should be peeing my pants or something, but instead I was just so fascinated with the fact that there was a city in the Netherworld. Music pulled my attention, and I peered over my shoulder just in time to see a male demon kissing the side of a female demon's neck as they stood out front of what looked like a nightclub.

Gross.

But I couldn't look away. I'd never seen a female demon before, and thank God for that, because it was horrifying. She had black wings that were patchy and looked like they'd been burned. The lower half of her face was normal-ish, but the upper part was gruesome. It looked like her brain was growing outside of her head and she had three pairs of eyes.

I shivered, looking away, keeping my eyes forward for the rest of the walk.

"Where are you taking me? Why did you bring me here?" I tried to get anything out of the dude so I could prepare myself for whatever was about to happen.

The dragon-demon said nothing.

"If you want money—"

The pressure on my arms released, then in a split second the black scaled creature was before me, hands on either of my shoulders. I was simultaneously relieved to have feeling in my arms again, and yet horrified to be face to face with this monster.

"Say. One. More. Word," he snarled, and his nostrils flared. I swear I could see teeth inside of his giant nose holes. I pinched my eyes and mouth shut.

He chuckled, delighting in my fear, and hooked a clawed hand under my armpit, dragging me forward at a faster pace than before. When I popped my eyes open, I noticed that we were heading toward a building made out of black glass, black metal, and black stone. It was like the building itself was a dark hole, snuffing out any light that dare try to penetrate its shadowed walls.

"I better get promoted after this," Trilok growled to himself. "I've been a level eight for two hundred cycles."

Promoted? Like he kidnaps a Watcher and gets more demon powers? Or becomes a level nine?

Before I knew it, we'd reached the front of the building. Everything was so dark I had a hard time distinguishing a door from a window, from a sheet of black stone. The building was like a modern castle, six stories high with clean lines.

The two doors opened and a woman stepped out. Delilah perhaps? She was a beautiful woman, not like the demon I'd seen before. This one looked human but for the red tinge to her eyes. Demon-possessed human maybe? It was getting harder for me to tell.

Then it hit me.

Shade. Was she a Shade?

Her hair was half red on the right side and black on the left. She wore a black silk pantsuit and reminded me of a secretary for some reason. She had that know-it-all air about her.

"Is this her?" the woman asked.

He nodded. "Tatum Powers. Just as Master asked."

She let her eyes rake over my body, stilling on my eyes.

"Good work, Trilok. You'll get a promotion for this. Go see Accounting. I'll take it from here."

"Yes, Delilah," the scaled demon said with a grin, and then backed away.

She snapped and black shadows flew from her fingertips and then formed an interlocked chain.

"What—" I started and then there was a bite at my ankles. I hissed, looking down to see two cuffs and a short length of smoke-like chain tethering them together.

"Can't have you running off before Master gets home." She smiled and my throat went dry.

Her teeth were black as oil.

I wanted out of this nightmare. I glanced behind me, but Trilok was long gone, off to reap his stupid promotion, and I was stuck here with Cruella, chained at the ankles.

"I can get money," I whispered to her, and she tipped her head back and laughed.

"Oh, honey, there's nothing you have that I want." She grasped me by the upper arm and yanked me forward and into the building. I had to take small steps since the chain between my feet was so short. I stumbled forward as she corralled me toward an elevator and then all but shoved me inside. Stepping in behind me, she reached out with a pointed red fingernail and pushed the button for the sixth floor.

"It's nice to finally meet you. Gave us quite the chase around here." She gave me a side look and I just stared at her in confusion.

Was she really trying to be all chatty? The psycho just cuffed my ankles!

"Yeah, it's great to meet you too. Highlight of my night really," I said dryly.

She pinned me with a glare. The elevator dinged before opening. Red marble floors ran the expanse of the room as she stepped out, yanking me by the arm. There was a male demon sitting in a chair by the elevator. With his gray skin, squished nose, and leathery wings, he reminded me of a gargoyle. Two small white horns grew out of his head right above each of his pointed ears.

"Tell him she's here," the woman said, and he nodded, looking me up and down before he stood and got into the elevator. I really wished I'd worn a longer dress.

The entire room was made of heavily tinted glass. The city lights and volcano glowed in the distance. It was kind of beautiful, in a creepy way I *never* wanted to experience again. We walked along the marble floors, Delilah's heels click-clacking as we went.

If she could manifest chains from her fingertips, what else could she do? I shivered to think about it as I racked my brain to try and remember if that was a Shade power. We came to a giant set of black onyx doors and she waved her hand and they swung open slowly as if by magic.

Okay, maybe she wasn't just *a Shade.*

Could she be a demon? If so, she had to be a level ten right? According to the poster Drea had given me, only level ten demons looked this human.

The doors opened into a grand room with twenty-foot ceilings and black iridescent flooring that felt like walking on an oil spill. The sconces on the wall were black as well, and the paint was black. I was sensing a theme here.

At the back of the room were two high thrones that were, surprise, black—one of them more opulent than the other with gold accents and giant clawed armrests. The smaller of the two had touches of red ruby and—

I gasped when I noticed a small figure crumpled on the ground in front of the less imposing throne. The black cloak she wore almost completely camouflaged her in the monotone room, but when I looked closely I could tell it was a woman by the delicate hand that peeked out of the covering.

Her face was almost entirely shaded by her hood; only a few strands of pale hair were visible. A peek of creamy white skin drew my eye, and I noticed her ankles were bound, same as mine.

"Sit," Delilah ordered, and then suddenly a chair materialized behind me, knocking into the back of my knees, forcing me to obey.

Delilah walked over to the woman, who sat up now, but still shielded her face and hair with the hood of her cloak.

"You're going to be good, right?" Delilah purred.

The woman nodded, the hood of the cloak bobbing up and down vigorously.

"Because remember what happened last time?" Delilah asked.

The woman whimpered and nodded again.

"Good." Delilah walked away from the throne and approached me.

"Now, Tatum—"

"Tatum?" The woman's voice was raspy, like she hadn't used it in a long time, but it held a note of wonder. She said my name as if it were familiar to her.

Delilah looked annoyed. She didn't bother turning when she addressed the woman. "Do I need to medicate you again? Because we can go back to that if you keep talking."

The woman pushed to her feet, her once timid and shrunken form went rigid and grew to its full height. Delilah didn't see it though, since she was facing me.

I watched as the woman reached up and pulled the hood slowly from her face.

Time stopped. Literally. Delilah froze mid-action as I stared into the eyes of...

My mother.

"You're dead," I croaked.

Unable to form a coherent thought as I peered at the blond hair, glassy blue eyes, and broken soul of the woman before me. Her face was streaked with dirt and red marks, and her eyes barely had any life in them, but I recognized her from the pictures I'd seen. That woman was my mother.

She stood, looking at Delilah with a wicked snarl. "We don't have time. I can't hold her for long."

Sweat beaded her brow as she stepped toward me, the chains at her ankles skimming on the hard floor as she scampered over to where I sat.

"Mom!" I sobbed. My heart catching up with my brain as I stood and rushed forward, crashing into her.

She whimpered and I froze, realizing she must be injured.

"Listen to me, Tatum." She pulled me back and grasped the sides of my face, her eyes getting bluer and more full of life by the minute. "You need to make a portal home. Now. You have the gift. Do it before he comes back and it's too late."

I shook my head, trying to focus on her words but failing, because *Holy freaking crap my mom is still alive!*

"Mom. Gran… she's—"

"Listen to me, child! He wants you, and once you choose Shade he'll have you forever. Siphon the power from the Netherworld and make a portal to go home. Choose Lumen. I've made so many mistakes in my life, but *you* were not one of them." Her eyes filled with tears.

My throat pinched with emotion. "A portal? How can I?"

A memory flashed in my mind then, of the level seven demon in front of the cemetery. It had gotten sucked into that rift in the air that had suddenly appeared. Had I done that? It had felt like it at the time, but Gage dismissed it. By the looks of it, my mom had spent the last seventeen years here as a slave of some sort, but if I could make a portal back to Earth, we would be going home.

"Okay. I'll try," I told her. I had no idea how to siphon power from anything or create a portal, but I was going to do my best to get us out of here.

My mom grabbed her temples and a thin trail of blood trickled down her nose.

"Mom!"

"Tatum, focus on your power. It's been inside of you all along. Just open yourself up to it," she said.

Delilah started to move, slowly like she was walking through molasses.

Crap. Okay.

I closed my eyes, settling my breathing and trying not to focus on the frantic beating of my heart. I felt for something, anything, and if I was being honest there had been something there in the cemetery that day with Gage. There was a buzzing of something just under my skin that I couldn't explain, but it had left me on edge since the cemetery incident.

Instead of pushing it away, I ran to it, and we crashed together, me and this power inside of me. My skin tightened as pure magic flooded my system. Goose bumps broke out over my arms, and I swear I started to *glow* a little.

What was this? How was this happening before my birthday?

I didn't have time to find out. Instead, I was motivated to get me and my mom out of here alive. Before the super demon, Apollyon, showed up.

Going on instinct, I lifted a hand in front of me and imagined New York City. A silver fissure cut a vertical line in the air before me. Reaching forward, I pulled the rift apart like I was parting curtains and the space in front of me changed. No longer could I see the black room in the demon world, now I was looking at the emergency exit of my apartment building. There was Chinese takeout sitting by the front door of the apartment to my right.

I burst into relieved laughter. *I did it!*

"Come on! Let's go!" I yelled at my mom as I looked over my shoulder at her. Pure grief crossed her face as she reached out and planted two hands on my back.

"I love you *so* much," she said and then pushed me.

"No!" I shouted, falling forward back into Earth and onto the carpeted hallway of Gran's and my apartment building. Reaching out to break my fall, I panicked and lost hold of that feeling inside that connected me to my powers. In an instant, that scary yet powerful magic fled my system.

"Mom!" I yelled, rolling onto my back immediately. I was just in time to see Delilah spring to life and smack my mom across the face before the sliver of the portal snapped shut.

"No, no, no!" I sobbed as my chest tightened. My entire

body went numb with shock as I tried to open a portal back, but nothing happened. Fatigue pulled at my limbs, but I tried over and over again as I screamed in frustration.

The door next to me opened suddenly and an older woman peeked her head out. Mrs. Baker.

"I called the cops, druggie!" she yelled, grabbing her Chinese food and slamming the door.

Reeling from the fact that I wasn't going to be opening the portal again anytime soon, I swayed on my feet, soul crushing exhaustion settling into my bones. It was like I'd run a marathon.

I sniffled, wiping my nose with the back of my hand, and stumbled into the emergency exit, shuffling down the stairs with my feet still restricted by the shadow chain. My legs grew weaker and weaker with every step.

What was happening to me?

I'd done something to my body by opening that portal. Depleted some sort of energy that I couldn't replenish. Either that, or I was too emotionally destroyed from leaving my mother behind in the Netherworld that I couldn't even stay awake. It wasn't until I hit the bottom floor that my brain caught up with me and I remembered I had a phone.

I pulled it out and dialed.

I should call Drea or the Lumen hotline. I should call people who cared enough about me, people who didn't make out with another girl in front of me.

But instead I ran to the guy with the tiny minuscule ember of goodness who could help free Gran, because at this point I couldn't bear losing both my mother and grandmother.

Gage picked up on the first ring.

"Tatum, where are you?" he shouted, voice filled with panic.

I peered at the cross streets, momentarily forgetting where I was. "Eleventh Ave and Prospect Park. I went to the Netherworld and made a portal to get back. I feel sick and sleepy. Something's wrong." My voice slurred and the street spun around me. "I know you hate me, but I need my gran. I need that talisman, I—" My brain shut off, and I started to fall backward. The only comforting sound before everything went black was the flapping of wings and the whisper of my name on Gage's lips.

CHAPTER
FOURTEEN

My head was killing me, and my stomach was trying to eat itself. I cracked my eyelids open, taking in an unfamiliar room with soft gray-blue walls. There was a simple wooden dresser at the foot of the white wrought iron bed I lay in. On it was a framed photograph of a woman holding a laughing black-haired, green-eyed child.

I blinked, opening my eyes fully. I recognized those green eyes.

"You're awake."

Gage's voice was a shock to my system, and I was instantly alert. Craning my neck to the side, I found him sitting in a tweed wingback chair. His hair was tousled and there were dark smudges beneath his eyes. It looked like he hadn't slept in a month.

"Wh—?" I tried to talk, but my voice cracked.

Pushing out of his chair, Gage stood and grabbed a glass of water on the nightstand next to me. I shimmied myself into a sitting position and then accepted the cup, taking greedy gulps to soothe my parched and raw throat.

"What happened?" I managed to ask after I'd had my fill.

Gage looked down at me, his face an unreadable mask. "You don't remember?"

Concentrating, I flipped through my recent memories like I was swiping through pictures. I was at the club with Indigo, the demon showed up, someone tried to choke me to death—which explained the sore throat—and, oh crap, the demon took me to the Netherworld, where I found out that my mom was still alive.

Worst of all, I'd left her there!

Throwing off the covers, I tried to jump out of bed, but my feet didn't cooperate, and I pitched forward, my face on a collision course with the hardwood floors. Gage's arms wrapped around me, and he hauled me up. We stood pressed against each other, chest to chest, for an elongated pause, before he guided me to sit on the bed and then stepped back. The butterflies that I couldn't seem to control around Gage started to flutter, but then I remembered what happened between him and Claire at the club and they disappeared instantly.

I cleared my throat. "Gage, I have to get back to the Netherworld. Right *now*."

Pressing his lips together, he folded his arms across his chest. "Yeah, that's not happening."

I narrowed my eyes. "I wasn't asking permission."

Gage pointed downward and I dropped my gaze to the

ground, where I could clearly see the black manacles cuffing my ankles and the short length of smoke-line chain tethering them together.

Crap.

Rubbing my face, I groaned. I'd forgotten about those. At least it wasn't clumsiness that had me falling out of bed.

"How do you figure you're going to be able to get back there?" he asked.

"Actually, I have a way."

Closing my eyes, I centered myself and tried to make another portal. There was a slight stirring inside, but it wasn't very strong. I couldn't seem to meld with my magic like I'd done before. Despite the disconnect, I raised my hands and tried to part the air to create a portal back to the Netherworld. After a fruitless five minutes, I heaved a frustrated sigh.

Gage stared at me like I'd grown an extra head. "What was that?"

"That was me trying, and failing, to open a portal." I glanced down at the shackles. "Maybe these things are draining my power or something? I feel like I need to recharge." Or siphon energy from something again. I kept that last thought to myself. Taking energy from anything sounded uber creepy, but stealing power from the Netherworld—as my mom suggested I could do—was just downright wrong.

He shook his head. "A portal? We've already been over this. Neither Shade nor Lumen can open portals. Not to mention that your powers haven't even been bestowed on you yet, which will only happen on your birthday once you choose a side. You *can't* create a portal."

"I *did*, Gage!" I slashed an impatient hand through the air. "How do you think I got home?" I didn't really know the ins and outs of portals, I only knew I'd somehow gotten myself from the Netherworld back to Earth, so I was determined to go back the other way and save my mom. "The important thing is that I *can* get from one dimension to the other. That's how I got out of the Netherworld. My mom showed me how."

Gage's brows drew together when I mentioned my mom, but he didn't interrupt.

"And remember when the rift opened in front of the demon chasing us through New York? I think I did it then too. I opened a portal that day right in front of you and that bull demon was sucked into it. I *felt* it happen, I just hadn't realized what I'd done at the time. Think about it, why would something that took the demon away appear so suddenly like that? The timing alone was too perfect."

Gage rubbed a hand over his mouth while my words sunk in. After what felt like an eternity, he finally nodded. "All right, then."

"You believe me?" I needed confirmation before I started to breathe easy.

He shrugged. "There's always been something different about you. I sensed it since day one. I see no reason why that should change now."

Different? Was that different good, or different weird? I shook my head. That didn't matter right now.

"Tell me everything that happened," he ordered, and I did. From the minute I got sucked through the portal, to first seeing the Shadow City, meeting Delilah, and finally my mom.

"And you believed your mother was dead all these years?"

I nodded. "Yeah. My gran said she died in a car wreck a few days after I was born. But maybe she lied to protect me? I won't be able to ask her until I get your father's talisman and break the curse." Gran got extra agitated whenever anything even close to supernatural was brought up. Now that made sense.

Gage looked confused. "As far as I know, your mom died in a Lumen attack. I mean, she was a legend at school, and that's what they said."

Yeah, I'm sure they did, to cover up the fact that she was really a prisoner in the Netherworld.

"And you're absolutely sure they said *Apollyon* was the one after you?" Gage asked, switching gears.

"Positive." I nodded.

A particularly colorful cuss flew from Gage's mouth.

"That's really bad, isn't it?"

"It's not good," he confirmed.

We both fell silent. I don't know what was going on in Gage's mind, but the weight of what happened over the last day settled heavily on my shoulders. Visiting the Netherworld and finding out Apollyon was trying to capture me was terrifying, but my gran, and now also my mom, were my first priorities.

As my mind wandered, so did my gaze. Cream colored curtains covered the only window in the room, blocking my view of the outside. The door to the room was ajar, giving me a peek at the space beyond, which had a vaulted ceiling with thick wooden beams. It felt like we were in a bungalow rather than a New York apartment.

"Where exactly are we?" I asked.

Gage ran his tongue over his lower lip and then crossed to the window, pushing apart the thick drapes to let the sunlight in. I saw trees and a small, manicured backyard. "Long Island. Glen Cove to be exact," he said.

Nope, wasn't expecting that.

"That's random. And whose house is this?"

Turning back around, Gage leaned against the windowsill. "Mine."

I studied the picture of the boy and woman across from me. I had picked up on the resemblance in the boy's eyes earlier, but now it was obvious it was Gage and his mother. Gage was probably only three or four in the photo. The toddler version of him was mid-laugh, his face alight with joy. His mother had him snuggled close and was looking at him with adoration.

"Is this your mother?" I reached for the photo, and he jumped up and snatched it from my grasp, laying it face down on the dresser.

"Yes. But she's gone now."

Silence filled the room, and I felt intense amounts of guilt that my mom was alive and his was dead.

"How old—?" He cut me off.

"I was eight. She and my little baby sister died during childbirth. Satisfied?" he growled.

Geez. That was the saddest thing I'd ever heard. No, I wasn't satisfied.

"So, is this like your secret love nest or something? Where you bring all your women for some alone time?" I tried to change the subject. I meant the words to come out jokingly, like I was asking but didn't really care, but instead I sounded a tad jealous. Apparently I wasn't over him making out with Claire right in front of me and a little of my bitterness was showing.

Gage tilted his head. The sharpness of his gaze said he saw right through me. "I've never brought anyone here before. *Ever.* My own father doesn't even know about this house."

Oh. *Oh.*

We fell silent again, and it wasn't the comfortable silence that sometimes happens between two close friends. It was the awkward kind when the room fills with so much tension that even the air starts to feel thick.

"Any idea what to do about these?" I wiggled my feet, causing the smoky chains to move.

"I can help with that." Gage released a sigh and came to

stand directly in front of me. "But it's going to be a little uncomfortable."

I didn't like the sound of that. "Uncomfortable, how?"

Gage cracked his neck, and then pushed one of his sleeves up to his elbow, revealing the thick brown leather cuff that ringed his right wrist. I don't know if all guys' forearms were sexy, but Gage's certainly were, and dang it, those butterflies were back from the dead.

Loosening the straps that held the cuff in place, he slid it off his hand, revealing an inch-wide gold band that ringed his wrist. He flipped his palm face up and there was a green stone with an iridescent sheen embedded in the gold.

"Your chains are made of demon magic," Gage said. "I have to use my own magic to break them."

His own magic? Demon magic? I mean, he did get his magic from Apollyon, right? That made me sad, but I somehow kept forgetting that he was a Shade working for the bad guys.

"What is that?" I asked, mesmerized by the luminescence of the green stone at his wrist.

"My talisman."

I felt my eyes grow wide as I looked from Gage's talisman to his face.

"Really?" I kind of wanted to ask him if I could touch it but thought that would be too weird. It would probably zap me or something.

"My father's magic has grown strong over the years, so

he only uses his talisman for his most powerful spells. Unlike him, I always keep mine on me."

"So back to this 'uncomfortable' thing." I lifted my eyebrows, waiting for an explanation.

"You'll see," Gage said, irritatingly vague.

He crouched down in front of me, and since I was still in this ridiculously short black dress I had to force myself not to squirm under his regard. He was getting a face full of a whole lot of leg right now.

Thank God I shaved recently.

Gage busied himself loosening the laces on my shoes. The tips of his fingertips caressed the back of my calves as he saw to his task of removing my boots.

He's mean. He kissed Claire. You don't like him. I looped the mantra in my head, hoping to slaughter those butterflies.

Once done, he took both of my feet in his hands and then skimmed his fingers past my ankles until he could grasp my legs right above each shackle.

I didn't know if he was doing it consciously, but his thumbs began to rub light circles on my shins, sending a delicious wave of heat up my legs and throughout the rest of my body. I was thankful he didn't look up because there was no way he would have missed the flush on my cheeks. Nothing had really happened, but so far this entire thing was starting to feel incredibly intimate. I wasn't sure I minded; the butterflies certainly didn't.

With his head bowed and his attention focused on the chains, he started to speak words I didn't understand. As the low tones of his voice rumbled from his chest, the manacles circling each ankle started to heat up.

The warming metal wasn't bad at first, but it quickly began to scald. A crack appeared in one of the shackles, so whatever he was doing was working, but I had to bite my lip to keep from yelling or jerking from Gage's hold. My skin felt like it was on fire.

After only a few more moments, I realized that Gage severely undersold this experience by calling it uncomfortable. I would have gone with excruciating, but I was determined to endure whatever I had to in order to get these off. I wasn't going to be of any use to my mom or Gran until these chains were removed.

A whimper leaked out from the back of my throat when the pain intensified, and Gage's head snapped up. His gaze landed on my face, and he took in every ounce of pain I was trying to conceal. Resolve colored his features.

"It's powerful magic. It doesn't want to let you go, but I think I can break it with a few more minutes," he said through gritted teeth.

A few more minutes of fire licking my legs. I wasn't sure I could endure that. My eyes filled with moisture and Gage frowned.

"I'm going to try something to help with the pain." He slid a hand farther up, cupping my leg behind my knee and turning his wrist so that his talisman was pressed against my calf. The ankle shackles continued to heat, but through the haze of white-hot agony I saw a bead of sweat trickle down the side of Gage's face as he squeezed his eyes shut to concentrate. This was costing him as well.

The pain started to ease. The blistering heat at my ankles morphed into a soothing warmth that ran up both legs to my torso and down my arms. It was a pleasant sensation which left my muscles feeling like a masseuse had spent the better part of an hour working on me. I sagged in relief and sighed.

When I glanced down to let Gage know I was okay, I saw that he wasn't. Sweat dampened his hair, his jaw was clenched, and a fine tremor shook his body.

"Gage, stop!" I yelled, and tried to pull away, but the stubborn mule just growled and tightened his grip. More nonsensical words spilled from his mouth, and another jolt of the tranquil warmth shot through my body, tempting to lull me into submission, but I wasn't having it. Whatever Gage was doing to take away my pain was obviously causing his own, and I wasn't okay with that.

I was about to yank my legs again when the chains and shackles that bound my ankles cracked and then shattered, the bits turning to smoke and then dissipating into the air. The relief of having them off was instant.

Gage slapped a hand to the hardwood floors to keep himself upright, panting at my feet. I quickly slipped off the bed and onto my knees next to him. His breathing was labored, and small spasms shook his frame.

"I'm fine," he said and weakly tried to brush my hands off.

"You're not," I insisted. "What just happened?"

Despite his protests, I helped him to his feet and then to sit on the bed.

"It was just strong magic. Harder to extinguish than I thought. I'll be fine in a minute." His hand shook as he reached for the discarded leather cuff on the bed between us.

I snatched it up and then took his hand in my own, placing and then securing the cuff over the talisman for him.

I studied Gage as he ran a hand over the cuff, adjusting it slightly so it completely concealed the metal band beneath.

"Did you take my pain?" I asked.

He poked a tongue in his cheek, rolling it before answering. "You wouldn't have made it through the rest of the spell otherwise. I'm used to it."

"Used to it?" I was almost frightened to know what that meant, but I couldn't help but ask. He wouldn't meet my gaze and I realized I wasn't going to get an answer.

Emotion welled in my chest, and before I had a chance to overthink, I went with it. Taking Gage's face in my hands, I pressed a soft kiss to his cheek. As I pulled back, he tilted his head in surprise and our lips brushed across each other.

I caught my breath, shocked at my own boldness.

It was a quick kiss, chaste and meant only to convey my gratitude, but the accidental caress of our lips stoked a fire in his eyes.

There was something between Gage and me, an attraction that had been there from the very start. Deep down I'd always known that all we needed was the tiniest of sparks to ignite the fire between us.

That brushing of our mouths, for as trivial and innocent as it was, lit the inferno, and I knew, just from looking at Gage, that he wasn't ready to snuff it out.

Despite the passion I read in his eyes, Gage lifted his hand achingly slow, giving me an opportunity to flee… perhaps even expecting me to.

But I wanted this—this inevitable moment between us. I wanted it just as much as he did.

He skimmed two fingers over my upper and then lower lip, before sweeping his hand past my cheek and burying it in my hair. Cupping the back of my head, he tugged me forward. I offered him zero resistance and swayed toward him, my eyes fluttering shut when his breath feathered over my mouth.

An unbidden image of Gage allowing Claire to kiss him rose in my mind, hitting me like a head-on collision and smashing the embers of my growing desire to bits.

He would be so careless with my heart; I wasn't sure I would *survive* kissing him.

"I can't." I ripped away from Gage, going as far as stumbling to my feet to put distance between us.

Lifting a hand, I pressed it against my lips.

As I stood there, chest heaving, I watched an array of emotions play across Gage's face. Confusion. Hurt. Anger. And then—as he rebuilt his walls—nothing.

With a nod, he stood and headed toward the bedroom door. It wasn't until his hand was on the knob before I found my voice.

"Gage," I called, but then my words failed me. I didn't know what to say.

He stopped, but only half turned. All I could see of his face was his profile. "Don't sweat it, Tate." His voice was brittle and cold. "I fed you too much of my magic during that last spell. It can do funny things. Make you feel certain ways. That wasn't the first time it's happened to me."

Ouch. I knew he was only brushing off the experience because he wasn't comfortable being vulnerable, but that barb hurt. Especially when what made me pull away was the memory of him with someone else.

Gage left, and I stared at the door long after he slammed it shut behind him.

I was still sitting on the bed, trying to figure out how my life choices had led me to this point when a door burst open in the other room and I heard Drea howl, "Where is she?"

Jumping to my feet, I rushed barefooted from the bedroom and into the main living space. Drea stood inside the entrance, weapons clenched in each hand as she scanned the room. Marlow, Skye, Jacob, and Dash were crowded behind her.

"Hey, Tatum," Marlow called from behind Drea. "Good to see you still in one piece."

Spotting me as well, Drea quickly stowed her dagger and axe back on her arms before rushing me.

"Girl, you have got to stop running off with demons," she said as she squeezed me in a hug. "You're going to give me gray hair."

The rest of the group filed into Gage's living room and

took turns giving me hugs or fist bumps and telling me they were glad I was okay.

"What are you guys doing here?" I asked.

"I called them," Gage said from behind me. I turned to see him leaned up against the doorframe, watching our group.

My stomach bottomed out. He'd changed his clothes, and his hair was still damp from a shower.

His gaze landed on me and stuck. My lips started to tingle, and as if he knew what I was feeling, his green gaze dropped to my mouth before bouncing back to my face.

I cleared my throat. "I thought you didn't tell anyone about this place."

He shrugged. "I was getting tired of it anyway. It's about time I found a new safe house."

"Hmm." I didn't believe him. Bringing me here and letting *Lumens* know about it was a big deal. He really was going to have to find a new safe house after this.

"Should I start the gutting now, or later?" Drea asked as she marched up to Gage.

Gage lifted an arm and gestured toward me. "As you can see, she's in one piece. And if I'm not mistaken, you were there too when she was taken."

"Yes, but you were the one who promised to protect her. You should have never left her side."

"What were you doing anyway?" Jacob asked as he flopped onto Gage's couch and put his dirty feet up on the ottoman, leaving streaks of mud on the white fabric. There was a hard glint in his eye, one that said he'd like nothing more than to get under Gage's skin. "Flirting with redhead Barbie in the alley when the demon attacked?"

I gasped. Claire.

Gage's head swiveled in my direction. Fury flashed over his expression before he wiped his face of emotion and then returned his attention to Drea. "No. Claire had already left. I was looking for Tatum. I assumed she had a head on her shoulders and fled the club. I didn't realize she was still in there until I found Indigo."

I plopped my hands on my hips. "Excuse me for having a conscience. Something Shades seriously need to look into growing. People were hurt, they needed us, and every Shade just tucked tail and ran from the club… including *you*."

Gage's eyes flared. What, did he not like that I insinuated that he was a coward? Well, too bad.

The clanking of plates and opening of drawers drew all our attention to the open concept kitchen. Dash looked back at us from under the hood of his sweatshirt. A piece of what looked like bologna hung out of his mouth, and a smattering of random food sat on the counter in front of him.

"What?" Dash said. "I was hungry."

Kitchen. Food. I was starving.

"Food," I mumbled, scuffling forward like a zombie.

"Peanut butter and crackers in the pantry. Cereal too but no milk," Gage said as he pointed to a cupboard behind me.

I tore open the pantry door and grabbed everything I

could, including some expired Pop Tarts. Putting everything onto a plate, I shoveled it into my mouth. "Can we order pizza?" I asked through a mouthful of crackers.

Drea frowned at me. "How long were you out?"

"Only a few hours. She gets like this after healing," Gage spoke from his spot against the doorframe, watching me behind his judgmental green eyes.

She gets like this.

"Healing?" Marlow asked from the far end of the living room where she and Skye were inspecting Gage's collection of framed photographs. Both Drea and Gage shared a look.

Whoops. Cat was out of the bag.

"I got a cut, it healed. Then I got hungry. No biggie." I took an angry bite of the stale Pop Tart while pinning Gage with a glare. He'd denied it, but he probably was flirting with Claire outside while I was attacked by a demon. I could see where his loyalties lay. I couldn't believe I almost just kissed him back in the room.

That would have been a huge mistake.

"Like… *supernaturally* healed?" Marlow pulled her little demon scanner from her back pocket.

Drea gasped as she smacked Marlow's arm, forcing her to lower the device. "Don't you dare! She's not possessed."

I backed up a step as I eyed Marlow's scanner. That thing better not go off anywhere near me.

Jacob dropped his feet from Gage's furniture and leaned forward with a frown. "She shouldn't be manifesting powers until her birthday, and not until after she's chosen her house *and* gone through one of the ceremonies."

"I told her that already," Gage growled.

"Well, I got some powers early. Big deal, okay? Can we focus on Gran and my mom?"

"Your *mom?*" Drea asked, her brow creased in confusion.

I quickly gave them the rundown of what happened while they all listened, completely absorbed in my story. Their faces ranged from shock to horror as I went on about my time in the Netherworld and Shadow City. Only Dash seemed unperturbed. Gage just tapped away on his phone like he was bored.

By the time I'd finished, Drea had worn trails into the carpet. "Your mom's alive?"

"Yep."

"Apollyon wanted to see *you?*"

"Yep," I confirmed.

"Why do the demons have it out for her?" Jacob asked the room.

"Probably the same reason she heals," Skye inserted. "Maybe she's special."

I shifted uncomfortably, spooning a mouthful of peanut butter into my mouth. "It doesn't matter. I need to get Arthur's talisman, save my gran, and then get my mom back."

"Your gran might have answers as to how your mom is still alive and why Apollyon would want to kidnap you,"

Marlow added. "She still hasn't woken. The healers don't think she will until you choose, or we heal the curse."

My stomach tied into even tighter knots at that.

"My father most likely stores his talisman in his penthouse," Gage spoke up. "He doesn't need it for rudimentary magic like I do. He's a master Shade. But he's on business in London so we have to wait until he gets back."

Dash barked out in snarky laughter. "Wait until he gets back? I like to rob places that are uninhabited."

Dash seemed like the kind of guy who had experience robbing places, as mean as that sounded.

Now it was Gage's turn to laugh. "You think you could get within a hundred feet of my father's house without being killed? No, we have to be invited."

Dash pulled the hood away from his face, and I was shocked at how handsome he was. He spent so much time hiding behind that hoodie, now that he'd finally fully revealed himself I was a bit speechless. Dark wavy hair fell to his chin as he glared Gage down with steel gray eyes. But I could see why he covered himself up so often. A long scar ran from the top of his ear, along his jaw, to the bottom of his chin. I'm sure he was self-conscious of it, but I thought it was sexy.

"Then get invited," Dash snarled. "He's your daddy."

Gage was still, the muscle in his jaw ticking. "He's a glorified sperm donor. He would never let me in there without him around."

Drea frowned. "Didn't you grow up there?"

Gage cut a frosty glare to her. "I've lived at the academy my whole life, first in London and then here."

Boarding school? My heart dropped into my stomach. No one to put him to bed at night, no one to put Band-Aids on his booboos. Even with all of Gran's memory issues, she gave me a beautiful childhood.

"Call your dad," Jacob demanded, coming to his feet. "Tell him Tatum is thinking of becoming a Lumen. She's undecided and you really want to wow her with a date in his penthouse. We all know that's a plausible story, because you've done it before." Unbridled disgust flashed in Jacob's eyes. That girl Britt must have meant a lot to him.

Gage narrowed his eyes at Jacob but didn't do anything else as he seemed to consider it.

"He might say no," he finally said, his voice even and controlled, not rising to Jacob's bait, but not refuting the insinuation either.

I frowned.

"Don't let him," Dash responded. "I know how men like him work. They are all ego. He would rather die than lose Tatum to the Lumens, especially if she's wanted by Apollyon."

Gage shook his head. "We haven't considered the possibility that he might be working with Apollyon, and as soon as I say I have her, demons will show up to take her again."

"Then we'll have to be quick. In and out." Drea rested her hand on a sword at her hip.

Gage looked at me. I couldn't read his expression, but I

was just about to publicly grovel when he spoke. "You'll get me proof that you've destroyed the voice recording?"

Drea's mouth popped open. "Wait, you're only helping Tatum because she's blackmailing you?"

Gage shoved his hands in his jeans pockets. "Of course. Why else?"

"Why else indeed?" Drea lifted a brow, suspicion evident by the look on her face.

"We might be able to get in with only an invitation, but it will take a team of us to get out with his talisman. It's not like I can recruit any of my friends to help," Gage added.

"You get us in, and we'll be your team," Drea confirmed, and the others nodded, even Jacob.

I didn't feel worthy of this kind of loyalty right now. My emotions were all over the place.

There was a knock at the door and all five Lumens plus me grabbed our weapons and brought them forward. Mine was a spoon, but I was ready to throw down if needed. Scoop someone's eye out.

"Relax. It's pizza. I was worried Tate would start eating my countertops if I didn't feed her," Gage spat.

His words were ugly, but his actions were sweet. He wasn't bored on his phone; he was ordering pizza. One of the butterflies tried to take flight in my stomach but I pushed it down, crushing its wings with visions of Claire and Gage making out.

Die, butterflies. Die.

After paying for the pizzas, Gage dropped five large

boxes on the counter and told us all to dig in while he went to the back room and called his dad.

I was on my fifth slice when that story about growing up in a boarding school, coupled with him losing his mom so young, wormed its way into my heart.

Gage was broken, and dang it, I really liked a good project.

"This might be a trap," Gage said for the tenth time.

We were two blocks from his dad's Manhattan penthouse. Drea and the others were following us, but sticking to the shadows, ready to jump to action when they were needed. Gage said Arthur had been all too eager to get me into his house where he'd told Gage to keep me safe until he could get home. It was totally a trap, but also the only way I was going to save my gran.

"Then it's a trap," I declared, slipping my arm into the crook of his.

Drea had loaned me a pretty red silk dress that thankfully went mid-thigh and actually covered my butt. Gage and I now just needed to pose as a couple on a date for all of his father's cronies who were watching.

"He said he would disable the security system remotely and be here in… " He glanced at his watch and then shook his head in disgust. "We probably only have like forty-five minutes to pull this off."

"Then let's go." I pulled him across the street.

Out of the corner of my eye I saw Dash and Jacob scurry down an alleyway, then I heard the beating of wings.

"See you up there," Drea whisper-screamed, and disappeared around the corner with Skye and Marlow.

Operation Steal Arthur's Talisman was in full effect. We passed one more block and Gage slowed, stopping us in front of a fancy building with a glass door lobby.

Gage nodded to a front doorman. "Hey, Mickey."

Mickey nodded curtly and opened the frosted glass door. "Long time no see, son." I recoiled slightly, flinching at the sight of the black shadowy snake around Mickey's neck.

My palms were sweating, and I wasn't sure I could trust myself to speak, when Gage paraded me across the shiny obsidian floors and up to a bellhop desk.

"I'm Arthur Alston's son," Gage told the demon sitting behind a bank of computer screens.

I swallowed hard, trying not to look into his slitted pupils. He looked human but for the snake-like eyes and black scales, both of which reminded me too much of my most recent captor, Trilok. This demon's nose was broader, and he had patches of peach human skin poking through the dark scales. It was as if he were turning into a human or something. Maybe a level nine?

I shivered involuntarily, and Gage cleared his throat.

"ID," the demon growled.

This guy must have been new, because Gage didn't seem to know him like he knew the doorman.

Gage produced an ID and the man scrutinized it before looking up at me, nostrils flaring. "And this is Tatum Powers?"

I bristled at his casual mention of my full name. Gage went very still. "Yes. My date. Now, if you will excuse us." Gage plucked the ID from his hand and stepped away from the counter, heading for the elevator. The demon picked up a phone and started speaking into it.

Gage pressed the button for the elevator. "It's definitely a trap," he whispered so quietly I almost didn't hear him.

"I don't care," I shot back.

Take me back to the Netherworld. I would be able to get my mom, then.

The elevator door opened, and Gage tugged me inside, giving the demon guard a nod before hitting the penthouse button. The guard flipped a switch on his desk and then the elevator doors shut, and we started to ascend.

"Drea—" I started when Gage suddenly moved forward, pressing his lips to my neck and catching me off guard.

"We're on camera," he whispered into my ear. "They can hear you."

My brain short-circuited then. I knew he was just trying to get the message to me without being heard by the guard on the elevator camera, but *holy yum*. His lips trailed across my neck, his breath splashing over my collarbone as heat shot through my body.

With one last brush of his lips on my skin, he pulled back and then I was met with his burning green gaze.

"I'm sorry I kissed Claire in front of you. It was a shitty thing to do," he said.

I froze, I hadn't actually expected an apology. "It was."

His brow furrowed, and I opened my mouth to say more when the bell on the elevator dinged and we jolted to a stop. When the doors flew open, I was ready for anything—demon attack, Netherworld portal, his dad holding a sword. But instead I was met with a gigantic open room oozing so much opulence I could only stare in shock, my mouth hanging open.

The floors in here were white quartz with a gray vein running through them, and flecks of... I leaned in close... *gold*.

An open entryway gave way to a living room which was decorated with blues, creams, and golds. It was not my style at all, but it had a charm to it.

"My dad dropped the protective wards," Gage muttered, looking up into the corner of the room. I followed his gaze and noticed a small camera propped in the corner. The red flashing light blinked, and I chewed my lip. "But I'm sure he's still watching," he added.

Where was Dash? He was supposed to—

We were momentarily plunged into darkness, and then the lights flicked back on. I glanced at the camera again and there was no red light. He'd taken out the security cams.

"Go time." Gage dropped my arm and rushed forward, through the glitzy apartment and back to the sliding glass door. I followed him, trying not to focus on the jaw dropping view of downtown.

A blur of white and gold feathers streaked through the air and then Jacob and Dash both dropped onto the balcony with Drea and Skye in their arms. Marlow was our lookout on the ground and would notify us if she saw Gage's dad or any demons.

Gage threw the door wide open, and the boys retracted their wings as they set Drea and Skye down and then stepped inside.

"I have Marlow on speaker," Jacob informed us as he looked around the space, taking it all in.

"All clear down here," Marlow's voice came through his cell phone.

"Nice crib." Skye ran her hand over the back of the sofa, and Gage looked at Drea.

"Did you get it destroyed?" he asked her, wanting to verify that I couldn't use the voicemail of him calling in the demon attack against him before moving forward with our plan.

Drea nodded, handing him her phone. He read something on her screen and then sagged in relief, nodding to the back of the apartment when he passed it back to her.

"My father's office is this way."

Jacob and Skye stayed back, light weapons drawn, while Dash and Drea followed Gage and me to a set of double doors.

Gage indicated a keypad. "Battery operated. You can't bring it down the same way as the cams."

Dash chuckled at that and pulled out some little black zipper case. It was the size of a book, filled with tiny wires and screwdrivers and… nail scissors? Taking a pocketknife, he popped the panel off of the wall and Gage stiffened. "Careful, don't damage the casing. I need this to look like his talisman was already missing when I got here."

Dash looked up at him. "You really think he'll believe that?"

Fear crossed Gage's face and I chewed on my lip, pulling him to the side while Dash worked on the door.

"What?" Gage asked in an annoyed tone.

"If you really think your dad will find out it was you and hurt you…. I won't do it," I told him. "I can find another way to get it that doesn't involve you."

Gage froze for a second, barely breathing, not even blinking, just staring at me, expressionless. "I can handle my old man. You just save your gran."

He moved to step away from me and I caught his arm. "After tonight, when I get the talisman—"

"You go back to Lumen Academy, have your ascension ceremony, and have a nice life." His jaw clenched as he ground his teeth together, but there was a hint of vulnerability in his eyes. He didn't mean it.

I stepped closer to him, letting my body brush up against his. "Come with me," I whispered.

His sharp intake of breath was audible, and he looked at me in shock.

"Got it!" Dash muttered, and then the doors opened.

Gage and I were stuck in a stare down. I was going to Lumen Academy, and I didn't want to give up on him, give up on that spark of goodness I saw inside of him. He blinked, shaking his head as if coming out of a daze, and then brushed past me, moving into the office.

A deep sigh escaped my chest. I wasn't going to give up on Gage, but I did need to focus on the task at hand.

I stepped into the space and moved around a large oak desk to a shelf of books behind.

"What is the talisman?" I asked Gage, knowing he'd probably withheld this information from me until I made good on my promise to destroy the evidence.

"I don't actually know for sure, but—"

"You don't know for sure?" I shrieked. "Are you kidding me? All this risk and you don't even know exactly what we're looking for?"

Dash and Drea riffled through papers and drawers, ignoring our spat.

"I didn't grow up with him like a normal dad! I told you that!" he yelled, and I instantly felt bad.

"Okay, you're right. I'm sorry." Anxiety made me extra cranky.

Gage walked over to a painting and stared at it with his head cocked to the side. "I remember him playing with a black pearl a lot when I was little. Back when my mom was still alive. I suspect it's that." He pulled the painting off the wall, and we all stared at a safe built into the wall. "Bingo."

Every single one of our heads swiveled in Dash's direction. The Lumen chewed his lip, inspecting the safe. Moving forward, he placed his hand on the metal door.

There was a pop and Dash's body was thrown across the room and into the opposite wall. Drea shouted and ran to him. A trickle of blood flowed from one of his nostrils and both his ears. Shaking his head, he wiped at the blood under his nose, smearing it across his cheek as Drea helped him to his feet.

"What happened?" I asked.

"Demon magic." Dash looked to Gage. "I can't crack the safe until the ward around it is removed. None of us are experienced enough to do that, so you're going to have to."

Gage paused, indecision clear on his face.

"You can do that, right?" I asked.

His gaze swept to me and held. A muscle in his jaw jumped, and then he nodded. "Yeah, I got it."

He turned to the safe and lifted his hands, muttering another round of nonsense words as his fingers poked and prodded at some invisible points. It looked like he was shocked a time or two, because his hands kept spasming. He pulled them back a couple of times to shake them out.

"I'm almost there," Gage announced a few minutes later.

Dash nodded. "Good. I'll need my other kit once you're through. It's in the duffle on the patio."

"Got it!" Drea answered and bolted from the room.

Not thirty seconds later, Drea was back, Jacob in tow.

"It's down," Gage said and stepped away from the safe to make room for Dash.

A fine layer of sweat now dotted Gage's brow and I noticed a tremor in his hands as he rubbed the cuff concealing his talisman. He didn't take the leather covering off this time like he had with me, and I wondered if that was because Dash and Drea were in the room.

He caught me watching him and quickly shoved his fists in his pockets. I frowned, concerned he was hurt or injured from removing Arthur's protection ward, but knowing he was too stubborn to ever admit it if he was.

"So, not to make anyone panic or anything, but Arthur just stepped out of a cab," Jacob informed us as he looked down at his phone screen. Gage went rigid.

"With a super creepy dude," Marlow added over the cell phone speaker.

Dash cursed and then went into blindingly fast mode. He tore open his other kit and pulled out a doctor's stethoscope, placing the metal circle to the wall of the safe.

Okay, we straight-up just went *Ocean's Eleven* on this robbery.

Gage crossed the room, stepping in front of me. "Change of plans. You have to trash the place. I'll say someone showed up right after we got here, and the thieves took you and the talisman."

I frowned. "No. Come with us."

He shook his head. "The doorman saw me. If I turn on

my own father, he'll kill me." He pulled me aside. "Besides, I don't belong in your world, Tate." Leaning forward, he placed a kiss to my earlobe. "Please. Just go."

Agony tore at my chest.

Drea started toppling books and throwing things across the room. "Text your dad now. He's likely in the lobby. Tell him it's already been trashed, and we were waiting for you when you got up here with Tatum."

He nodded, pulling out his phone.

"Got it!" Dash called and popped open the safe.

Gage hit the send button on his phone and then stepped up to the safe. Peering over his shoulder, I took in the contents. Stacks of money, a bar of gold, a picture of Gage's mom... black pearl. I reached for the pearl, snaking my fingers around it, when a jolt of pain ripped through my arm and right into my head. I yelped, dropping the pearl, and the room swam as dizziness overtook me.

"No!" Gage grabbed me. "What hurts?"

"My arm... my head."

"Protection spell. I don't have time to remove it." His eyes were wide.

I swallowed hard. "I'll be fine. Magical healing, right?"

I grabbed it again, whimpering at the pain it sent down my spine, and stuffed it into my purse. Even though I was no longer touching it, the talisman must have some magical energy field, because the pain in my head increased until I felt sick.

"Get her out of here!" Gage roared. "They're coming!"

Drea grasped me by the arm and tried to pull me away.

"Gage, come with us. You don't have to live this life. You have a choice! Every day you have a choice!" A sob formed in my throat. The bastard had grown on me. I wasn't going to leave without him.

A darkness fell over his features, and he looked at me with absolute desperation. "My choice was taken from me the day I was born."

"I don't believe that!" I yelled, tears running down my face as Drea dragged me away.

Gage stepped over to Dash, squaring his shoulders. "It was a break-in and kidnapping. It needs to look real."

Dash nodded once and then fisted his hand. Reeling back, he socked Gage right in the nose. The crack of bone filled the space, and my heart broke in two. Why wouldn't he leave? He could come with me and never look back.

Because he's broken and broken people think they have no options.

Gage crumpled to the ground, holding his nose, and then we were all running. Drea pulled me along as my headache got worse and handed me off to Jacob.

"Gage. Please. Don't do this," I begged one more time, as Jacob tucked me into his chest and his golden wings snapped out.

On his knees, with crimson blood covering his shirt, Gage looked up at me. His dark wings snapped out, and for a glorious second I thought he was going to fly away with us. Then we were plunged into darkness, every light in the space extinguishing, even the lamps in the streets.

He was helping us get away. Covering for us while his dad likely would step out of the elevator any moment.

When Jacob lurched into the air, I wasn't ready to say goodbye. I wasn't ready to be done with Gage and those green eyes. I wanted more of the butterflies.

CHAPTER
SIXTEEN

I watched the Lumen healers work on Gran from a viewing area outside the room. We'd gone straight from Arthur's penthouse to Lumen Academy. I ran his talisman to Aurelia and begged her to remove the curse. With a few shouted commands, Aurelia had an unconscious Gran wheeled out of her room on a gurney and into the Lumen equivalent of an operating room. The healers first removed Arthur's protection spell from the talisman before they started working with it.

I knew the Lumens working on her for the last several hours were only trying to help, but removing a curse was more brutal than I'd prepared myself for. I was assured Gran was unconscious and felt nothing, but every once in a while her body would flinch, or her back would arch when one of the Lumen healers would peel a ribbon of black smoke from her body using Arthur's talisman. It was as if the curse didn't want to let Gran go. Watching was like having my heart cut out of my body while I was still awake, but I refused to leave her side.

The healers were two women of average height and looks, but they were powerful. Arcs of buttery yellow light shot from their fingertips as they cut the shadows in half and the curse left Gran's body. Every time a shadow was snipped in two, it tried to reenter again, but these women were fierce in their protection of my beloved grandmother. Filigree tattoos swirled on the tops of their hands as they bent light, guiding it into Gran's body.

Aurelia laid a hand on my shoulder, startling me. "Tatum, you need to rest."

I read the concern in her eyes. I shook my head and then went back to watching Gran. "No. I need to be here. And then once they've lifted the curse, I'm heading back to the Netherworld for my mom."

"I don't think that's the best idea," Aurelia said, her words soft for my benefit.

I cast a sharp glance in her direction. "I'm not leaving her there. You didn't see what I did. They're not—" My throat tightened, and I had to clear it before I could go on. "She's not being treated well. I'll go alone if I have to. I think I'm rested enough to open a portal to the Netherworld myself."

I wasn't exactly sure that last part was true, but I wasn't giving up. If it took me hours or even days to open a portal, I was determined to do it again.

A crease formed between Aurelia's eyebrows and she

gently shook her head. "I'm not trying to stop you from going after your mom. I know that's something you'll eventually need to do. I'm only suggesting it would be wise to make a game plan first." Aurelia gestured toward the viewing window. "It will probably take a few days for Joelle to recover. When she's up for it, you can talk to her about what she knows about your mother. Maybe she'll be just as surprised as you were to find out she's still alive. On the other hand, she may know more than any of us. There's so much mystery surrounding you and your family. Joelle just disappeared one day, left her students, her apartment, all of us. And when your mom chose to be a Shade, she cut off contact with us, so no one even knew she was pregnant with you. Having some light shed on the situation may give you an idea of what you're up against so you can be better prepared."

I ran my teeth over my lower lip as I watched the Lumen healers pull another dark strand from Gran. The color seemed to be returning to her cheeks, and she didn't flinch this time as the piece of the curse was removed.

"Besides, we don't know much about this ability of yours to open portals, but if it's anything like closing portals, it's dangerous work. I've studied my entire lifetime to learn how to close them and I still run into hiccups. You were lucky you weren't sliced in half the first time."

Sliced in half!

As anxious as I was to help my mom, Aurelia had a good point. I needed to have a real and truthful conversation with

Gran. Even if she didn't know that mom was still alive, she'd be able to tell me why they turned their backs on the Watchers and kept me in the dark all these years.

"There's something else to consider as well," Aurelia went on. "You have less than a week before your eighteenth birthday. When the curse is broken, you'll have the freedom to choose your house, then your gifts will be bestowed on you. You've already presented abilities beyond what a regular Watcher would ever be capable of at your age. I can only imagine how powerful you're going to be after you ascend."

Aurelia reached out and rested a hand on my shoulder. "Demons are strongest on their home turf. You're going to need every bit of advantage you can get if you want to travel to the Netherworld and bring your mom home."

With a sigh, I hung my head, knowing everything she said was right. My heart was telling me to run to the Netherworld and break my mom out right now, but I'd be doing so half-cocked. It would be wiser to gather as much information as I could beforehand and make a solid plan. There was so much I still didn't know about being a Watcher, demons, the Netherworld, *or* Avalon. Getting a boost of strength, or whatever juiced-up abilities I might inherit by becoming a full-blown Lumen wouldn't hurt either. I'd been dying for some of those fancy tattoos.

"All right," I finally admitted. "I'll wait until after I ascend and can talk to Gran."

My mom had survived the Netherworld and all its

horrors for the last seventeen years. She was going to have to hold on for a little while longer.

Aurelia's shoulders sagged in relief. "I'm glad to hear it. In the meantime, I'm going to arrange for you to get as much private tutoring as possible. Drea and her friends can handle the textbook material. And I know more about portals than any Lumen in the city, so I can work with you on trying to figure out your portal-making powers. We're going to try to cram eighteen years of early childhood Lumen training into the next six days. If you're going to the Netherworld, I'm going to make sure I've done my best to prepare you. And I won't let you go alone."

My heart filled. Aurelia really did care. But she was also letting me make my own choices. Growing up with Gran wasn't bad. She made sure I was cared for and knew that I was cherished, and I loved her for it, but what would life have looked like if I'd grown up knowing I was a Watcher? There'd always been a pit in the bottom of my stomach that said I was somehow different. Even before I quit school to take care of Gran, I never had good friends. There was never anyone I clicked with like Drea, or even Indigo. I was lonely, and knowing what I knew now, it seemed it didn't have to be that way.

Why did Gran hide me from this world if it was always going to catch up with me? Maybe she was trying to protect me, or maybe the curse had kept her from telling me the truth. As soon as Gran was awake, I was going to find out.

"Thanks, Aurelia. I really appreciate it."

The corners of Aurelia's mouth lifted, the smile reaching her honey brown eyes. She really was a stunning woman and the resemblance to Drea was uncanny.

"Your mother, Emery, used to be a good friend. I was crushed when she chose to become a Shade, but that didn't mean I stopped caring about her and hoping for the best. I know if our situations were reversed and I was separated from Drea, that Emery would do whatever she could to help my daughter." Aurelia reached over and squeezed my hand. "I want to see her back safely as well."

"I'm going to get her back," I said with conviction.

Aurelia nodded in agreement. "I believe if anyone could do it, it would be you. I'll help in any way I can."

She reached next to her and lifted a brown lunch bag and handed it to me. "If you won't rest, at least eat."

I took a sniff. Did I smell bacon?

Aurelia left after I thanked her for the food and assured her I would eat it. There was an apple, some carrot sticks, and a BLT sandwich in the sack lunch. Digging in, I turned my gaze back to Gran and the Lumen healers working to remove the curse, but my thoughts drifted to my mom and what she might be enduring right now, especially since she'd helped me escape. Apollyon seemed to be going to an awful lot of trouble to capture me. He couldn't have been happy that I slipped through his fingers, and logic dictated that he would take it out on my mom. The thought soured my gut, and although the hunger pangs in my stomach didn't subside, I put down the half-eaten sandwich.

"Don't worry, Mom," I whispered. "I'll be there soon. I promise."

The Lumen healers worked on Gran for another four hours. There was one scare when they used Arthur's talisman to pull a band of dark curse from Gran's forehead and she seized. The healers concentrated some sort of light magic from their hands on her head and stabilized her. After that chunk of curse was removed, it was like it knew it was beaten and gave up. The healers were able to peel the rest of the curse off Gran within the hour and then it was over.

Gran remained unconscious for the whole process. She was sleeping soundly now in a recovery room, and even in slumber she looked a solid ten years younger. I, on the other hand, picked up every one of those years. She'd given me such a scare that I wouldn't be surprised to look in the mirror and see a couple of gray hairs.

Gran's room in their recovery wing had a nice street view and lots of light that Gran would love when she woke up. But the room was only set up for one person, so the little bit of sleep I managed to get was sitting upright in the world's most uncomfortable wood chair. Everything ached.

"You look rough," Skye said from the doorway. Drea smacked her on the arm, and Marlow rolled her eyes.

"Learn some tact, Skye," Drea said as the three girls walked into the room.

Skye pointed to my head. "Come on, it's true. Just look at her hair."

I lifted a hand and tried to run it through my hair, but I couldn't get my fingers through the strands without hitting snags. I was still dressed in Drea's red dress, and there was a layer of fuzz on my un-brushed teeth. Skye might be lacking tact, but she was probably right about how I looked.

Drea lifted her gaze upward and shook her head.

Marlow stepped forward and offered me a bundle of clothes and a brand-new toothbrush and paste. "We thought you'd like to get into something a little more comfortable."

I accepted the items gratefully, expecting them to be more borrowed items, but recognized the vintage Bon Jovi tee folded on top. I fingered through the fabric and found my favorite pair of jeans and slip-on Vans.

"These are mine," I squealed. It had been several days since I'd been in my own clothes.

"We went to your apartment and packed up your stuff," Drea said with an apologetic smile. "I was worried your landlord would throw it all out if we didn't grab it."

I'd forgotten we were being evicted. With everything that had happened in such a short period of time, almost everything from my old life had slipped my mind. It was a good call to contact Sal and tell him I'd be off for a couple of weeks.

"Thank you," I said, and meant it. "If you hadn't done that, I'm sure Mr. Daniels would have eventually put our stuff on the curb."

Drea nodded, her smile turning genuine. "We have some boxes of your things in my room at the dorm. You'll be my new roomie—at least if that's okay with you. Everything else is in storage here at the academy. I can show you later in case there's something you need."

My eyes started to cloud. I blinked rapidly to keep the tears from slipping over. "I'd love that. Let me go change," I said and then fled to the small en suite bathroom.

I emerged a couple minutes later feeling clean and refreshed. Skye eyed my shoes and scrunched her nose, clearly not impressed, but I didn't care. I felt more like myself in my worn clothes and my hair twisted on top of my head than I had since this whole ordeal began.

"My mom already has a schedule made up to get you caught up on all things Watcher related. If you're okay leaving your gran, we can get started now."

I glanced at Gran sleeping peacefully in the bed. There was an IV attached to her hand, giving her fluids. The healers didn't think she'd be awake for at least a day or two while her body adjusted to being free of the curse. After that, they cautioned that she'd most likely be weak for a while. I hated leaving her, but this was truly the best time.

I took a deep breath. "Yeah, let's do it. Let the cramming begin."

"Okay, so it goes novice, junior, senior, principal and *then* master?" I asked, making sure I had the correct sequence of Lumen hunter hierarchy correct. The past few days had flown by with all of the studying and training I'd been doing.

Drea and Marlow nodded helpfully.

"So, you guys are all junior hunters, but I'm a novice?" That was disappointing. Just another area I needed to play catch-up in.

"Well, not even that if you want to get technical," Skye said as she added another coat of bubblegum pink polish to her nails. "Watchers between the ages of twelve and sixteen are novices, but seeing that you haven't had any official training, you wouldn't be considered a hunter at all."

I scrunched my nose. That was a bit insulting. Skye was laying the truth bombs on thick today.

"Don't get hung up on titles," Drea interjected. "The terms are just something we use to determine what level of demon it's safe to go after. If the demon is higher than a level four, we junior hunters are supposed to hang back and call for backup. You're getting a crash course right now, but I've seen you in action with zero training and you've done great. I'm sure you'll get promoted to junior hunter in no time after you ascend to get your abilities."

Marlow nodded, agreeing with Drea. Skye just blew on her nails. I wasn't even sure if she was listening anymore.

"But wait, I've seen you guys fight demons higher than a level four. The demon at *Wings* was covered in scales and had a tail, so he had to be at least a level eight according to the chart… right?" I shivered, and tapped the paper in front of me, remembering his yellow eyes with slit pupils, and all those teeth. I would happily live the rest of my days without meeting up with him again.

A wicked smile grew on Marlow's face. "We don't always like to do as we're told. Sometimes it's better to ask for forgiveness than permission."

"Corrupting Tatum already, are we?" Jacob asked as he entered Drea's dorm room, where the girls had been bombarding me with information for the last two hours.

Dash trailed behind him, tipping his head in greeting when our gazes connected. I gave him a small finger wave to acknowledge the gesture.

"Not all of us," Drea sighed.

"Break time?" I asked hopefully. And by break time I really wanted to know if it was mealtime. I'm pretty sure I could eat my weight in bacon right now.

Jacob shook his head. "Not yet. You have a workout, followed by weapons training—"

"That's with me," Marlow piped up. Bringing her hand to her tattooed arm, she slapped her palm over a serrated dagger. When she pulled her hand back, the dagger peeled away from her skin and became real.

That was a *really* useful party trick that I wanted in on. ASAP. I knew I wouldn't be able to ascend until my birthday, but did I have to wait until then to be able to store weapons on my skin? Probably.

Jacob looked down at his phone, his finger passing over the screen as he read something. "I think after weapons training you might get a—oh wait, nope. You have to meet with Theo, then to go over the basics of Lumen and Shade magic. It looks like she scheduled in dinner at around eight tonight."

I pouted.

"What is that?" I asked.

"Aurelia made a schedule for you," he answered with a shake of his phone.

That was really thoughtful. I was glad and thankful she was doing her best to get me ready for my trip back to the Netherworld, and to start schooling here, but what I really wanted was a snack.

"Come on." Jacob waved for me to get up. "We'll hit up the academy's gym. Grab some clothes and you can change in the locker room."

After snagging my workout clothes from a drawer Drea had emptied for me, I waved goodbye to the girls and followed Jacob and Dash out of the dorms and next door to the academy. I quickly dressed in the modestly decorated locker room, so different from the state-of-the-art changing room and spa at Shade Academy, and met Jacob by a row of exercise equipment. Dash was on the other side of the gym pounding a punching bag with his bare knuckles, hood pulled over his head. Dude definitely had some skeletons in his closet.

But who was I to judge? I had my own.

"What am I learning first?" I asked.

"The most important part of demon fighting is endurance," Jacob answered, gesturing to an ancient looking treadmill.

Sword fighting… yes please. Martial arts… sign me up. Hand-to-hand combat… bring it on. Running… *hard pass.*

I eyed the machine with a heavy dose of disgust. "Please no."

Jacob laughed. The sound rumbled deep in his chest. He probably thought I was kidding. I really wasn't, especially not without food.

"Come on, hop on up. We'll just do a thirty-minute jog as a warm-up."

"Warm-up?" I didn't think I was capable of running for that many consecutive minutes, and I had less than zero desire to test that theory.

Ten minutes later, I was limp walking on the treadmill, holding a hand to my side where a stitch had formed.

"No more," I wailed.

Jacob was sprinting full-out on the machine next to me, not even a hint of perspiration glistening on his brow.

"Oh, come on, you've barely even—"

I yanked the red string which brought the whole thing to a stop and then glared at Jacob. "Feed me or *suffer my wrath.*"

He chuckled, pressing the buttons until he came to a slow stop. "All right, one quick trip to the cafeteria. They have twenty-four-seven pizza and chicken fingers."

My mouth started to salivate. "Dude, if you'd told me that earlier I would have chosen Lumen on day one."

Jacob waved to Dash and made a motion with his hand that looked like he was eating. Dash nodded to let Jacob know he understood and then went back to pounding on the punching bag. His hits were hard and solid. I was surprised the bag hadn't split.

Jacob and I left the gym with smiles on our faces. My legs felt like Jell-O, but the fact that I was walking toward food made it easier. When we got to the cafeteria, Jacob had me sit and told me he'd grab me a plate with one of everything. He was chivalrous, which made me think of Gage, who was basically the opposite of Jacob in every way.

Pulling out my phone, I decided to send him a text.

Me: *How are you?*

The three dots appeared, indicating he was writing a reply, and the butterflies took flight in my stomach all over again. The dots disappeared and the butterflies turned to hornets.

Me: *I'm safe. Gran is healing.*

I added.

Three dots. No dots. Dots. No dots.

Dang it, Gage. Just write me back!

"Food for my lady." Jacob's voice pulled me from the agony of watching my phone. I was under the three-dot anxiety spell and I couldn't take it anymore. Gage would write when he was ready. I just hoped he was okay, and his dad never found anything out.

One look at the slice of cheese pizza, three chicken tenders, tater tots with ranch dressing, and all thoughts of Gage flew from my mind.

"This is what I need," I moaned, and started to shove food into my mouth.

Jacob chuckled, shaking his head. "Don't overdo it. The last thing I need is you barfing on the brand-new training mats."

Whatever. I could easily take down this plate and still be hungry. I'd always been a healthy eater, but lately, as I got closer to my birthday, it was like I couldn't get enough calories.

We ate in comfortable silence before heading back to the gym, where Jacob, Dash, and Marlow tortured me for the next three hours.

I was in a love-hate relationship with this place, but I mostly loved it.

I
t had been four days since they'd removed Gran's curse.
She spent the first two days in a coma and the last two
in and out of consciousness. Tomorrow was my birthday,
and I hoped to find her awake and lucid when I stopped by.
I'd just finished dinner and was hoping it was enough to
tide me over for a few hours.

"Good luck!" Drea called as I left our shared dorm room.
They'd brought a twin bed and desk in, and Drea had even
been helping me fix up one of the studio apartments in the
family housing for Gran. It was within the Lumen
compound, so I could see her every day if I wanted. So far,
I'd set up her bed, nightstand, and even brought her favorite
pillow. Drea even dragged that bistro table set two blocks
from the Lumen storage unit. Aurelia said Gran could stay
as long as she needed, forever if need be. The kind of weight
that took off of me was too hard to describe. I'd been
hustling for so long to make ends meet, to provide for Gran,

that now that we were both taken care of, I could finally breathe.

I took the elevator to the first floor and stepped out onto the street, making my way to the healing center a few doors down.

Checking my phone one last time, I growled when I saw there was no reply.

Gage still hadn't texted me back, despite my five follow-up messages, and I was starting to take the hint. He didn't want anything to do with me now that I'd made my choice and the evidence had been deleted.

It stung, not gonna lie. Those days with Gage were infuriating but also special. I felt like we understood each other on a fundamental level. I wasn't ready to let him go. Or give up on him.

The sun, just setting, threw a splash of color across the sky in golds and yellows as people walked home from work. Before I knew it, I was at the healing center, where Rose was on duty at the front.

"How is she?" I asked her as I signed in and attached my visitor's badge to my top.

Rose grinned, her dimples in her cheeks popping. "She's awake. Fully lucid and asking for you. I was just about to call you."

The shock ripped right through me, and I burst into tears of joy. Taking off running down the hall to her room, I almost slammed into the healer who was stepping out into the hallway.

"Oohf." I skidded to a stop.

Healer Francine smiled warmly at me. "We just scanned her. No remnants of the curse left behind. She's very coherent, and I've brought her up to speed as much as I could to fill the gaps of her memory from when she was unconscious."

Tears streamed down my cheeks as I pulled Mrs. Francine into a hug. "Thank you for everything. Seriously, I will always be grateful," I managed to eke out.

She pulled back and smoothed my hair. "You're more than welcome, my dear."

Without waiting another moment, I burst into the room and took in the sight of my beloved gran sitting up and eating a chocolate chip cookie. There was a healthy glow to her skin I hadn't seen in years. Her bobbed hair was shiny and now browner than gray, and even though she was sitting, her frame looked strong.

When she saw me, she dropped the cookie onto a napkin on her lap and opened her arms. I bolted forward, closing the distance as I sank into her embrace. Sobs racked my body as her arms tightened around me.

"I was so scared," I cried. "I almost lost you."

I wept, letting it all out as the emotional roller coaster from the past few weeks finally caught up with me. Gran just held me, patting my back through it all. When I felt like I'd cried every tear I had in my body, I pulled back and wiped my eyes.

"I'm so proud of you. That couldn't have been easy.

Aurelia stopped by and told me about everything you did to break Arthur's curse on me." Gran squeezed my shoulders. Her eyes glistened as she looked down on me.

I nodded. "It's fine. I'm just glad you're okay. But, Gran, I have to tell you something. Mo—"

"Me first." She broke her cookie in half and handed it to me. "Pull up a chair, honey. This might take a while."

Telling her my mom was still alive could wait. She'd waited years to be clearheaded. I needed to hear her out.

Standing up from the edge of her bed, I walked over to the far wall and dragged a chair right up next to Gran. Taking my cookie, I nibbled at it and looked at her expectantly.

She sighed, looking tired already and she hadn't even spoken. "Arthur's curse was one that got worse any time I tried to tell you the truth."

I knew it! That bastard.

Gran shook her head. "I tried a few times when you were twelve, but it just deepened my confusion, and I'd wake up with the stove on or forget where I left my keys. That's when I knew I would have to be careful."

My heart broke at the fact that this whole time she'd been cursed, and I had no idea.

Gran wrung her hands together. "I thought maybe his curse only applied to you, so once I tried to come here to ask for help, but when I got within two blocks of the place I blacked out and woke up at a police station."

"Oh, Gran." I grasped her hand and squeezed lightly. I

remembered that day. I was fourteen and had gotten a call from the police station that Gran was found at a park mumbling about shadows and things. I'd lied and said my mom would come with me to get her, and then I'd walked in and picked her up myself. I'd told the cop my mom was circling the block looking for parking. It was the first time I realized she had a serious problem.

Gran frowned. "As your birthday drew nearer, I didn't want you to be left in the dark, so I tried to tell you bits and pieces of what to expect, but it only made the curse's hold on me tighter."

"It's okay," I said. "I was lucky enough to meet some Lumen friends on the subway. They helped me through what I was seeing."

She nodded lightly. "Tatum, now that I can speak freely, I have some information that might be distressing."

A lump formed in my throat. I knew there had to be a reason that Arthur gagged my gran from speaking about the Watcher world, and now I was scared to find out that reason.

"Tell me everything." I leaned toward Gran, because without the truth I wouldn't be able to move forward.

Gran picked at her cookie, not eating it. Cookies were our thing. We could polish off a dozen in a day. If she wasn't eating, it was because what she was working up to tell me was bad. Really bad.

I braced myself.

"Your mother was the light of my life," Gran started, and I totally remembered the fact that she was still alive.

"Gran... she's alive. I met her. In the Netherworld."

Gran's entire face dropped. "What did you just say?"

"Gran, I met her! I talked to her. She got me out."

Gran didn't look shocked, she looked... angry. "You went to the Netherworld!" she yelled, and I flinched.

Okay, Gran was back with zero problem with hollering at me. "I was kidnapped. I didn't go on purpose. And did you hear me? Mom is alive!"

Gran frowned. "That can't be. I identified her body for the police after her crash. I went to her funeral."

I took her hand, forcing her to look at me. "Then it was a trick. I met her. She's kept as some pet to Apollyon. They have her chained, but I'm going to get her out."

Gran's entire body froze, her hands clamping down on mine. "You met Apollyon?"

I shook my head. "Mom got me out before he could get there."

Gran's brows drew together.

"Emery's alive?" A small sob escaped her throat.

Poor thing had been through enough shock and trauma the past few days. I didn't want to do any more damage to her fragile and healing memory.

"She's alive," I promised.

Gran suddenly looked at me with desperation. "You must never go back there. Not even to get your mother."

I reeled back in shock. "I… Gran, I have to. It's my mom. He keeps her in chains!"

Gran clamped her teeth shut and anger flooded her features. "Your father took enough from me when he took Emery. He *won't* take you too."

Chills erupted on my arms, and I stood so fast the chair toppled over. I stepped away from the bed as if it were crawling with shadow snakes.

"My fa-father?"

She never spoke about my father. Now I realized it was the curse. Gran swallowed hard, clutching her little chocolate chip cookie as if it would make whatever she was about to say a bit sweeter.

"Apollyon. Tatum, your father is the ruler of the Netherworld."

No…

No. No. No. No.

The room spun around me as panic crept in. My heart rattled against my rib cage and my breath came out in short bursts.

"Tatum, calm down." Gran dropped the cookie onto her lap and held out her hands for me.

Why was it so hard to breathe? It felt like I was sucking air through a pinched straw. Black dots danced at the edges of my vision.

"Apollyon. Is. My. Father?" I barely got the words out.

Gran frowned, nodding once. "Yes, dear. He lured your

mother from me with poisonous lies, all in an effort to make an heir. Why? I don't know. It wasn't until she was pregnant with you that she realized how evil he truly was. She didn't want Apollyon to get his hands on you, so she came to me for help."

An heir. I was the freaking *heir* to the Angel of Death?

That had to be why I was so different from the other Watchers. Why I could make portals, heal, and eat like a football linebacker without gaining an ounce.

I couldn't handle this. "Gran. I gotta get some air. I'll be back in an hour, okay?"

She looked at me with concern, but then relented. "Okay, honey. I'll be here."

I stumbled from the room, feeling like the walls were closing in on me. The second my feet hit the pavement, I ran through the dark Manhattan streets.

I guess I'd lied when I'd told Jacob I didn't like running. In this case, it was the only thing keeping me from full-blown panic.

My legs burned, my lungs screamed, but I didn't care. I pumped my arms harder as I covered the twenty or so blocks to Shade Academy. When I finally slowed, I was wheezing and ready to drop.

My dad was Apollyon. This wasn't happening. No wonder my mom was kept there.

Was she his wife? Judging by the chain on her feet and broken demeanor, I would say no.

Fumbling for my phone, I texted Gage, one last cry for help.

Me: *I'm outside, in the alley by the Mediterranean place. I need to talk. Something happened. It's bad.*

Those three dots appeared, and then were followed by an actual response.

Gage: *Coming. Don't be seen.*

I could almost hear his throaty growl through the text, but relief spread through my limbs. If anyone would understand being born of darkness, it was Gage. I ran my fingers through my hair and adjusted my sports bra under the glow of the streetlamp.

A figure moved at the end of the alley. Gage, shrouded in a baseball cap, walked toward me. He passed the first streetlight and it dimmed to nothingness, then he passed another and took the light from that one too. By the time he reached me, the light overhead flickered a few times before plunging us into the soft glow of moonlight.

"Are you insane? You'll be killed on sight," he growled, head tipped down and avoiding eye contact with me.

I bristled at his demeanor, hugging my arms. Were those fading bruises on his neck?

"Gage, look at me," I begged.

I was in a really fragile place. I hoped my cracking voice conveyed that. I needed soft Gage, not prickly Gage.

He lifted his gaze to mine and I gasped. Two black eyes shone on either side of his nose, and there were stitches above his eyebrow, just under the brim of his hat. His chin was black and blue, and the bruising pattern around his neck looked like fingerprints.

This wasn't from when Dash punched him to make the break-in look real. "Are you okay?"

"Why are you here, Tate? Other than because you have a death wish?" he snapped.

My fragility slowly turned to rage. "Because I need your help. I need to talk. I just found out—"

"I'm done helping you. Take a hint." He yanked his baseball cap down so that it would better cover his face and spun to walk away.

I wasn't going to let him go.

Running forward, I grasped his upper arm and yanked him backward. He hissed as if I'd caused him pain and I let go.

"Gage, who did this?" If he said his father, I would never forgive myself.

"What do you care? You're a Lumen now, you shouldn't even be on this block."

My mouth popped open. "What do I care? Gage, don't do that. You know I care about you."

He shook his head. "Just go, dammit! I don't want to see you ever again."

Tears pricked my eyes and my bottom lip quivered. "Why?"

"Haven't you figured it out by now?" Gage stepped closer, nearly pressing his body up against mine, and I held my breath for a moment.

"What?" I snapped, no longer sad, fully wanting to throat punch him for being such a jerk.

"You're my weakness and I *can't* have a weakness," he growled, looking down at my lips.

He was more broken than I realized if he thought caring for someone was a weakness.

I stepped forward, pressing my body flush with his, and tipped my chin up so that I could look directly into his eyes.

"You're so stubborn, I hate you sometimes," I said through clenched teeth. I knew I was pushing him to the brink, but I didn't care. I wanted to shove him over the edge and watch his stony resolve crumble in front of me. Consequences be damned.

His hands came up to rest on my hips, sending a blast of warmth through my body from the point of contact as the muscles in his jaw clenched.

"You have *no* idea," he said through gritted teeth. His fingers flexed at my sides as fire flashed in his eyes.

I growled then. The tension and frustration between us had reached critical mass.

The throaty noise finally ignited something in Gage. He cupped the back of my head, tugging me forward. We crashed into each other, and I offered him zero resistance, pressing harder into him.

Our lips clashed with an urgency I'd never felt before. His mouth was a drug I couldn't get enough of.

On instinct, I sucked Gage's lower lip into my mouth, and he groaned.

Walking me backward, I followed his movement until my back hit the brick alley wall. Wrapping his free hand around my lower back, he hauled me upward and I looped my legs around him, hooking my ankles at his lower back, but it wasn't close enough.

His hand skimmed over my hip until it met the bare skin on my stomach, the contact sending a jolt of awareness throughout my body.

Skating a hand over his shoulders, I reveled in the feeling of the muscles beneath his shirt. Our tongues intertwined in a frenzy of desire as all of the rage and adoration I had for this idiot mixed into one giant fevered moment.

Gage dragged his mouth from mine, trailing kisses up my jaw to my neck, and I released a soft moan when he found a sensitive spot beneath my ear.

Bringing his mouth back to mine, he kissed me with so much passion it stole my breath and made me never want the moment to end.

But just as quickly as it started, he suddenly pulled back, as if shaking himself from a daze, and dropped me to my feet.

Holy epic kiss. We could have been kissing like that all along?

I was only sorry we waited until now to figure that out.

Chest heaving, I brought my fingers up to touch my swollen lips and grinned just as Gage took two giant steps back.

He shook his head. "I shouldn't have done that."

A frown pulled the grin right off my mouth. "I'm glad you did."

He shook his head adamantly, a look of defeat on his face. "Tatum. Go home. Be a Lumen. Forget me."

He called me *Tatum* for the first time, and for some reason it stung.

Now was the absolute worst time to cry. I wanted to be strong and not let him see how hurt that made me, but I was so raw from what Gran just told me that I couldn't stop the single tear that slipped down my cheek.

"Apollyon is my father," I blurted.

Gage froze, unmoving, unbreathing for a full minute. I expected him to ask me to tell him the whole story, but instead he just said, "You're sure?"

I nodded.

"That makes sense," he said. "And all the more reason for you to get the hell out of here and stay with the Lumens. Don't come back here again." He turned, giving me his back.

"You're a real prick, you know that?" I shouted at his retreating form. "The one person I wanted to talk to when I heard this news was you!" I picked up an empty soda can and chucked it at him.

He stopped, spinning around and storming back at me, anger all over his face.

"Why? Because you thought the darkness of Apollyon would make you more like *me*?"

Guilt wormed its way into my gut, and Gage shook his head, his next words sounding tortured. "You don't see what I see? You're all light and goodness, okay? You could never even be a tenth of a Shade, no matter *who* your father is. People aren't born bad, they become it."

Grief ripped through me so unexpectedly then. He was talking about himself. He thought he was bad, that he'd become his father?

"Gage, you're not—"

His wings snapped out so fast I yelped in shock, stumbling backward, and Gage glared at me. "Come around this block again and I'll turn you in."

He kicked off the ground and shot into the sky like a rocket.

Emptiness filled my body. I wished I'd never met Gage Alston.

CHAPTER
EIGHTEEN

I was dressed in black battle leathers that were covered in sleek armor. Shiny silver plates hugged both shoulders and shielded my shins, and a fitted breastplate lay against my chest. Other bits of armor were speckled over my arms and legs, but not too much to make the coverings feel bulky. The gold ceremonial sword that was sheathed at my hip completed my Ascension getup.

I was surprised when Drea brought me the garb, expecting to be clothed in a flowy white dress or something equally virginal for my visit to Avalon to meet an angel. But once I got over the feeling that I looked like a professional cosplayer headed to my next Comic-Con, I had to admit I looked pretty badass. Full princess-warrior garb beat damsel-in-distress costume any day of the week. At least it did in my book. Drea had said that I was a demon hunter and warrior now, so I needed to look the part.

As I walked with Drea to the Ascension Sanctuary, I was

glad for the armor. I was nervous and confused, and the silver plates strapped to my body helped boost my confidence and make me feel protected.

Last night had been hard. I understood that Gran couldn't tell me about Apollyon because of the curse that had been placed on her, but I was struggling to come to terms with the truth of my parentage. Gran said she wouldn't push me, but I couldn't bring myself to have another conversation with her about Apollyon, which was ironic because now that she finally could tell me everything, I couldn't bear to hear it.

"Are you excited?" Drea asked.

Normally a family member would escort you to the Ascension Sanctuary, but Gran still wasn't strong enough to leave the healing hospital, so Drea was standing in for her, which I was grateful for. As we walked out of the dorms on the bottom floor, we stepped into the courtyard and I plastered on what I hoped was a convincing smile and nodded, hoping she didn't know me well enough yet to see through the facade.

Truth was, that doubts had plagued me since my conversation with Gran last night. Gage said people weren't born bad, but did I really believe that was true? I wanted it to be. I'd always lived my life that way. Even with Gage I never thought he was inherently evil because of who his father was, but what if I was wrong? What if there was some gene Apollyon passed on to me that meant I'd never truly be good? A black mark on my soul I could never wipe clean.

Would the angels in Avalon even accept the daughter of the Fallen Angel who was the ruler of the Netherworld as one of their own?

We strolled through the hidden garden in the center of the Lumen compound. A breeze carried the fresh smell of the newly-budded roses, making me momentarily forget we were in the middle of New York City, and a peaceful feeling settled over me. By the time we reached the stairs at the base of the Ascension Sanctuary, I felt a tiny bit better.

I spotted the Angel Gang standing off to the side, leaning up against the library and a huge grin broke out on my face. Dash, Jacob, Skye, and Marlow all gave me a wave.

"I told them not to stand too close and embarrass you," Drea warned.

"Go get 'em, girl!" Marlow hollered across the entire garden, causing my cheeks to pinken.

"Lumens for life, baby!" Skye whooped.

Drea chuckled and turned me toward the sanctuary steps.

My gaze drifted up the gray stone staircase to the opposing dark wood double doors, the only entrance and exit into the one-room structure from what I could tell. Two Lumen guards stood at each side of the door, hands on the hilts of their swords, which hung from scabbards on their hips. I chewed on my lip as I took in the ornate filigree etched into the stone around the entrance, and the battle scenes of angels in full armor. Their spread wings were carved into the panels of the twelve-foot-tall doors.

"Hey. It's okay to be nervous," Drea said, giving the guards a nod.

I tore my gaze from the Ascension Sanctuary and turned to Drea. She had a soft look of understanding on her face that just about broke me.

"No, I'm not—" I started, but then stopped myself. Even though we'd only known each other a short time, Drea had proven several times over what a solid friend she was. I didn't want to lie to her. "Yeah, I'm nervous. The last couple days have been extra hard."

She nodded in understanding. I confided in Drea about my conversation with Gran, and also that I ran to Gage afterward and what a huge mistake that had been. She was of course super understanding, in typical Drea fashion. We'd stayed up talking half the night last night, but I didn't share my fears about ascending.

"This is a big day, Tatum," Drea wisely said. "You've had to take in a ton of information about our world in a very short period of time. It's only natural that you'd have anxiety. The Lumens who choose to ascend have years and years to make their decision. You've had less than two weeks. Give yourself a break."

"What if they don't want me?" The vulnerability of my statement was punctuated by the tremble in my voice. The day of their eighteenth birthday was the day most Lumens looked forward to more than any other, yet here I was practically shaking in my boots, ready to bolt in the other direction at any moment. The tranquility the secret garden had brought me was now gone, doused in fear.

"Oh, Tatum, they will. They do." She pulled me into a hug that I could feel despite the armor wrapped around me. When she drew back, she searched my gaze. My eyes were watery with unshed tears. Now that I'd verbalized my fear, the waterworks demanded to be unleashed.

"It doesn't matter who your parents are, or what they did. You *don't* inherit darkness. Watchers are blessed with free will, just like humans. You are your own person. Despite whatever ties you have to Apollyon, you're choosing light over darkness, and that's what really matters."

A single tear leaked from the corner of my eye, and I let it slide down my face rather than brush it away. Taking a deep breath, I let the truth of Drea's words sink in, and for the first time in days hope bloomed in my chest, pushing out the fear, the anxiety, the feeling that I was somehow less than. This time, the smile that lifted the corners of my mouth was authentic.

"Thanks. I really needed to hear that."

"That's what friends are for." Drea winked and then turned me toward the sanctuary. "Now, get in there and get your Ascension on. We have a wicked birthday party planned for you tonight that we can't start until you go get all suped up with angelic powers. Between you and me, I'm secretly hoping you get wings bigger than Jacob to shut him up about his."

I looked over at the Watchers and grinned. Jacob was talking to Dash and showing him something on his phone. Marlow and Skye waved to me.

I perked up even more. "A party? Will there be cake?"

"You'll have to wait and see," Drea said with a cheeky grin and a sparkle in her dark eyes. "I'll be out here the whole time. I'll see you when you get back."

She wasn't going in with me?

I guess it was kind of a private thing, but I wasn't ready to let go of my comfort person just yet.

"Okay… see you when I get back." From Avalon… which was where angels lived… and basically made it Heaven.

No big deal.

Nodding, I set my sights forward and gave the guards a small wave. They stepped away from the door, giving me full access to the building as the nerves in my stomach tightened. One final whoop from Marlow and Skye across the garden and I was ready. Sucking up all the courage I could muster, I marched up the stairs, opened the double doors, and walked into the building. The doors swung shut behind me, cutting me off from Drea and the others, dampening the regular New York street noises.

There weren't any overhead lights in the sanctuary, but there didn't need to be because the spinning vortex against the far back wall cast light throughout the entire space. In contrast to the reddish portals to the Nether-world, the one in front of me was a mix of whites and blues. A faint breeze, tinted with the scent of flowers and sunshine, wafted from the portal. Lyrical notes, faint enough that I couldn't quite hear the melody, tickled my eardrums.

I caught my breath as a wave of peace washed over me. Something in Avalon spoke to my heart, calling out to me.

I took a step forward. Whatever anxiety I was still holding on to just drifted away in that moment.

"You feel the call, don't you?" Aurelia's voice wasn't loud, but she startled me. I'd been so entranced by the purity of the vortex to Avalon that I hadn't even noticed she was there.

She moved from the corner of the room to stand next to me, clad in a white robe that covered her from neck to toe. I was relieved to see her. Going through this completely alone wasn't ideal.

"It's beautiful." Unshed tears welled in my eyes. "Can I?" Now that I was here and felt the flow of energy, I couldn't wait to go to Avalon and see what it was like.

Aurelia gestured to the portal. "Absolutely. I'll wait right here."

I swallowed hard, stepping forward and giving her a small smile.

I was about to enter a portal into the upper realms of the universe. No biggie.

It was like the blue and white light was magnetically pulling me forward. I almost couldn't stop myself, and I didn't want to. I wanted to run and jump into it feet first.

Reaching forward, the tips of my fingers grazed the

portal, and I could feel warmth from the dimension beyond. I was about to take that last step when the ground shook.

There was a loud bang on the roof, and I looked up to the rafters, expecting to see a hole in the ceiling.

"What was—?"

Unearthly shrieks rang out from the other side of the sanctuary walls, and the hairs on my arms stood up. The ground rumbled, and an alarm sounded somewhere inside the Lumen compound.

"The sanctuary is warded," Aurelia yelled over the noise, her face betraying the smallest amount of panic. "Nothing can get in here."

That meant something was out there. Another demon? The same alarm from the night of the demon attack in the gym started to blare.

"But Drea and the others are outside!" Panic gripped me as I stumbled away from the portal.

A trickle of wood and stone rained down on us as something up above tried to smash and claw its way in.

A fist pounded on the sanctuary's large wooden doors.

"We're under attack!" Drea yelled, her voice muffled.

Glancing at Aurelia, I saw the spark of fear in her eyes before she shut it down. "Go, Tatum," she called to me, as she took off toward her daughter. "We'll hold them off. Get to Avalon!"

There must have been some sort of noise dampening magic on the sanctuary because the moment Aurelia pushed through the doors, the sounds of battle increased tenfold, and then cut off again when the heavy wood panels swung shut.

Were the demons attacking now in order to stop me from going to Avalon? I knew for a fact this wasn't the first time Apollyon sent demons after me. It made a scary sort of sense that he'd try to stop me from becoming a Lumen. I felt stupid for not considering that this could happen.

I looked back at the portal to Avalon, my heart tugging me in that direction, but then another loud thud came from above, shaking the whole building.

I couldn't do it. I couldn't walk through that portal knowing Lumens were being attacked, knowing Drea was being attacked, all because of me.

Even without my full powers I could still help.

I glanced down at the gold sword sheathed at my side and grimaced. With any luck, this beauty would have some demon-slaying mojo in the blade.

Spinning, I sprinted for the doors, shoving through them and into a war zone.

Holy hellfire and brimstone.

The air was thick with sulfur and smoke. Demons were pouring into the area from three separate newly cast portals as Lumens ran from the surrounding buildings to defend the compound against the assault. Battles between Lumen and the shadowy monsters raged throughout the beautiful, once tranquil, courtyard.

I spotted Aurelia shouting orders. She had quickly shirked out of the white robes, revealing she was dressed in battle gear beneath. I guessed you had to be prepared for anything in this line of work.

Her husband, Theo, stood behind her, guarding her back. He cut down any demon that tried to get to her. Drea was on her left, doing the same.

It was chaos.

An orange fireball whizzed through the air in front of me, close enough that the heat from the blaze warmed my face, and I stumbled backward. The fireball splashed over the chest of a Lumen warrior I didn't recognize, engulfing him. His scream of agony reached me, and I gasped as several people ran to his aid, forcing the Lumen to the ground to try to put out the flames.

If Hell were ever unleashed on Earth, *this* is what it would look like.

I scanned the battleground, unsure of where to jump into the fray, until my gaze snagged on one of the red and black portals. Demons were filing out of it two by two as more hunters reached the ground floor to join the battle. Adults and teens descended into the garden. It was all hands on deck.

An idea came to me then. If I could open portals, then was it possible that I could use the same power to close one?

I looked toward Aurelia again, the only Lumen who had the power to shut the portals, but she was surrounded. The demons seemed to have targeted her, purposefully keeping her busy so she couldn't close the portals anytime soon.

But I hadn't been noticed yet.

Setting my sights on the closest portal, I started toward it, only to have a figure drop out of the sky and land in front of me. Jacob tucked his golden wings behind him as he straightened.

"What are you doing?" he yelled at me.

I gestured to the portal behind him. "I'm going to see if I can help."

"No." He stuck his hands out to stop me. "You have to get to Avalon. You haven't ascended yet. This isn't a normal demon-Lumen brawl. This is all-out war. They're here to stop you from getting your powers."

"Exactly why you need my help," I growled, ready to shove him out of the way if I needed. "This is all my fault."

The rest of my Lumen friends appeared. Marlow, Skye, and Dash were all armed to the teeth. There was a streak of red blood marring Skye's perfect face, but besides that the rest of them looked unharmed.

"What are you doing, Tatum? Get in there," Marlow said to me.

I grunted in frustration. We didn't have time to argue.

"I want to try to shut the portals," I quickly explained.

Marlow tilted her head in interest and Skye nodded.

"It might work," Skye said. "She opened one from the Netherworld back to Earth with some portal mojo. Maybe she can close portals too?"

I glanced to Dash, but he was watching for threats.

"With us guarding her, we could give her a chance to try," Marlow added.

That's right, girls stick together.

"They'll just open another one," Jacob yelled.

"But it takes them time. Time we need to win the battle," Marlow growled. "They've probably been working on these three portals all night long in the Netherworld."

Jacob snarled. "Fine," he relented. "I'll protect you from the air. The rest of you fan out around her." He then took off without any further argument. When I looked up, I noticed over a dozen shadowy flying demons.

Crap.

With a round of nods, we all fell into position. It was harder to get close to a portal than I expected. Demons, mostly levels fives and sixes from the looks of them, attacked en masse as we pushed forward.

Marlow used double pickaxes in each hand, both lit with Lumen energy as she slashed out a path for us forward. She sliced through the demons with the help of Skye and some random fellow hunters I didn't recognize.

Skye used a semi-automatic crossbow to defend the group, letting bolts loose on demons in the air and on the ground, careful to avoid Jacob.

I pulled my blade free and held it before me, ready to defend myself if charged at.

We moved forward as one cohesive unit. A guttural battle cry rang out to my right and I turned just in time to see that it was Dash. He held twin daggers and went after the higher-level demons, leaving the smaller shadow demons for Marlow to take care of. When the daggers couldn't get the job done, Dash used his fists and raw strength alone. It was brutal but effective. His tattoos swirled and glowed every time his fist landed a punch.

It took at least five minutes to get in front of the portal. By that time, the courtyard was overrun with demons. My eyes watered from the combination of sulfur, smoke, and ash pouring from the open mouth of the churning portal.

"You're up," Marlow called over her shoulder to me.

Now that I was close, I could see the distant Shadow City gates and steaming lava ruins of the Netherworld in the center of the portal, beyond the swirls of red and black magic. My heart squeezed at the sight of Shadow City. My mom was somewhere in that city, but now wasn't the time to rescue her. I would need all my angelic powers to face whatever horrors the Netherworld was going to throw at me. That much had been made clear today. I was in no way ready for some big demon battle. I just hoped my mom understood that.

On the other side of the portal, a group of demons appeared in the distance, running toward us and snarling with angry expressions.

Sucking in a deep breath, I closed my eyes, relying on my friends around me for protection. I did what I could to center myself in the midst of the chaos around me, finding that well of energy inside that I'd tapped into before.

The same buzzing sensation I felt before rose to the surface and I welcomed it, melding with the magic even more fully than I had in the Netherworld. I felt a pulse of energy from the sanctuary building and wondered if I was somehow siphoning power from the portal there. The electric power flowed through my body like blood through my veins.

I smiled, knowing I had control, and then opened my eyes to see there was a slight golden glow haloing my entire body. Lifting my hands toward the portal in front of me, I directed my magic, holding back for a moment while it built, and then let it loose with a warrior's cry.

The power I unleashed was so intense that it blew my hair backward. Streams of fire so dark purple it almost looked black shot from my palms and slammed into the center of the portal.

Holy crap. Purple fire was coming out of my hands!

Within seconds, my fire spread over the opening and licked around the edges, engulfing the passageway from the Netherworld completely. Tortured screams sounded from within the void, but I didn't know what to make of that. Was my power blasting into the Netherworld and somehow the demons in it?

I hoped so.

Gritting my teeth, I threw all that I could into closing the portal. I didn't know or understand how to control my gift, but through sheer willpower alone I was determined to stop any more demons from pouring into our world and attacking the Lumens.

My magic was part of me, and even though I'd only accessed it a couple of times before, I instinctually began to use it to do my bidding. But even knowing what my intent was, I let out a soft gasp of surprise when the portal actually started to slowly shrink.

"She's doing it!" Skye shouted from somewhere behind me.

I resisted the urge to look back at her, and instead kept my gaze focused on my task. Before long, the portal was only the size of a basketball.

"Almost there," I whispered to myself, and then a body dropped next to me.

Keeping my hands up and the purple fire focused on the portal, I glanced over to see a leather-winged demon stand to his full height. Two black horns jutted from his forehead. His skin was marbled, tan mixed with patches of dark fur, but his body was clearly that of a man. The only other mutation were the long claws that tipped each of his fingers.

Holy ugly bat demon from Hell! He was a level eight at least.

Ducking his head, the demon pointed the tips of his horns at my middle and prepared to ram me.

I quickly looked back and forth between the portal that I continued to pound with purple fire and the demon preparing to rush me. The passageway was almost gone, and not a single demon had slipped through since I'd first hit it with my power, but if I stopped what I was doing before it completely closed, would it open back up? On the other hand, if I didn't defend myself against this demon, he was going to gut me.

A blur of gold dropped in front of me then.

"Sorry, I let this one through," Jacob yelled, and then rushed the demon like a linebacker.

They clashed and went down together in a ball of limbs and wings. The black-winged demon went at Jacob with his claws at the same time Jacob hammered him in the face with his fists. Red and black blood spattered the ground around them. I couldn't take my eyes off them until I caught Dash sprinting toward the pair. He'd help Jacob, so I didn't need to worry.

I breathed a sigh of relief and returned my attention to the portal. It was barely the size of a baseball now and still shrinking. The moment before it disappeared completely, it exploded, as if putting up one final fight before shutting completely. The blast of energy threw me and everyone else in the vicinity backward. I landed on my side a solid twenty feet from where I'd been standing. Pain shot up my arm and hip, which had cushioned my fall, but I hardly paid it any mind. Scrambling to my feet, I scanned the area, but the portal was gone.

"You did it!" Marlow shouted. There was a cut on her forehead that wet her black hair and dripped blood down the side of her face, but she didn't seem to notice.

"But there's still two more," I said, pointing to the next closest portal. A steady stream of small level one and two demons slithered from the black and red vortex. That portal was spitting so much smoke I couldn't even see the Netherworld beyond.

"You still have juice left in you?" Marlow asked.

"I think so." My hands shook slightly, but I think it was from an adrenaline rush.

"Then let's take care of those as well," Jacob said as he limped toward us. He was covered in gashes and scratches but had a huge smile on his face. The demon he'd defeated lay on the ground behind him, a shriveled husk of skin and bone, which slowly turned to smoke, and after a moment dissipated into the air completely.

Gross.

"That was badass," Dash said as he and Skye rejoined our group.

As a unit we limped, slashed, and fought our way toward the second portal. When we reached it, Marlow slew the smaller shadow demons that slithered out of the void, and then ducked out of the way for me to blast it with my purple fire once again.

Rather than my power waning, it seemed to multiply. It took half as long to shut this portal, as I was getting used to funneling the energy. The second portal exploded when it died as well, but I shouted a warning right before it happened and ducked. It knocked us off our feet, but at least we were ready for it. I landed on my back this time; the wind knocked out of me. I blinked up at the sky, seeing some flying demons and Lumens battling in the air as the clouds darkened.

Dash's face appeared above me, his hood having been blown off his head from battle, his dark hair sweat dampened. The scar at his temple and chin looked dark red and angry. Reaching down, he hauled me to my feet and opened his mouth to say something, but claws clamped onto both of my shoulder plates and lifted me into the air. I gasped, catching only a glimpse of the shock splashed across Dash's face as I was pulled skyward.

Some sort of two-headed demon beast had me in its grasp. One of the heads was a dragon and the other a horned goat. Its animal body was a mix of scales and fur.

I dangled from its hind legs as the demon flapped its giant bat-like wings and we shot skyward. In mere moments, we hovered over the top of the tallest Lumen building.

I looked down and caught a glimpse of a man standing on the opposite side of the street as the academy. Serpentine shadow demons wound around his torso. He stared straight up at me with a smirk on his lips.

Arthur.

The bastard. He knew this would happen and had come to Lumen Academy to what... watch the show?

I ripped my gaze off of Arthur when the beast flew even higher. I had limited mobility in my upper body but managed to grab the handle of the golden sword at my hip. Yanking it free, I jabbed wildly at the demon's underbelly. A river of black blood splashed down on me when I sliced through its flesh. The smell was vile, and I struggled to keep myself from retching.

Stabbing it again, I sunk my blade deep into its flank.

The creature shrieked and released its hold. And then I was free falling toward the ground.

A scream ripped from my throat. I was high enough that my body was going to splat like a blood bag when I reached the hard earth below.

Arms wrapped around me suddenly and I came to a jarring stop.

"Gotcha," Dash said into my ear.

Looking over my shoulder, I took in his face and then the wings that arched behind him. I hadn't really noticed his wings before, but now I took note they weren't full white. Veins of gray weaved throughout each of them.

A flash of gold streaked by me as Jacob took off after the two-headed demon that had dropped me and, somehow, despite getting stabbed twice, still wasn't dead.

Dash glided us safely to the ground near the third portal that I had yet to close. Marlow and Skye were already defending a space in front of it, ready for me to get to work.

The courtyard was a complete disaster. The battle raged all around us. Part of the community center was on fire, and there were plenty of injured lying on the ground, but it looked better than before—the odds were turning in our favor. Closing two of the portals had forced the demons to funnel through only one to enter our world, and that had to have helped.

"One to go. You got this!" Marlow shouted, and she was right. I *did* have this. I'd passed out after creating the portal back to Earth when I was in the Netherworld, and now I felt pure energy running through my veins. I glanced at the closed doors of the sanctuary and felt the tug of magic from deep inside. Being near the portal to Avalon was feeding my power somehow. I could sense it.

After having called on it twice today, I now had the feel of how to move the energy back and forth inside me, and how to focus it in one place before commanding it to leave me.

Standing before the black and red swirls, I blasted the third and last portal with everything I had. A torrent of dark purple fire shot from my hands straight for the vortex, ashing a few level one and two demons who got in the way. I definitely wasn't sad about that.

Peace out, suckas.

I smiled as the portal started to shrink. It was working, we were going to do this.

I realized too late that my mental celebration was premature. Suddenly the portal bounced back to its original size, a force from within pressing back against my own magic, startling me. I lost control of my powers; the nearly black fire sputtered. From the smoky void, a bolt of dark lightning shot toward me, and I dove out of the way, hitting the ground face-first. Rolling over, I watched a figure emerge from the angry portal.

I felt his power smother me like a heavy blanket before the smoke dispersed enough to see his face clearly. His energy was dark and oppressive, pressing against me, making the fine hairs on my arms and the back of my neck stand on end.

He strode forward, muscled and at least seven feet tall, with a folded set of black feathered wings arching behind him. His face was handsome, almost spellbinding. He had light blond hair, piercing blue eyes that were ringed in black, and a sharp chin. He looked angelic.

My heart thumped in my chest, beating against my rib cage almost painfully.

I don't know how I knew who he was, but I did.

Apollyon had arrived.

CHAPTER NINETEEN

The ruler of the Netherworld, my father, strode forward. Thick black chains of smoke trailed behind him and wrapped around his feet as he walked.

Huh. That was interesting. Even the ruler of the Netherworld was chained? But why?

The demons must have felt the same dark power I had, but rather than being filled with revulsion, it whipped them into a frenzy.

I wanted to cover my ears against the shrieks and calls they made, but terror locked my muscles and joints.

Apollyon's gaze trailed over the violence and carnage around him, and the corners of his mouth lifted in a wicked smile, one filled with bloodlust and pride.

Forcing myself to move, I scrambled to my feet, instinct telling me to run and hide. Despite the clashes between demons and Lumens throughout the courtyard, my actions caught his attention.

Oh crap.

"I think that's above level ten," Marlow squeaked next to me, looking down at the gadget in her hands. The light blinked wildly, and *Error* scrolled across the screen.

That's definitely above a level ten, I wanted to say, but my vocal cords were knotted.

Apollyon's gaze locked with mine and recognition flared in his eyes.

"Come with me, daughter. You don't belong here. Your place is by my side." Apollyon held out his hand, as if it were an offering, even though his words were a clear command.

There were gasps as he outed me as his daughter. I glanced around, and any Lumen near me scattered. Even Marlow, Skye, and Dash took several steps back, their faces painted with a mixture of disbelief and horror.

Shame blanketed me. I wanted to disappear in that moment. The other master hunters and Lumens present didn't yet know about my parentage. When I'd told Drea, she'd offered me nothing but unconditional support, but it was clear from the looks of fear and distrust from the Lumens around me that I wouldn't get treated the same from everyone.

"You see how they react," Apollyon said, poking at my insecurity. "You'll never really be one of them. You're *mine.*"

"You *are* one of us!" Drea shouted as she broke through a group of Lumens and ran toward me. "Don't listen to his poisonous lies!"

Apollyon didn't even look at Drea, he just held out his hand in her direction and then she went flying.

"Drea!" I lunged for my new best friend, but Jacob dropped from the sky and caught her before she could hit the wall.

The chains at Apollyon's feet pulled taut. "Come with me now!" he commanded, his voice shaking the windows in the buildings that ringed the courtyard.

Aurelia, Theo, and one of the other master hunters were slowly moving to flank him. I was worried someone was going to get hurt. He could clearly toss people with a mere flick of the wrist, so why wasn't he forcing me? And why wasn't he stepping more than a few feet away from the portal? Maybe it was the chain.

"You have free will," a familiar female voice shouted from deep inside the portal. "He can't take you by force, but his demons can. Once you're a Lumen, not even his demons will be allowed to drag you back to the Netherworld."

I couldn't see her, but I knew it was my mother. The blood drained from Apollyon's face upon hearing her voice, which only strengthened my conviction that it was my mom.

"Mom!" I rushed forward, only making it a few feet before hands grasped my upper arms and yanked me back.

"No," Dash growled in my ear.

"Come with me and I won't hurt your mother." Apollyon smiled a sadistic grin that said he had plans for her otherwise. The demons were closing in, and I didn't want anyone else to get hurt.

Suddenly, my mom appeared in the open portal. Her lip was bleeding, eye black and blue, hair a stringy mess, but she looked madder than hell. In her hands was a thick, black, smoky chain, swirling and moving as if it were alive.

"Tatum Angelina Powers, I know your gran didn't raise a fool," my mother declared in an authoritative mom voice. "I *command* you to go to Avalon and receive your ascension blessing." The next instant, she yanked the chain with supernatural force and Apollyon's legs swept out from under him. Before he could regain his footing, he was hauled backward into the portal, and then it snapped shut with a crack, the grass beneath it burning.

The words she spoke slammed into me, and I nodded. Becoming a Lumen, getting the tattoos and weapons and powers, was the only way I was ever going to be able to fight Apollyon and save my mom.

The demons remaining in the courtyard roared back to life, but now that they were no longer funneling out of the portals in droves, I felt better leaving the Lumens to deal with them.

"Tatum, go!" Drea screamed as Jacob dropped her right on top of a level two bat chimera demon. She sliced its throat with one clean swipe and then landed on her feet in the garden.

Kicking off from where I stood, I bolted through the garden, weaving in and out of the melee. Demons and hunters slashed at each other like mad. There were broken windows, scorched grass, and the sounds of battle all around me.

Reaching the sanctuary's double doors, I checked over my shoulder. Aurelia was racing up the steps. When she joined me, she turned to face the battle.

"I won't let anyone in. I swear it on my life." She held her glowing blue sword aloft and looked out at the advancing demons.

That was the thing though, I didn't want anyone to protect me with their life, but it didn't seem like there was anything I could do about that now.

Pushing all of that aside, I burst through the doors and ran across the room. When I reached the portal I leapt without hesitation into the swirl of blue and white, letting the feeling of peace come over my body and saturate my very soul.

I was airborne for a moment, there was a flash of golden light, and then warmth kissed my skin as my feet touched the ground. My surroundings slowly came into focus, and when I realized I was standing before an angelic being with a twelve-foot wingspan, I dropped to my knees and bowed my head.

I knelt on a glass bridge. Through it I could see waterfalls, trees, lakes, and rivers down below. Underneath me, snowy white doves flew in and out of marshmallow fluff clouds as I stared in wonder at the world that was Avalon.

The deepest peace I'd ever known fell over me. Tears

welled in my eyes as I bowed my head and took in the wonderment. Gran's healing, my mom, my father being Apollyon, and even Gage didn't bother me here. It was like I left all that stuff back at Lumen Academy.

"Hello, Tatum," a deep yet gentle voice called above me.

I looked up into the gaze of the seven-foot angel now standing before me. His eyes glowed light purple, and his skin was a bronzed gold. His long blond hair hung over his shoulders, and I couldn't help but stare at his armor. The sword at his hip was nearly as tall as me. His golden breast-plate and wrist cuffs gleamed; his thigh protectors wrapped around solid muscle. I thought I looked badass and battle ready, but that was nothing compared to this dude. This being was built for war.

I pushed to my feet on shaky legs.

"I'm Cael, and we're all so glad you're here." He smiled warmly at me, and a chorus of cheers rang out behind him. I moved slightly to the side and peered through a gap in his white feathered wings to see a golden castle at the end of the glass bridge. It appeared to be floating in the sky and was like nothing I'd ever seen before. The cheering figures in and around the glistening fortress were small blips, too hard to make out, but they screamed and thrust their fists into the air enthusiastically.

"What's the excitement all about?" I asked.

He tilted his head as he regarded me, his gaze full of affection. "It's for you, beloved child. We thought we almost lost you to the Shades."

A sob formed in my throat and tears welled in my eyes. The angels of Avalon were cheering for me? Tears spilled over and ran down my cheeks.

"I would never choose Shade," I assured him, sniffling, "I just had to save my gran."

He nodded once. "Admirable."

I was about to reply when I caught a hint of color in the sky and peered up. I gasped when I saw the stained glass overhead. This place was breathtaking.

We were chilling on a glass bridge in the sky, but there was stained glass above us, trapping the clouds inside the most colorful dome I'd ever seen. It was like all of the artists in the world got together and created this masterpiece of a place.

"Sorry." I shook myself, facing him again. "This is all just... so much. I don't know how to process it all at once."

His warm smile deepened. "Common reaction actually."

"I'll bet. Sorry if I'm late, I had a bit of trouble getting here." I reached up and rubbed the back of my neck nervously.

His smile faltered while sadness crept into his gaze. "We saw that. I'm sorry we could not be of service."

I frowned. "Yeah, why are you guys all hanging out up here when the demons are ravaging Earth?" The second it flew from my mouth I regretted being so blunt. "I'm sorry, I didn't mean it like that—"

"You did. And that's okay." He chuckled softly, and I sighed in relief, thankful he was amused by my candor and not annoyed. I wasn't looking to go to Avalon and get smote by the first archangel I met. "We used to travel to Earth freely and check in on the humans there. We would help in any way that we could. But unfortunately it's become so filled with darkness and evil, the dimension no longer supports our form. Our bodies simply cannot pass through the portal to Earth without being irrevocably harmed."

Whoa. Earth was so messed up that even regular angels couldn't go there anymore? Man, if that wasn't a reality check, I didn't know what was.

All levity bled from Cael's gaze and a sinking feeling settled in my gut, warning me that whatever came next was going to be heavy. "Watchers were created to protect Earth and its inhabitants from evil if the angels of Avalon were ever unable to do so themselves. The hope was always that Watchers would lead relatively normal lives, thriving with the rest of humanity and never knowing their true lineage, never needing to be called to action. For many thousands of years that was the case, but not anymore. Humanity's free will opened the door to darkness. By distorting the truth with lies, and tempting them with wealth, Apollyon took advantage of the situation and swayed some Watchers away from their true missions and made them Shades. Watchers of light, the Lumens, are truly the only ones holding the darkness at bay."

"Is there truly nothing you can do to help us?" I asked. It didn't seem fair that Apollyon's demons were allowed to ravage Earth but the angels of Avalon couldn't help with the fight. Even just a few of these suped-up angels would surely help tip the scales in the direction of good.

Cael's mouth pinched as he shook his head. "I'm afraid not, but there's hope that will change one day. Right now, we can only gift you with powers and help guide you."

I peered past Cael to see the angels had quieted, and now flew up and around the castle, some holding swords and other spears. What did they need weapons for in this place? Wasn't the battle on Earth? I frowned, and he seemed to read my expression.

"We have our own challenges. Even in Avalon," Cael said, causing goose bumps to break out onto my skin. "But that's not for you to worry about. You're here now." He clapped his hands together. "And we're so glad you've chosen to become a Lumen."

Reaching out, he placed one of his hands on each of my shoulders. His hands were so large they completely engulfed the shoulder plates, and his thumbs brushed my neck. Heat poured from his palms, through my armor and down my back, where it settled along my spine.

"I have a very special mission for you, Tatum, one set apart from any other mission given to another Lumen. Something that we are aware is a lot to ask." His tone was gentle, but his words scared the crap out of me. But he was a living, breathing, feathered angel, so I wasn't going to deny anything he asked of me.

"Whatever it is, I'll do it," I assured him.

He beamed with pride, and the heat between my shoulder blades turned into a burning sensation. I winced and opened my mouth to ask what he was doing to me when he said, "Would you trust me if I told you that you aren't ready to know exactly what it is yet? Only that it involved eventually defeating Apollyon?"

When an angel asked if you trusted him, you obviously didn't say no. But *defeat Apollyon?* That was a big ask. I opened my eyes so wide they felt like they were going to fall out of my head.

"Defeat the ruler of the Netherworld?" I yelped. That sounded like something fit for Aurelia, or someone much more advanced.

The buzz from his touch intensified, and I was about to shrug out of his grasp when a cool balm from his palms went right to the heated skin on my back.

"It's a lot to ask, but only you can do it. As Apollyon's daughter, you alone have the abilities needed for this task."

I knew it. I knew some of Apollyon's darkness had leaked into me. "But you won't tell me how?"

He smiled. "In time."

"And if I complete this mission?" I chewed my lip.

"Only then can the balance be restored to Earth so that we could go there again. We could help the humans and bring peace to all who live there."

I squirmed. "I mean, Apollyon moves stuff with a flick of his hand, I'm not sure—"

"Oh." The angel grinned, his hands still on my shoulders

as small vibrations of energy pulsed through me. "Are you worried you won't be powerful enough?"

I nodded. The ruler of the Netherworld against *Would-You-Like-Ketchup-With-That?* Tatum. There was a clear winner there, and it wasn't me.

He released me and the power fled my system, leaving me feeling dizzy and worn out.

"Tatum, if you do not fulfill your mission, Earth will fall into a darkness that will be beyond repair," he stated bluntly.

My mouth popped open. "Wait, what? Surely there is someone else—?"

"There is not. But it's your choice." He crossed his arms and his biceps bulged.

Way to put the weight of the world on a barely eighteen-year-old's shoulders. But I couldn't let the world fall into darkness on my account.

"Of course I'll try, but I'm going to need the works. Wings, tattoos of light, weapons." I held out my arms for him to give me the good stuff and gasped when I looked down at them. They were covered in thin white glowing arcs and swirls.

I peered over my shoulder and cried out in surprise when I saw two white transparent wings hanging off of my back.

When he was touching me, he was giving me my powers. Mind. Blown.

"It's done? I'm a Lumen?" I asked as a giddy feeling

bubbled up inside of me.

The cheers in the mansion behind him started up again, and angels flew up into the sky.

I was so humbled by their excitement, it nearly brought me to my knees again. "So you'll tell me my mission soon?"

Cael grinned. "It was an honor to meet you, Tatum."

Well, if that wasn't a polite no, I didn't know what was.

"Thank you," I managed to say through the lump in my throat.

He nodded and I started to turn around.

"Tatum," he called after me.

I spun, facing him, and swayed a little, still not used to the wings. They might be translucent, but they still had some weight.

"No one is irredeemable. Remember that." His violet gaze held mine as confusion swirled in my mind. I had barely opened my mouth to ask what he meant before I was being sucked backward into the same portal that had brought me here.

I landed back in the sanctuary, my ankle twisting awkwardly on the uneven stone floor and a tingle of pain shot up my leg. A swirl of tattoos lit up on my arm and then the discomfort disappeared.

Whoa.

Drea! My friends. I had no idea how long I was gone and if they still needed me.

Rushing forward and out the double doors, I stopped when I was met with the cheering crowd of my fellow Lumen.

They were battle weary, covered in blood, but screaming their heads off in joy.

"You got wings," Drea grinned, and then rushed toward me.

I opened my arms and wrapped them around her after she slammed into me. Laughter bubbled out of us both as she pulled back and checked out my tattoos, comparing ours.

She pointed to one swirl. "Whoa, what's this one do?"

I frowned. "Aren't they all the same?" They looked like hers to me.

She chuckled. "It's angelic script, we learn to read it as children. This one is healing." She pointed to one swirl. "This for speed." She pointed to a tighter swirl with a tail coming off the back. "Weapons. Light magic—"

"Let her breathe, daughter." Aurelia stepped up behind Drea and pulled me into a hug. "Good job, kiddo."

"Thanks." I smiled but then peered at an injured hunter being carried away behind her and the grin slipped from my face. "People are hurt."

"They are." Aurelia nodded. "But it is a pleasure to protect those ascending to Avalon and cause for celebration." She bowed slightly and emotion clogged my throat.

Before I could respond, Jacob walked over with a grin. "Wings? That means you'll need flying lessons."

"Yeah, she can get them from Dash. He's a better flier." Drea put one hand on her hip.

I smiled, trying not to think of the injured or the carnage littering the courtyard, instead I focused on the warm welcome from my friends. I was a Lumen now and Aurelia was right, it was to be celebrated.

Marlow, Skye, and Dash were next, timidly stepping to our little group. Marlow was the first to speak. "Hey, sorry we kinda got spooked when—"

"The Ruler of the Netherworld said he was my father?" I offered.

Skye tossed her hair over one shoulder. "Yeah, that *was* slightly disturbing. But you're one of us now."

"Forgiven?" Dash asked from where he hid behind his usual black hoodie.

I smiled. "Forgiven."

Drea pulled her fingers into her mouth and whistled. Every hunter in the courtyard turned in our direction.

"It's party time!"

Whoops and cheers rang all around me and then I was being hoisted into the air and carried back to the school.

The carnage around the courtyard was a reminder of the battle we'd undertaken today, but for what happened in Avalon, it was worth it.

Three hours later, I had showered, changed, and stuffed myself with five slices of pizza, two cupcakes, and three glasses of sparkling cider. Even Jasmine and her twin brother James were at my party. I was glad to see that Jasmine was fine after being injured by the serpentine demons during the attack last week.

Drea pointed to Jacob. "Your face when you saw her wings! You were *so* jealous."

Jacob frowned. "Was not. Dash has wings too."

"And you hate it." Drea tossed a cherry at his head, but he jerked to the side and caught it in his mouth, giving her a wink.

Dash leaned into me slowly. "You know they will retract with a simple thought. If you're done showing them off."

Oh they would? I hadn't even noticed them. I was starting to get used to the weight. Unlike Dash's and Jacob's, which were made of feather and bone, mine were made of light and smoke.

I thought of them sucking in my back and they retracted, sending a tingle down my spine. Drea and Marlow jumped a little.

Marlow grabbed her chest. "Warn us, dude! That's freaky!"

I burst out laughing and thought about opening them again. They snapped out, cutting through the air, and Jacob grinned. "See. They're fun, huh?"

"Braggers!" Skye yelled. But then she lifted her hand and

wiggled her perfectly manicured nails in the air and sparks of light danced over her fingers.

Cool.

I was about to try to show off another new power when my phone buzzed.

"Be right back." I slipped out of the cafeteria where my birthday party was being held and pulled out my phone. Maybe it was Gran. When I looked down at the screen, I frowned.

Indigo?

"Hello?" I picked up.

A sob ripped through the other end of the line and chills broke out on my arms.

"We're outside Lumen Academy. He's dying," she wailed.

I froze. "What? Who?"

"Gage!" she screamed.

Something took hold of my heart and squeezed. Gage. Dying.

My wings snapped out of my back and then I was running.

We were on the third floor, and I wasn't wasting any time if Gage was dying. The window at the end of the hall was open to the city below.

"Tatum!" Drea yelled, but I ignored her and leapt onto the windowsill, yanking the screen off and throwing it to the floor inside of the building.

When I looked down, in the glow of the streetlamp I saw

a sobbing Indigo hovering over a body that was covered in blood.

"Gage!" I yelled and then jumped.

In hindsight, I probably should have taken a flying lesson first. The crisp night air swirled around me, and I instinctively flapped my wings as my hair whipped around my face, covering my eyes. Fear sliced through me as I wobbled left and right, dropping fast. It wasn't a graceful descent, but I didn't die, so that was something.

Not caring who saw me, I slammed my boots onto the concrete next to Gage and took in the horror before me.

His entire gut was split open, and I could see his intestines.

"No!" I fell to my knees, gathering him in my arms. "What happened?"

Indigo sobbed. "Arthur. He found out about the talisman. That Gage helped you. He'd been dumped in the alley behind Shade Tower to die." She sniffled. "Gage wanted to see you. He told me to bring him to you. He made it this far, and just collapsed."

Her words cut through me like knives.

It was late, and thankfully the streets were devoid of people, but being seen was the last thing on my mind.

"We need to get him to the healing center." I tried to heave him in my arms, but he was too heavy.

His glassy eyes looked around as if searching for someone.

When he finally found my face, a slight grin pulled at his

lips. "Tate. You did it." He looked at the light wings behind me and a tear fell from my cheek.

"Help me carry him," I screamed at Indigo, and tried to lift him again.

"No," Gage said stronger than a moment ago. "No Lumen healer can fix this."

Pure panic flushed through me. "Gage."

The resignation in his voice scared me.

"Tate." Gage reached for me, his fingertips dripping with blood as he touched my chin.

"I should have left with you. I should have said yes." His voice had lost its momentary strength and was now breathy.

I couldn't hold it back anymore. A sob racked my chest and I let it free. "Please don't go."

I stared down at him, feeling completely lost as his life bled out onto the concrete.

"You..." Gage rasped, and his chest rattled with blood. "...were the first one to make me feel like I wasn't irredeemable."

I froze. *Irredeemable.* The memory of the angel Cael saying nearly the same thing flooded my mind. I thought it weird and random at the time, but what if...

Had the angel foreseen this very moment? Was he trying to tell me something? A wild thought ran through me just as Jacob and Dash landed behind me.

"Tatum, what's going on? Is that—?" Jacob cut off when he saw Gage over my shoulder.

"Help me grab him." I stood and hooked my arms under Gage's arms.

"But—" Jacob argued, looking at the state Gage was in.

"I got you, bro." Dash stepped up and grabbed Gage by the ankles. "Where to?" Dash asked me, and I wanted to cry for the amount of trust and complete ride-or-die I saw in his face in that moment.

Bless you, Dash. Silent but loyal.

"Sanctuary," I told him. I stretched my wings wide, and we kicked off the ground.

Gage groaned as we took flight. We looked like two drunks carrying a bloody corpse. It was wobbly, messy, and probably horrifying to any human watching, but it was the only way to do this quickly. We soared over the building, my wings getting stronger and steadier with each flap.

"Let me help." Jacob zoomed into view, putting his hands underneath Gage's back to support his middle. "Drop the wards," he yelled at someone below.

I'd forgotten about that, but I didn't bother searching for whoever Jacob called to. I just prayed they'd figure it out in time. There was a shimmer in the air for a second and I wondered if it was the wards dropping.

I glanced down at Gage to make sure he was still breathing just as his eyes rolled into his head and he went limp.

"Hurry!" I screamed.

We sailed over the roof and then descended way faster than anything I would ever try on my own. We didn't have any resistance, so I was going to assume the wards against Shades entering the compound had been dropped.

Slowing upon landing so that we wouldn't jostle him more, we touched down right in front of the double doors to the Ascension Sanctuary.

A Lumen warrior ran toward us, sword drawn. "Get that Shade out of here," he barked.

"You can't bring just anyone in here. It has to be approved by the Lumen masters," Jacob told me softly.

There was no time for that.

"Step aside or answer to the angel Cael, who has approved this mission." I sort of lied, but I was pretty sure this was what Cael meant when he said no one was irredeemable. Gage wasn't hopeless, and maybe the angels could heal him.

I'm not sure it was even possible, but if anyone could heal him from near death it was an angel of Avalon, right?

The dude blinked at my casual use of the archangel's name but didn't move. I was just about to set Gage down and pull my sword when I heard a familiar voice behind me.

"You heard her. *Move!*" Aurelia shouted and the dude jumped into action, opening the door for me, and stepping aside.

I didn't have time to thank Drea's mom. Jacob, Dash, and I just shuffled Gage into the room and beelined it right for the portal. With each step, the vortex's normally white and blue light grew gray. When we were not six feet from it, black shadows began to bleed into the portal.

"What's happening?" I asked Dash.

"He's a Shade, Tatum." The way Dash looked at me, with such pity, it made me sick.

No. This had to work.

"What do we do?" Jacob looked to me.

I glanced up toward the sky, the heavens, Avalon, whatever.

"Please save him. He's good. Deep down he's good," I said, and then grunted with all my might and pushed Gage into the portal.

The second his head hit the now gray and black swirling energy center, his body jerked and then he was sucked all the way through. I moved to follow him, and the portal snapped shut, going from a giant opening to nothing in seconds. My mouth dropped open as I stared at the crack in the stone wall that was once covered by the portal.

But that didn't make sense. This was a permanent portal. That meant it didn't close, ever.

But just like that, it was gone. Gage was gone.

I turned to Dash, who stood there with his hands still in a position to hold Gage, mouth hung open. Then I looked to Jacob, who stared back at me, eyes wide.

Okay, this was definitely not normal.

"What happened? Where is the boy?" Aurelia's voice called from behind me, and I swallowed, facing her with shame and horror.

"He's... gone."

I threw a Shade into a portal to Avalon and broke the one thing that was considered holy in this place.

Crap. Not cool, Tatum.

But even though that was bad—and I would need to answer for it—I wasn't sorry.

Was Gage alive? Would they save him?

I didn't know, but I had to hope. Sometimes hope is all you need.

SHADOW ANGEL: BOOK 2

www.ShadowAngelBook2.com

PLEASE WRITE A REVIEW

amazon   goodreads

SCAN TO REVIEW

Reviews are the lifeblood of authors and your opinion will help others decide to read our books.

If you want to see more co-written books from Leia and Julie, please leave a review on Amazon.

http://Review.ShadowAngelBook1.com

JOIN THE FAN CLUB(S)

Get involved, make some friends, and get exclusive sneak peeks before anyone else.

🤍 Leia & Julie

ACKNOWLEDGEMENTS

A big thank you to my amazing co-author Julie for being so lovely to write with and having such creative ideas. You deserve a pet otter. Thank you to our editors, beta readers, my ARC team and everyone involved in making this pretty baby be the best it could be. A special thanks to Lucas Hall for the amazing interior formatting and graphics.

~ Leia

A giant shout-out to my talented co-author, Leia Stone, for being such an amazing writing partner. Leia's brain is a giant "idea machine" that I stand in awe of on the regular. Authoring can be a lonely career, but I had such a blast creating the world of the Watchers and crafting Tatum and Gage's story with her. And better yet, I know I now have a lifelong friend.

Also a wet sloppy kiss to my hubby, Lucas, for all the hard work he puts into all of my books and for making a place-holder cover that was almost too good. Love you babe, now and forever.

~ Julie

ABOUT LEIA STONE

Leia Stone is the USA Today bestselling author of multiple bestselling series including Matefinder and Wolf Girl. She's sold over two million books and her Fallen Academy series has been optioned for film. Her novels have been translated into five languages and she even dabbles in script writing.

Leia writes urban fantasy and paranormal romance with sassy kick-butt heroines and irresistible love interests. She lives in Spokane, WA with her husband and two children.

www.LeiaStone.com

ABOUT JULIE HALL

Julie Hall is a USA Today bestselling, multiple award-winning author.

She writes YA paranormal / fantasy novels, loves doodles, and drinks Red Bull, but not necessarily in that order. Julie's daughter says that her superpower is sleeping all day and writing all night . . . and well, she wouldn't be wrong.

Julie currently lives in Colorado with her four favorite *people* - her husband, daughter, and two fur babies.

www.JulieHallAuthor.com

BOOKS BY LEIA STONE

LeiaStone.com/books

BOOKS BY JULIE HALL

Fallen Legacies Series
www.FallenLegacies.com

Life After Series
www.LifeAfterSeries.com

Made in the USA
Middletown, DE
01 February 2022

59301927R00217